Praise for

The Temptation of Adam

"An honest, emotional, funny, romantic, dark, hopeful, musical gem of a novel. I know that's a lot of adjectives, but it'd be a disservice to leave any out."

—Adi Alsaid, author of *Let's Get Lost* and *Never Always Sometimes*

"*The Temptation of Adam* is the sort of novel you finish and immediately wish you could read again for the first time. It's profound without being preachy, funny without pandering, and thoughtful in a way that few debut novels manage. Dave Connis is a writer to watch."

—Bryan Bliss, author of *Meet Me Here*

On the surface, *The Temptation of Adam* is the story of a teenaged boy with *teenage-boy* problems, but the true brilliance of this novel lies in the way it uses heartache, humor, and music to reveal LOVE as both Healer-of-Wounds and Kick-in-the-Pants toward greatness. Highly recommend."

—Nic Stone, author of *Dear Martin*

"Dave Connis's *The Temptation of Adam* confronts a difficult topic with honesty, humor, and heart. The friendships and love that form amongst the misfit cast of teens trying to overcome addiction are an important reminder of our power to destroy or give hope to those tangled in our messy lives."

—Randy Ribay, author of *An Infinite Number of Parallel Universes*

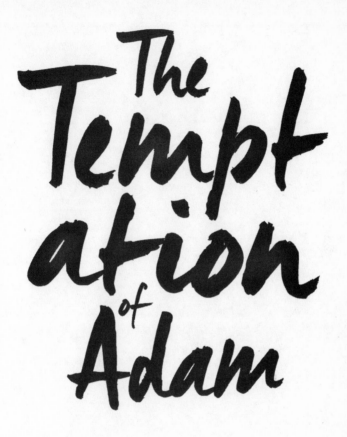

The Temptation of Adam

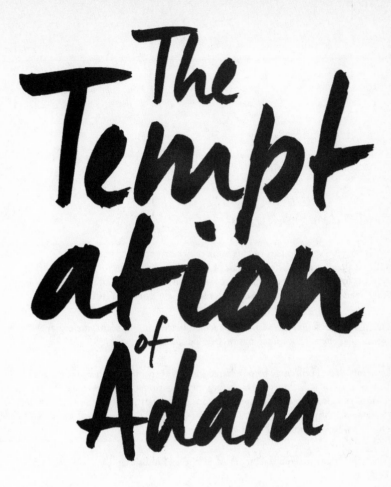

The Temptation of Adam

DAVE CONNIS

Sky Pony Press
New York

Sky Pony Press books may be purchased in bulk at special discounts for sales promotion, corporate gifts, fund-raising, or educational purposes. Special editions can also be created to specifications. For details, contact the Special Sales Department, Sky Pony Press, 307 West 36th Street, 11th Floor, New York, NY 10018 or info@skyhorsepublishing.com.

Sky Pony® is a registered trademark of Skyhorse Publishing, Inc.®, a Delaware corporation.

Visit our website at www.skyponypress.com.

10 9 8 7 6 5 4 3 2 1

Library of Congress Cataloging-in-Publication Data is available on file.

Cover design by Sammy Yuen
Interior design by Joshua Barnaby

Print ISBN: 978-1-5107-0730-6
Ebook ISBN: 978-1-5107-0732-0

Printed in the United States of America

To Asa. You're always enough.

OUR FIVE O'CLOCK APPOINTMENT

I sit outside of the principal's office awaiting the guillotine of high school justice.

My phone buzzes and I pull it out of my pocket. It's Addy.

> Dad just told me you're in trouble at school?

I groan and collapse my head into my hands. My sister *would* be in town when something like this happens to me. The only person who actually matters is about to find out I'm getting expelled. How charming of you, Life.

> I guess.

> You guess you're in trouble? What happened?

> I'll tell you later @ Pritchett's.

> Will you actually tell me or is this one of your famous avoidance techniques?

Bryonie Welch walks by the office. Her curly blond hair bounces a bit as she stops in front of the door. I don't feel very plucky, so I just watch her as she flips me off, slides a note beneath the door, and keeps walking. I stare at the note for a little while before picking it up.

Dear Adam Hawthorne,
This is your first warning.
Sincerely,
The Anti-Adam Order

There's an order out for my destruction?

Well, don't the giggles abound.

I am now super pissed. The evils unleashed upon me were calculated *and* formulated?

I cuss, shoot out of my chair, and storm toward Principal Johnson's door. I have evidence of a conspiring enemy; I'm prepared to restate my case and secure an acquittal. I raise a fist, ready to pound down the door, but I hear Mrs. Johnson say, "That may be true, but it's a miracle that Miss Howard's parents aren't going to press charges."

I pause and press my ear against the door.

"Tracy," Mr. Crotcher says, "I'm begging you to accept this proposal. Please."

Awesome. Mr. Cratcher—I call him Mr. Crotcher—is the last person I want bargaining for my soul. Mr. Crotcher is Bothell High's bio/chem teacher *and* a friend of my family's. What was left of my family, anyway. He's been waiting for this day since I started high school, the day he could exact his chem-tastic revenge. This revenge covered a multitude of grievances because Mr. Crotcher and I went back.

Way back.

Back before The Woman left my dad. Addy had been in one of his advanced chem classes when his wife, Gabby, passed away. Despite a few faults, Addy is the best of the Hawthornes. Better than me. Better than my dad. Better than The Woman by miles. Because Addy is who she is, she invited the newly widowed Mr. Crotcher over to dinner every Tuesday night.

Our rivalry started my second year of middle school, the first dinner night he attended. A song came on through the radio in the kitchen. I loved the song so I tapped my fork to the beat on my plate—and he told me to stop. I didn't even know the guy, and there he was telling me *not* to do stuff. In my own house. I decided I didn't like him, and he's been Mr. Crotcher ever since.

On the first day of high school, I was accidentally late to his class because I got lost and wound up in the wrong wing. When I finally found the classroom, he assumed I was just a miscreant and pulled me aside to give me a "you have so much potential" speech laden with mysticism and quotable one-liners about humanity. At the time, The Woman had just left my dad, so Crotcher's "potential" bucket'a'bull pissed me off. It was like he'd judged me to be one of those chronically late kids who needed a mentor as soon as he'd seen me tap my fork on my plate. So, after that, I felt the need to make being late for his classes a thing forever more.

It turned into some sort of unspoken war.

Instead of curing my tardiness by reporting me to a school authority like any other teacher would, he just made frequent calls to my dad to inform him of my shortcomings. This was a major oversight for Mr. Crotcher because, even though he knew a ton of formulas, he didn't know the fundamental formula for my dad:

THE GREG HAWTHORNE FORMULA OF LESS THAN
Greg's care for Adam < Greg's care for getting The Woman back

"This is an incredible offense, Colin," Mrs. Johnson is saying. "We could permanently expel him for this."

Mr. Crotcher sighs. "That's not what he needs. I know him. I know his father. Approve this. Call West Seattle High if you desire some success stories from some of my other mentees."

Why does Mr. Crotcher always think he knows what I need? What about my fork tapping made him think he knew the ins and outs of the Adam Hawthorne blueprint? Was it possible that he was the leader of the Anti-Adam Order? Maybe he led the AAO in discussions on how to screw me over while dissecting cats in class.

"This is a cycle, Mrs. Johnson," Mr. Crotcher says, "and I'm sure I can help."

Silence.

Finally, Mrs. Johnson sighs. "Okay."

"You'll let me do this program?"

"Yes, but he'll still have a eighty-day suspension. At the end of that period, we'll assess the situation again. If your program doesn't work, we may have to take further action."

"Thank you, Tracy."

"I'll let you handle it from here," Mrs. Johnson says. "I've got enough to worry about as it is."

I walk back to my seat, pissed, and pull out my phone. This whole situation makes me think too much, so I calm myself by skimming through an expertly curated porn playlist I have saved for later tonight. There's no thought involved in that.

A minute or so later, Mrs. Johnson's office door swings open. I click off my phone as Mr. Crotcher pushes a wad of papers toward my face.

"I've called your dad and updated him on your current situation."

"You sure he listened?"

"Read over this." He holds out the paperwork. "This is your situation report and discipline outline."

I take them with an aggressive snatch.

"Bring this home and have your dad sign it. If he wants to request a hearing for you, he needs to do it by tomorrow morning. However, to be candid, the evidence is so stacked against you it would be a waste of everyone's time if he did."

This crack about "evidence" is the biggest joke someone could've made. There was no evidence. I almost don't care if I get expelled. I'm an academic anomaly, a sultan of study poised for slaying the entry-level job world with my eventual overpriced college degree. I could find another school.

"You have an eighty-day suspension," he says, "and we will meet every day of it at five a.m. Then, every Monday and Friday at seven thirty p.m., you will meet with what I call a Transparency Forum, a group of guys who get together and talk about what's happening in their lives." He pauses to give me the chance to add something, but when he realizes my lips are zipped—nay, glued, nay, welded together—he continues. "Also, every Thursday night, you will attend a public addiction group based on AA's twelve-step program with your Transparency Forum."

"Why do I have to go to an addiction group? That's a bucket'a'bull. I'm not addicted to anything."

"Sure you are," he says, his voice laced with annoying calmness.

"No. I'm not. You know nothing about me."

"I know you have porn waiting for you tonight. I know your social activity has declined to a halt over the last year. I know you sit alone at Pritchett's. I know neither your father nor your sister know anything about what's going on with you."

"You've only seen me at Pritchett's once."

"Perhaps, but seeing you once at Pritchett's has no bearing on my *seeing* you. I've been around a while, Adam. The look of a human searching for something they can't find is as evident as where the sun shines."

"So you're stalking me?"

He smiles, taps the papers in my hand, and turns to leave. "Make sure you have your dad sign those papers. Bring them with you tomorrow to our five o'clock appointment."

WALK AWAY

Settlers of Catan.

I was always red. The Woman was always blue. Addy and Dad never cared what color they were, which was probably why they always won. *Settlers* was the go-to family board game. You traded resources to build cities and roads. You got points for building specific things or hitting certain achievements like having the longest road.

The Woman and I never won. No matter how hard I tried to come up with new strategies, Addy always got the longest road or dad always magically figured out how to upgrade all his settlements to cities without anyone noticing.

One night, we were playing and I felt something nudge my hand under the table. I looked up from my deck, and dad was whisper-singing, "You can't always get what you want, but I can get you what you need." I grabbed the thing nudging my hand—two ore cards. I hadn't gotten any since the beginning of the game, and I could literally do nothing except sit and complain about the inefficiencies of the Catan economy. For the rest of the game, he slipped me ore cards and I avoided stealing any of his routes.

He won because I let his territorial expansion go unchallenged, and then we fake fought the rest of the night and Addy was cry-laughing and The Woman was, too, and . . . I say all this because Mr. Crotcher said he told my dad what happened at school, and I'm certain it won't matter. There was a point in time, the ore-card-sliding, fake-fighting time where it mattered, but *Settlers* was now just a dusty box in the corner of the dining room. I barely get slid a "good morning" *over* the table these days. I figure I'll go home and, as ususal, nothing will happen, and after I ride out the tortures Mr. Crotcher has for me, things will go back to where they were.

I walk outside. Stupid papers still in hand. What do you do when you're expelled from school and have nothing to do? Go to Pritchett's—home of the best milkshake this side of that one chick's yard, possibly in America—and sit. Definitely *not* go home.

"Hey, Genevieve," I say, patting my black 1990s Buick Riviera on the rear passenger's side window, which is proudly hand-crafted entirely out of duct tape. I may feel like utter hell, but Genny has only ever been the best, and she deserves all the love I can muster.

Inside, I settle into my seat and try to forget about everything by turning the radio on. Top 40 comes through the speakers. I frown and hit preset button number one. The sound of my daily enlightenment washes me away in a wonderful wave of perfect, publicly funded noise.

Marry me, NPR.

At a stoplight, in the middle of NPR's *All Things Considered*, I pull out my phone and do some searching and favoriting of some more porn videos to watch later on. A few seconds later, the driver behind me honks his horn, and I look up to see the light's turned green. I favorite two more videos before putting my foot on the gas pedal. The Hyundai driver honks again and speeds around me, nearly hitting my front bumper when he swerves back into the lane. I watch him disappear before returning to my screen to favorite one more video before I turn into the parking lot of Pritchett's.

I walk inside, find my booth, and for the next three hours I sit and work through two baskets of waffle fries covered in cheese and gravy and a milkshake. I look for more porn videos. I ignore calls from my dad. It's a great afternoon.

At around 7:30, Addy walks into Pritchett's. It's weird to see her here. She hasn't been in here since she moved to Portland with The Woman two years ago. That and she randomly showed up last night. I'm not complaining. Addy might be the only person I ever want to be around. Still, seeing her here is weird. Like, brings me back to the old days where I almost think things could be whole again.

Hahahaha. Right.

She showed up last night at ass o'clock, so I hugged her and went to bed, but today, after we hug and she slides into the booth, I finally get a chance to look at her. In the light, I notice her usually short blond hair has gotten even shorter, stops-right-above-her-ear, bangs-almost-hang-in-her-eyes short. She's wearing a gray long-sleeved shirt that says Coalweather Construction.

I point at it. "They're giving you fancy gear now, huh?"

"A perk of moving up to project lead," she says. "Now I get to build houses *and* boss people around."

"The fact that you like both of those things so much is weird." I smile then reach for a fry. "No one believes me when I tell them my older sister's a construction worker."

She waves a hand. "Please, lil' bro, like you've talked to anyone since the divorce."

I roll my eyes. "A—don't call me 'lil' bro.' B—I talk to Myself all the time, and he gets me. He gets me so much I might ask him out on a date."

Addy goes to respond, but her phone rings. Jefe/Boss flashes her screen. She mouths, "Gotta take this," then stands and starts talking about roof trusses. She steps outside, which I take as an opportunity to make my final porn selections.

I finish a black cherry and toffee shake as I look out the front window to see if Addy's showing any signs of getting off the phone, but almost five minutes later, she's still outside.

Behind me, a familiar voice requests a booth for four. I look up from my table, and, sure enough, there's Mr. Crotcher by the host podium, flanked by a trio of high school kids. This must be my future, and it's comprised of a sixty-six-year-old man and a random group of teenagers. I know I shouldn't stare this long, but it doesn't help that one of the guys practically has an arm made out of spiky bracelets.

I'm about to go back to my playlist when Mr. Crotcher looks up. I think our eyes meet, so I look back at my table, cursing under my breath. A few tense seconds pass, and just when I think he might not have seen me, I hear, "Hey, Adam."

I don't look up. "Hi."

This is what he says: "I know it's before your given start date, but would you like to join the boys and me tonight?

Get a head start? Meet everyone? We're going over a book on addiction. The discussion should be wonderful."

This is what I hear: "Would you like to start your misery earlier than when I'm forcing you to?"

I shake my head. "No, thanks."

He casts a glance at my phone and sees a screen filled with the thumbnails of my porn playlist. "You sure?"

I slide my phone in my pocket. "Yeah. I'm really sure."

Addy finally comes back in. She's walking toward me. Now, I really want Mr. Crotcher to leave. I don't want her to hear anything he has to say, and I don't want her to see him and start talking.

"That's fine," he says. "Look, Adam, I know your mother leaving has hurt you deeply—"

"My sister is here," I say, pointing to her. "We're supposed to be hanging out."

Mr. Crotcher looks at her, smiles, waves, then turns back to me, taps a knuckle on the counter, and walks back to his table.

I cuss him out under my breath as Addy stops to hug him at his table with the other guys. They chat for a few minutes, and then she slides back into our booth.

"Aw, it was so nice to see him. I miss him. He's so smart. I don't have an elderly soul guide in Portland."

"Shouldn't have moved, I guess."

She rolls her eyes. "You and you—"

I stop listening when this girl walks past the booth. No. She's more than a girl. She's a mountain in the morning sun. A forest of trees in a northern fall. I swear she's the subject of every Michael Bublé song. Ever. A puff of tight, chocolate brown curls with a yellow hairband holding it back. The cutest nose ever put on a human.

Beautiful faice.

Loveloy legspdfpn.

Uhisoiasepuhn.

Addy snaps her fingers. "Lil' bro, do I need to send in a rescue team?"

"What? Hey, don't call me lil' bro."

She takes a sip of her milkshake. "Do I need to find out her name?"

That wakes me up. "Oh, nah. She's not my type."

Addy laughs. "BS! The formula for your type is girl plus that's it."

"Not true."

She stands. "Right. You tell yourself that, Papi."

"What's Papi? Addy . . . Addy, where are you going?"

She walks toward the apex of a woman, and I have no idea what she's going to do, and I don't know if I can watch her destroy my chance with the most beautiful girl in the universe, so I go back to my milkshake. As I turn, I make awkward eye contact with Mr. Crotcher. He doesn't know what I need. He doesn't know anything about me. No one does.

My phone buzzes.

> Her name is Desiree, but she goes by Dez and you literally need to marry her.

> I'll stick with a literal no marriage for now.

Adam . . . if you don't come over here, I'm going to propose for you.

Let me know how the wedding goes.

You're pathetic.

I've been given multiple awards for my extraordinary dignity,

thank you very much.

Any award received in France doesn't count.

Come back so we can finish our milkshakes.

Fine.

What? Addy doesn't say *fine*. I look for them and see Addy's head in the furthest booth away in the center aisle, sitting with the so-called Dez. Dez catches me looking, smiles, then holds up Addy's phone and wiggles it back and forth.

You're really missing out, Frenchie.

I smile back and somehow, despite myself, walking toward her. She has beauty like a tractor beam.

I walk over to her table. "Hey, I'm Adam, which you probably already know."

Dez doesn't respond. Instead, she types D-E-Z into Addy's phone, then holds it up so I can see it.

Addy motions for her phone. Dez gives it to her.

> Isn't she darling?

> What are you two doing?

Addy shows the message to Dez. Dez takes the phone back.

> Using mystique to lure you into a situation you don't understand, therefore disabling your ability to label our interaction. In other words, I'm giving you a judgment-free "Talk to Dez" card.

"You're welcome," Dez says as Addy slides out of the booth so an older man with giant glasses can take her place. He smiles and nods at me.

"It was nice meeting you two," Dez says.

Addy laughs. "Likewise. Come on, Gape-y."

"Thanks for the card," I say. "My French dignity appreciates it."

Dez laughs. "Au revoir, Mademoiselle."

As we walk back to our booth, Addy puts her hands over her eyes and says, "Oh my God, Adam. Why didn't you get her number? It really seems like you were born yesterday."

"Phone numbers don't jive with my stance on relationships."

"Do I even want to know?"

"Probably not."

"Tell me, then."

"I align with the wise, postmodern, Western philosopher 50 Cent. In his song, 'In Da Club,' he quotes a tenant of his life philosophy, 'I'm into having sex, not into making love.' When everyone is out for themselves, what's the point of love? Is love even possible?"

Addy looks at me with this half-smile, half-furrowed brow face, and I know I've said too much. I change the topic. "Did Dad know you were coming?"

We slide back into the booth, and even though she looks disappointed, she nods. "I told him a while back so he could make sure you weren't doing anything."

"You were home when Dad heard about school, right? Does he actually have emotions about the situation?"

She nodded. "The emotion you're thinking of is 'pissed,'" she says, turning on what I call The Addcent. "But no worries, honey, you will have life just the same."

Addy has talked in The Addcent since I can remember. Isn't any particular accent, but it's heavily influenced by the fact that she's fluent in Spanish and French. She learned French in high school, but she learned Spanish by working construction. That's one of the reasons her company keeps promoting her; she can talk to everyone. She's so used to switching from English to Spanish at breakneck speed on the job that that's become a habit off the job, too. I asked her about it once, and she just said, "Sometimes I think of words in Spanish and in English at the same time and that's just how it comes out."

Surprised that my dad is actually having a reaction, I ask, "Did Dad tell you anything he's thinking?"

She jabs a fork into a waffle fry as big as my palm and then folds it, gravy and all, into her mouth. She chews, regards, swallows, and then says, "Dad doesn't tell people things. Remember? You guys are twins that way."

I shrug and turn to look at the front of the diner.

Addy sighs. "Are you ever going to tell me things again?"

"I used to have things to tell," I say. "What happened at school's not a big deal."

She gives me not-a-big-deal?-then-why-are-you-expelled-for-eighty-days look, then asks, "Why'd you stop? Telling me things, I mean."

"I don't know."

"Yes, you do. What's wrong, Adam? Something's wrong."

"Really, it's nothing, Addy. I'm fine."

"If you don't tell me, who are you going to tell?"

This is exactly what my ex-friend Jason used to do—badger me with questions like this. That's why he's an ex-friend. I don't want them, and I don't want Addy to turn into Jason. Besides, Addy gave up her right to be told things.

"I'm fine," I say, standing. "Look, I've got to go. I'll meet you back at the house."

Addy's eyes glisten. "Adam . . ."

"I'll see you in a bit."

I still don't want to go home, so I hop in Genny and drive to downtown Bothell. I just walk around a bit with a to-go Thin Mint and Oreo milkshake sipping cookie chunks through the straw. The discipline papers are rolled into a tube in my pocket and they press into my thigh as I move. Downtown Bothell is undergoing a massive reno after a big fire, and every time I come here, I never know what will be done and what will be under construction.

I pass a swanky little chocolate store called The Chocomotive and see a woman inside. She's trying to hold a bag of chocolates, push a stroller, and open the door at the same time. I walk up to the door and prop it open with my foot.

The woman sees me, sticks the bag of chocolates in her teeth, and shoves the stroller onto the sidewalk. Once she's out of the store, she takes the bag out of her mouth and flashes me a genuine smile.

"Thank you so much," she says.

I just nod and pull my foot away from the door.

She unrolls the bag of chocolates and holds them toward me. "Here."

I reach for one, hoping to get something caramel-y, but right as my hand dips into the bag she says, "Your mother deserves a medal for raising such a gentleman."

I pull my hand out and walk away.

PULL AWAY

Is it weird that my dad's yelling at me and I'm kind of enjoying it? I don't think I've been yelled at for at least two years.

He crosses his arms. "Really, Adam? What do . . ."

Addy walks into the house. I look at her. She avoids my glance and lies on the couch, playing some game on her phone.

Dad slams his fist on the table. "If you think . . ."

When The Woman left, I came up with these two formulas in Mr. Crotcher's Bio 101 class.

ADAM'S FORMULA OF LIFE SCREWAGE A

People who think + life = get screwed

ADAM'S FORMULA OF LIFE SCREWAGE B

People who don't think + life = get screwed

I've thought about these a bit, not too much, just a bit, and come to a few conclusions.

My dad throws his hands up in disgust. ". . . You are going to go to everything Colin Cratcher has . . ."

Conclusion One
People who think = People who don't think

This seems true by logical deduction; however, I'm pretty sure it's false. Why? Because my dad's warier than I am about the bucket'a'bull life dumps on you from day-to-day. I mean, look at him. He's yelling, but the slouch of his shoulders and his half open eyes are saying "this is the last thing I need right now." Lately, what he thinks he needs is Nicholas Sparks. Yes. . . My dad *loves* Nick Sparks. He's read all of his books. Twice. But none of that romantic bucket'a'bull helped him when The Woman said she wanted a divorce. Getting your relational acumen from Nick Sparks is about the same as getting it from *Cosmo*.

Conclusion Two
There is a variable that doesn't change in either of the formulae: life, and that forces the equation to spit out the same sum.

So, according to Conclusion Two, it doesn't matter how you carry yourself, because somewhere between the plus and the equal sign in **Adam's Formula of Life Screwage A** and **B**, everything goes up in flames.

Sounds pretty accurate to me.

"If your mother were here . . ."

I stare at him. Is he really going to use The Woman as a discipline point?

"She'd be appalled. Come on, Adam why would you—"

"But she isn't here," I say.

"That's not the point. The point is women are—"

"People who leave you. It's all BS, Dad. You did everything right, and look at you. You've been reduced to reading Nicholas Sparks to figure out how to get her back. She's destroyed your life, and you did nothing but treat her like a celebrity. You cared about someone, something, and it got you nowhere. Same goes for everything else. Why bother?"

Addy's sitting up now. Staring at me. Hurt. I see it shimmer across the lines between her eyebrows. I see it in the tears pooling at the side of her eyes. I want to tell her "This isn't about you," but if I was honest? The pie chart of what *this* is about would have a slice, albeit a smaller one, designated to Addy.

Dad runs his hand through his silver hair. They come to rest over his eyes. When he says, "I've taught you better than this," his voice is muffled as it escapes from behind his palms.

He hasn't taught me anything in the last year that makes me think otherwise. He's barely looked at me since The Woman left. He's obsessed with being the best he can be for her, all while she's with some other guy. I refuse to end up like that.

With nothing else to say, I shake my head, leave my dad at the table, take the steps two at a time to my room, lock my door, and dig my computer out of my bag. This is me. This is how I relax. It's not an addiction; it's how I relax. Tell the guy who relaxes by doing the dishes after dinner that he's a dish addict and needs to go to an AA group for it. After today, I need a naked girl named Glitter to remind me that the world isn't just a useless pit of obnoxious misery.

—

There's a man in my room. This man looks like my dad. He never comes into my room.

Dad + my room = never.

"It's 4:50. You're late for Mr. Cratcher's."

"I didn't set my alarm for a reason," I mumble. "I'm sure you can deduce what it is."

"I'm sure you can deduce that this is me overriding that deduction."

"Dad."

"Adam."

"You've been ignoring me for the last year. You can't just get interested when all the fun starts."

"Adam, get out of bed, put your pants on, and go. We'll talk about my shortcomings as a father when you get home."

I make my way downstairs. Addy isn't here. I look out into the driveway. Her twenty year-old sky blue Ford F-150 is gone.

I made her leave. I hate myself.

I put together some breakfast, but Dad doesn't let me eat because I'm too late.

—

The early morning lullaby of NPR and random thoughts of that Dez girl distract me from my impending counseling session with Mr. Crotcher. I pull into his driveway, but I don't get out of Genevieve. I've never been early to his classes, so why should I be early to our love-is-all-you-need session? I pull my phone out of my pocket and send Addy a text.

> I'm sorry.

I stare at the screen, touching it when it tries to shut off, but after five minutes of staring, she hasn't texted back. It makes my brain and heart bicker back and forth like Gollum and Sméagol:

Addy's just trying to help you.

My feelings are mine, Precious. I'll hurts them. They'll hurts me.

Do you care?

Glitter doesn't hurts me. Gollum! She protects me, it does.

But you're still a mess.

Nothing changes mess until heart burns red and you are dead.

So why not feel as good as possible?

Yes! Gollum! That's it, it is. I swears.

I stare at Mr. Crotcher's front door. I don't think I've ever come here by myself. Back during the frequent dinners with Mr. Crotcher, we came here ia few times. After The Woman left, and took Addy with her, our interaction with the outside world died. It's not that we didn't want to go places; it's just that she robbed us of table conversation not based on the divorce. She turned dinner into a scratched CD, repeating, "How are you holding up?" or "How can I help?" or "I'm sure it's been hard."

I know people were trying to help, but that doesn't change the fact that certain kinds of tragedies—divorce and losing a limb being two examples—have a tendency to make people treat you like a toddler. Encouragement starts sounding like, "You're such a big boy for dealing with this," or "Wow, look at how strong you are. Good job eating all your food!" After a while, that kind of interaction gets old.

At 5:09, I climb Mr. Crotcher's stairs. As I ring the doorbell, I accidentally drop the discipline report paperwork. He opens the door while I'm scrambling to pick up the pages stuck to the railing slats before they blow into the street.

"Good morning, Adam," he says, his voice bright and wretchedly cheery. "Come in."

His living room is lined wall-to-wall with books. He has no TV.

Of course.

"You haven't been here in a while," he says. "Not since your mother left, correct?"

"Yeah."

"I've added a study studio in the attic, but that's about all that's changed. Haven't felt like changing much else. So," he continues, "you're starting everything on a Thursday. That means tonight is the Addiction Fighters meeting at the Civic Center. I really am sorry you won't get to interact with your Transparency Forum beforehand, but in my defense, we had an extra night last night so we could finish discussing that book before you joined, and you had a chance for introductions then. However, I have faith that tonight's group sharing time will be as good of an introduction as you can get."

We walk up a dark stairwell. The walls are covered with pictures of him and Gabby. I never met Gabby. Also of note, there are no pictures of kids. So either Mr. Crotcher and

Gabs didn't get down or they never had any. As a guy who doesn't have a TV in his house, my guess is the former.

At the top of the stairs, we turn left, walk down a long hallway, and step into his study. The room's wide and open. Instruments line the walls, and a computer desk the size of Noah's Ark sits in the far right corner. Behind the computer, by a rectangular window with a clear view of the neighborhood, is a small room. The door is open, and the inside walls are covered with gray cubes of wavy foam. A microphone rests in a stand pointed toward the back wall.

"Is that a recording studio?" I ask.

Mr. Crotcher nods. "Yes. It's taken me a while to decide which pieces of my equipment I wanted to switch from analog to digital. Digital equipment is much easier to work with and has an incredible amount of capabilities. However, I will always be of the opinion that analog equipment has a warmer sound more conducive to the kind of music I play. That's why, when I record, I use both."

I poke one of the gray sheets of foam. My finger disappears. "Why do you have a recording studio? Do all your . . . people . . . record with you?"

"No, no. Just you. It takes a poet to keep up with the demands of the studio. You've always seemed to fit the bill. Music production has always been a passion of mine. In a past life, I was a sound engineer."

That's not something you hear an ancient high school chemistry teacher say every day.

He points to the walls. "I mixed and recorded a few of Johnny and June's albums."

Tons of framed records hang around the room, Johnny Cash and Roger Miller among the names.

"You're about to lay into me for eighty days about how I need to stop wasting my life when you had the chance to be a music mogul in Nashville?" I've got to admit, the man just ascended a few levels of awesome in my head, but not enough to lose the name Mr. Crotcher.

"My life would've been a waste if I didn't choose to teach high school chemistry."

"Why would you choose teaching over being a giant in the music industry?"

"I'd just gotten engaged to Gabby and was in the process of destroying myself with alcohol and drugs. She made me choose between lives. Luckily, I chose her, and we left any trace of that old life behind to come here and build a life we *both* wanted. Our story is much more complicated than that, of course, but what isn't complicated is that choices change you. Especially the life and death ones, and life and death choices are exactly why you are here."

I study his clean-shaven face and note that he's incredibly dramatic.

He crosses his arms, his familiar sternness showing. "Here is what to expect from our meetings. I'm not going to ask you about your feelings, your father, or your mother, and we're not going to talk about what you did or didn't do. For eighty days, from five to seven a.m., you are going to help me record the album I've been working on for the last forty years."

Recording an album > talking about feelings.

"You've only recorded one album?" I ask.

"Indeed, though it has changed quite a bit over time. Can you sing?"

"Yeah, sort of, I guess."

"Do you play anything? Banjo? Guitar?"

"Guitar, but I'm not very good."

"It's no matter. You will probably make a better sound engineer and lyricist, anyway. Alright, let's waste no more time. You need to be brought up to speed on how to run a studio."

For the rest of our time together, Mr. Crotcher gives me a rundown of all the recording equipment. He tells me what things do, how things do what they do, and the difference between one thing and another. Eventually, we do some test recordings so he can teach me how to use the recording program. I record him singing a few times, and as much as it pains me to say, he has a good voice. I expected it to be shaky and outdated, but it's rugged and wise. If his voice was a thing, it'd be a solid hike in a rustic forest, or every character Denzel Washington has ever played.

At seven, he walks me to the front door and says, "See you at the Civic Center."

I leave my first morning with Mr. Crotcher without a single lecture or guilt trip. He didn't mention the fork tapping or tell me all about why I'm throwing my life away by being late to his classes. He didn't even mention our forever rivalry. I get in Genevieve and stare at Mr. Crotcher's house.

He's tricksy, that hobbits.

Maybe he's just genuinely nice.

He wants your precious. Gollum!

Maybe he can help.

Helping hurts us, it does.

You're right.

I text Addy another apology, turn on NPR, and pull away.

WE'RE GOING TO BE LATE

Dad comes to the Civic Center with me. It would've been miserable enough *without* him being here. I told him he didn't have to come a million times, but his only answer was, "I think I need it just as much as you." His presence has already changed my plans: we're early. I didn't want to be early. This is something connected to Mr. Crotcher, so I should be at least five minutes late.

Not only are we early, but also as soon as we walk through the door, he disappears in search of a bathroom so I'm left alone, with nothing else to do but take in the sights, smells, and sounds (mostly smells) of Washington's finest: the Bothell Civic Center.

The Bothell Civic Center is also on the city's list of things to be renovated. Construction cones litter the entrance and demolition is going on everywhere the light touches, which is good because the place was undoubtedly built in the seventies, and I don't think it's been redecorated since. It would be better if it were called the Creamsicle Empire, or The Palace of Linoleum Glare. As I look around, I feel slapped by the entire spectrum of tan, yellow, and orange.

The windows are caked with slick grime left over from the "make love, not war" era, and the fake grout of the linoleum floor is brown instead of white. Fluorescent lights line the ceiling. The Plexiglas surrounding them looks like transparent peanut brittle, all chipped and discolored. Thin sheets of decorative cork cover the walls. Cork. As wallpaper. Not the thing you stick in a wine bottle. There must have been a lack of intelligence among interior designers in the seventies.

I was forced here by the Anti-Adam Order. This is their doing. I sigh and pull out my phone to make a quick porn playlist. I call this "preventative maintenance." If I don't do this, I won't make it through tonight's meeting without puking in the middle of the Healing Circle.

"Are you looking for the Groupeth De Pain?"

The female voice makes me jump. I let out a silent curse, click my phone off, and turn around.

It's her. Dez.

Her hair shines like a chocolate sun. For some reason, seeing her this time is even more of a blessing than at the diner. Her face is childlike, but more mature than all of the girls in my class. Her clothes are thoughtful. She's wearing a gray, hooded pea coat, but it isn't buttoned. Underneath that, you can see an unbuttoned denim shirt and a gray tank top. A pair of sunglasses rests in her hair. She looks as if someone's taken all that's sexy and painted it on a human, one layer at a time. Something about her just tugs at me in a strange way, and I'm not sure what it is.

"Oh, it's you, Adam, hey," she says, like it's not weird to find me at an addiction meeting. "Is Addy coming? She was really cool."

I'm so taken off-guard, I forget to answer. No, Addy isn't coming. I chased her away and now she hates me.

"So . . . judging by the look on your face, you're new and in denial," she says with a smirk and then points down the hall. "Addiction Fighters is down this way. Just make sure you take care of your eyes." She slides the glasses onto her nose. "This place is a proxy for the surface of the sun. Come addicted, leave blind. For people who are addicted to porn, like me, it's the best cure ever."

I feel my mouth drop. Her honesty, wit, and posture take me completely by surprise, and the only thing I can think to say is: "You're addicted to porn? But girls aren't—"

"Into porn?" she interrupts. "Ha. You flatter the male species with your gender specific delusions. For your information, for every guy jerking it on the World Wide Web, there's roughly three-fourths of a girl going to town on herself. But I should be honest; my addiction is pretty complex. I'm addicted to porn, yeah, but only because I'm addicted to addiction. It's complicated."

Maybe this is why girls aren't into me. I don't say hello, I just ask them if they are addicted to porn. Not smooth.

"My last name is Coulter, by the way. Yours was Hawthorne, right?"

Desiree "Dez" Coulter. Even her name has an unrivaled sexiness. Just like at the diner, everything about her is an intense flirtation that makes me want to ask her if she wants to get a shake at Pritchett's instead of asking "Want to sleep with me?" I note the change and mark her as dangerous, but gorgeous, territory to approach with care. Kind of like a volcano.

"Yeah," I finally say as I attempt to get my proverbial feet back under me.

"Hi, Adam," she says in the most monotone way possible.

"Hi, Dez," I repeat in the same flat tone.

She purses her lips. "Already used to the dirge-form of greeting we use here?"

"I'm used to dirge tones. I live in a funeral parlor."

"Uh," Dez says. "No?"

I nod. "Yeah. No."

"No on the yeah or yeah on the no? You know what? No. You don't live in a funeral parlor?" Her tone rises at the end of parlor.

I do the same sort of tone rise with a "Yeah?"

She laughs, and Dad reappears out of a different hallway than he'd wandered down. He sees me talking to Dez and asks, "Who's this?"

She turns around, but I answer before she does. "This is Dez. We just met. She's addicted to porn and addiction in general."

Dad looks at me like I just stuffed a grenade into a baby rabbit's mouth.

"Aw, you should be proud of your son," Dez says, shaking my dad's hand. "He's blatantly honest and dirge-y already. He's going to do *so* well here." She winks at me, and I'm pretty sure I fall into an attraction coma.

She beckons us to follow her with a confident side nod. "Come on, I'll show you guys around."

Before I can take a step, Mr. Crotcher walks into the lobby with the guys I saw at Pritchett's. I recognize one of them.

He's a freshman, huge, white as Downy paper towels, and a starting varsity football player. His name's Mark, I think.

Mr. Crotcher waves at me, but then he sees my dad and his thick white eyebrows shoot up. "Greg, it's been so long. Are you joining us?"

Dad smiles and gives Mr. Crotcher a hug—the kind with the intense back patting.

"I think so," Dad says. "Adam and I both realized we need some changes."

"Father and son addicts?" Dez asks with this make-your-fingernails-sweat smirk. "Mr. Bunson's going to eat this up."

"Dez," Mr. Crotcher bows his head. "Good to see you. Is it a first or last line day?"

"Last," she says. "It is definitely a last line day. Hello, Knights of Vice." She waves at the three boys who came in with Mr. Crotcher, and they each take a few seconds to hug her.

This pisses me off, but I don't know why, and both the being pissed off and not knowing why is weird.

Mr. Crotcher grabs me by the shoulder and pulls me toward the other guys. "Adam, let me introduce you to the men of your Transparency Forum. This is Elliot."

A plump kid with a pair of hot pink headphones around his neck and swoopy blonde emo hair holds out his hand. "Hey, brother."

I guess it could be worse. He could be calling me "bro."

"Hey," I say.

"This"—Mr. Crotcher points toward a skinny Hispanic kid—"is Trey. Trey, this is Adam."

"Hey, Adam," he says.

"And last, but not least, this is Mark. He's the youngest and most in shape member of the Knights of Vice."

Mr. Crotcher looks at Dez like they have an inside joke.

"The name is gold," she says.

Mark doesn't offer me his hand. He just says hey.

"Hey," I say, thankful for his minimalistic approach to interaction. This kid's the best out of the bunch. I can already tell.

"Such dialogue. Much riveting," Dez says. "Come on, everyone, and Adam's dad, we're going to be late."

I WANT TO UNDERSTAND DEZ COULTER

Dez leads us all into a small conference room. I look for the circle of addicts holding hands, but all I see are people scattered among the four rows of chairs facing the podium. I haven't even moved out of the doorframe when a homeless guy named Eric introduces himself to me and my dad. He *quickly* tells us he struggles with alcohol addiction. When he asks me what I'm addicted to, I tell him Cocoa Puffs. He gives me a sympathetic look that makes me think he's forgotten he's the one with the addiction.

"You need tonight," he says. "It will help your denial."

A man with a thick mustache and Coke-bottle glasses, the man who met with Dez at Pritchett's last night, steps up to the podium. "Hello, hello, everyone."

"Hello, hello," the room responds.

Not even a minute into the meeting, and I've almost thrown up and punched a homeless guy. I take a deep breath and think of my playlists.

"If you could gather in your seats, we can get started."

I make my way to the front to sit next to Dez, but Mr. Crotcher waves me into a row with the Knights of Vice. I get to sit next to Elliot, "Brother of the Universe," and watch as Homeless Eric scores the seat next to Dez.

"Well," the man at the podium says, "welcome to Addiction Fighters. I'm Doug Bunson, but feel free to call me Doug. I see some new faces out there so I'll explain what we do here, and our basic structure." Doug pushes his glasses back up to the bridge of his nose. "Addiction Fighters is based off the Twelve Steps of Alcoholics Anonymous. Can anyone tell me what those steps are?"

Homeless Eric stands up. "One: admit our powerlessness. Two: believe in a greater power. Three: release our lives. Four: inventory our flaws. Five: confess our exact flaws. Six: be ready for God to remove our flaws. Seven: ask God to remove our flaws. Eight: be willing to make amends with those we've harmed. Nine: make amends with those we've harmed when possible. Ten: continue to inventory flaws and admit wrongs. Eleven: seek God in meditation and ask for power to carry out his will. Twelve: carry this message to others, and practice these principles."

Homeless Eric sits down like Hermione Granger after answering a question in class. This guy has to be a fraud. He's got to be here because he's addicted to the high of being a better addict than everyone else. Maybe that's his new way of making himself feel better.

"Very good, Eric," Doug says. "Addiction Fighters is here to help people struggling with addiction by practicing the steps Eric just outlined. We're an outlet for the soul. A judgment-free zone. As for our structure, each week looks a little different. Tonight, however, we'll have an extra-long time of introduction and sharing. I'll go first to give an example of how to share."

Everything else Doug says is lost on me. I'm sure it's some emotional story of how he found himself by coming here, and how happy he is to be a part of a group of people who suck at self-control. Instead of listening to him, I focus on Dez and organizing my playlists in my head.

I don't know how long I'm in my own world, but I snap out of it when Mark stands and walks to the front of the room. He hates this. I can tell by how small his steps toward the podium are. Maybe I could talk to him. Maybe he'd be willing to give me some advice on how to glide through Mr. Crotcher's program without dying of cliché addiction group-itus.

At the stage, he shares as quick possible. He winces throughout his speech, as though each spoken word is painful.

"I . . ."

Wince.

"Struggle with . . ."

Wince.

"Drug abuse. I'm nervous that I'm risking my chances of . . ."

Wince.

"Being a professional athlete."

When he finishes, he takes a breath of relief and returns to his seat. Elliot, Trey, and Mr. Crotcher pat him on the back like he just finished a marathon.

Just when I think this meeting couldn't get any more ridiculous, a woman takes the podium who's "addicted" to soap operas. She says she uses them to remove herself from her own problems. She knows she needs help because she refuses to talk to people unless they have the name of a character in her favorite show.

Soap operas.

Really.

Trey's addicted to sex, and in my opinion, that isn't a bad problem to have. I make a mental note to ask him how he gets women to sleep with him. Elliot's a self-harmer, which I saw coming with the hair, the calling everyone *brother*, and whatnot. Though it isn't surprising he cuts, it's strange because guys don't cut. Although, as soon as I think that, I hear Dez's voice in my head saying, "You flatter the male species with your gender specific delusions."

Speaking of Dez, she's walking up to the podium.

She clears her throat and lays a crumpled piece of paper on the podium. "I don't read whole books. I think you can learn enough by reading the first and last lines. For example, here I am in word form: 'We all have reasons for moving. I move to keep things whole.' That's the last line from *Keeping Things Whole* by Mark Strand."

I swear her voice sounds like the roar of a waterfall, like nature resides in her lips. She's smart. Can quote random lines from books. A true sultan of literary legacy.

Who is this girl?

"I'm Dez Coulter, and I'm addicted to addiction. By that I mean I'm addicted to the chemicals that come with addiction. That's why I cycle through everything you can possibly be addicted to: food, drugs, information, alcohol. Currently, I'm addicted to porn. I know it's only fueling my problems, but I can't stop. It's what I do. I move from thing-to-thing to keep myself whole. My addictions grow to a point where they don't create the necessary chemical reaction, so I move on to the next. It makes me a perfect storm, because by the time I get back to the addiction I started with, it's new enough to keep me going. I'll probably kill myself if I don't stop. Not because I want to, but because my existence is based on chemical pleasure. I'm a walking addiction clock, counting down to midnight, and I really want to stop before the arms swing too high. Thanks."

She steps off the podium and everyone claps for her. I'd probably be clapping if I weren't too confused to do anything but sit. How could someone so beautiful and perfect be so . . . messed up? More importantly, why am I even here? I'm not like these people. I'm not addicted to drugs, alcohol, or porn for that matter. I can stop thinking about it if I wanted to. It's just a nice release, which you need when you live in a world as shitty as this one. I don't need porn to survive. As a matter of fact, I'll prove it. I won't think about it at all tomorrow. Sure, I want to have sex, but what guy doesn't?

Dez returns to her seat next to Homeless Eric. He smiles at her, and they hug—for real hug—as though he understands her. I don't want to believe that Homeless Eric can understand Sexy Dez, but the look she gives him has undeniable soul. Suddenly, I *want* to be Homeless Eric.

I want to understand Dez Coulter.

AT ALL COSTS

I stare at my phone, waiting for Addy to respond to another apology attempt and avoiding my dad's constant looks. He's about to talk, but it's like his paternal vocal chords are rusted over with disuse and he can't figure out how he wants to start, so he keeps rubbing the back of his neck and taking deep breaths. Finally, he says, "I'm sorry I've been ignoring you. It wasn't intentional. It's just . . . I love your mom a lot, and I want to get her back."

I don't say anything. This is awkward. He hasn't actually said anything about The Woman since she left.

"I've been thinking that if I make myself better, if I can just figure out what she needs to see in me to be satisfied, she'll come back."

He clears his throat. He only does that when he's getting frustrated.

"I might be addicted to the hope of getting her back. Like it's my only motivator and maybe I'm too afraid to see what life without that hope would be like. You know?"

I don't know what to do, so I don't say anything. Dad and I used to be the joker type of father and son. If we went too deep, we didn't know what to do, but if we stayed too shallow, it just felt like we were failing. So, we got good at following up a dryly delivered, somewhat true fact with a master joke to keep it from going too far or deep.

The Formula of Well-Balanced Relations:
Statement of semi-truth + good joke = a safe and easy way to control acknowledgment of true feelings or thoughts

"Are you really not going to say anything?" he asks. "You've had plenty to say before now, yet, when I'm trying to apologize, you're silent. That's really unfair to me, Adam, and pretty hurtful."

"What do you want me to say?"

"I forgive you? You aren't a shitty dad? We'll get through this stuff together? It isn't fair for you to be pissed at me for being uninvolved, and then when I try to apologize, you become uninvolved."

He's right; I know he's right, but he also knows that we've never done this sort of honest thing, even before the divorce. This might be the first time he's ever apologized to me.

Dad sighs. "Ignoring your dad while he's apologizing isn't right, Adam."

"Dad, I'm sorry, and I forgive you, but I don't want you to overthink all of this and change everything about yourself. I just want you to look at me every once in a while. That's all. It's nice not having my dad always in my business." I internally nod at my use of The Formula of Well-Balanced Relations.

"But my not being in your business obviously went too far, because now you've gone off and—"

"I don't want to talk about it."

"Fine . . . but you're in trouble because of this major thing, so we have to meet in the middle. I'll figure out how to not disappear, and you have to let me interfere with some of your independence. I've given you too much."

"If there's one phrase no child wants to hear, it's *I've given you too much independence.*"

"Adam, do I need to remind you what you did? Why you're suspended from school?"

I physically can't say anything. It's like there's net in my throat catching all the words before they can come out.

"Anyway, what I'm trying to say is that some of your suspension is my fault, not all of it, but some of it. This is why I keep saying that we both need to change. I know I'm guilty, too, but I think if we stop blocking the world out all the time, we can do it together."

We pull into the parking lot of Pritchett's. I reach for the door handle, but he hits the lock button.

"I want your word that we'll change together. I'm serious, Adam. Our lives need a revamp."

"Okay." I press the unlock button, but Dad quickly counters.

"Adam, stop avoiding everything. That isn't how you fix problems."

"How would you know?" I snap. "You've always avoided everything, and suddenly you're like a bulldozer attacking the stuff that needs to be worked out full-speed with your loader down."

Dad rubs his eyes. "You're right. I just don't know how else to do it. I've never done this before, but it seems like your way of handling this isn't actually handling it. Mr. Cratcher's right. You need to start facing yourself."

"'Mr. Cratcher's right'? Damn. Are you in the Anti-Adam Order, too?" I reach for the handle a third time, and this time he doesn't fight back. "I—I have nothing to face," I say. "I'm fine."

"No, you're not."

"Dad, Mark's waiting."

"Adam, you're a smart kid when you want to be. Please use your intelligence to realize what you've done. This whole situation is an indicator that something's up with you."

"Bye." I shut the car door and head toward Pritchett's.

I don't get how all these people think I'm as messed up as the people at Addiction Fighters. I'm doing fine in school. Well, I *was* doing fine in school. I've never been in a fight. I've never done drugs. The societal factors that make a child "troubled" don't exist with me.

I, Adam Hawthorne, am a hub of fineness and solidity.

I walk into Pritchett's and see Mark sitting at a bar counter in a corner against the far back left wall. Not my normal spot. After Addiction Fighters, I asked him if he wanted to get a shake and he said yes. I did this un-Adam-like thing, asking someone to hang out, so I could get his thoughts on Mr. Crotcher's program and the Transparency Forum. I figured his distaste matched mine, and we'd probably have a decent conversation about how stupid this was. Now that I'm walking up to him, I have no idea why I thought this was a good idea. I feel my chest constricting. The words I thought I was going to say zip themselves into my throat.

"Hey," he says.

"Hey."

I sit down and look at a menu like I've never been here before.

"What do you think of the group?" he asks.

I put the menu down. "In my opinion, these kinds of programs are always shallow and forced. The people that experience 'change' are just addicted to encouragement and idealism. It's a bucket'a'bull."

"Better get used to it," he says. "If you play along with it, they'll leave you alone."

"So, I just have to act like I'm eating everything up, and Mr. Crotcher will think I'm fixed?"

"I guess." He pulls a cell phone out of his pocket to look at the time. His background is a picture of him pretending to choke a guy who looks just like him in a wheelchair. I laugh and point at it.

"Is that your brother? You guys look alike."

"Yeah, football injury."

"That sucks. So . . . how long have you been in the Knights of Vice?"

"Six months."

"Good lord, how's that possible?"

"I've been caught with coke three times. I've got to be with them for a year. Mr. Cratcher isn't that bad, though. He really does care."

"Seems like he's just bored because his wife's gone."

"Nah. He'll push your buttons, but he wants you to succeed. I just don't buy into all his 'humanity needs each other to survive' shit. I do just fine by myself."

"I get that."

Just like that, we run out of things to talk about.

The awkwardness of the moment almost hurts. I immediately regret asking him to hang out, and the look on his face is telling me he's regretting saying yes. I think being the only person in a room filled with five couples breaking up simultaneously would be less awkward than right now.

I fake a phone call. "Dad, I'm out with someone. Why do I need to come home?" I act like I'm pissed I have to go, but deep down I'm bubbling with joy.

I hang up the phone. "Sorry, man. We didn't even get to order anything."

"It's alright," he says. "I'll see you later."

"Sure."

Sorry, Mark, but we'll never have one-on-one time again. This was incredibly awkward, and I'd like to keep it from happening again at all costs.

WE WILL FACE OURSELVES

I'm in the Deception Pass State Park. The Deception Pass Bridge arches over water to my right, and I'm rooting around for cool shells under the carcasses of trees stripped naked in the Puget Sound and pushed onto the shore.

Addy is there. I'm telling her about a crush I have on a girl back at middle school. I'm telling her everything. How scared I am that if I say something, she'll tell me to leave her alone. She asks me why I'm so afraid of taking risks, but I'm in middle school so I'm not quite sure how to answer. I try and she must think it's good enough, because she goes on this long talk about how hard we hold onto these ideas of who we think we should be, and the whole time I just wonder how she got so smart and think about how lucky I am to have a sister who cares about me enough to tell me things that seem wise, but I don't understand.

The Woman and Dad appear at the shoreline. They're holding hands. That's when I know it's a dream. That I'm recalling the last vacation we went on. I try to stir myself awake, because I've been here before. It strikes me that Deception Pass Bridge is where truth always bends into sadness. The whole scene gets darker, as if someone put a filter over the sun. Suddenly, I'm sitting on the form of a bare tree and my whole family is pushing me into the water. Dread fills me as I drift into Puget Sound and watch my family wave on the shoreline. After a while, trees swallow their waving with a leafy maw, and all that's left is wilderness. Then the wilderness turns to the expanse of the Pacific Ocean, and I'm all that's there. I know this so deep that my bone marrow aches. There are no boats. No whales. No life at all.

Just me and salt.

—

A portal to hell—my alarm clock—opens on my nightstand, putting me in a scramble to close my computer before my dad comes in. I hadn't planned to fall asleep while staring at a picture of a curvy human version of Genevieve—the sexiness of the human version affirms I made the correct name choice for my car. I guess that's what I get for staying out late with awkward humans.

I hit the snooze button and turn over in my bed, ignoring the Deception Pass dream for the millionth time. I also attempt to ignore the fact that I'll be seeing Mr. Crotcher's face at a time too early for early birds over the next eighty-eight days.

My door squeaks open. It's my dad. "Adam, it's time to go to Mr. Cratcher's."

I don't turn over. "Can you revive your interest in raising me at like, lunchtime, instead of ass o'clock in the morning?"

"Hey," Dad says, "can you not beat me up with my mistakes every time we talk? I feel bad about it. You know that. At least give me a chance to work on it."

When I told him I wanted him to be around, I was just hoping for a "Hey, Adam" in the morning. I didn't think I'd hear *all* his thoughts about life and The Woman. It's a lot to handle out of nowhere, but his honesty's making it so I can't help but feel for him. He's trying, I guess.

"Wow, someone's sensitive," I say.

"No, someone's just extremely insensitive. Get up."

"Okay, okay."

I stand and shake my head. Today, I'll prove I'm not addicted to porn. I won't watch any videos, think about it, or make any playlists.

I've got this.

I run my fingers through my hair to get it back to its state of light brown craziness, throw on a gray and white long-sleeved shirt, slim-fit khakis, and my gray Vans. Downstairs, I grab a bowl of Cocoa Puffs and sit at a table lacking any sign of Nicholas Sparks.

"Whoa," I say, "where's your boyfriend this morning?"

"We broke up. I want to stop focusing on getting Mom back. It's time for a change, for the both of us. I think you getting suspended somehow was a great thing for us."

"A: I was framed by the Anti-Adam Order. B: that's a funny thing to say."

He raises an eyebrow before digging around in his milk for his last puffs of cocoa.

"A:"—he shakes his head—"you have to face what you've done eventually. B: you know what I mean."

C: I didn't do anything wrong, but whatever.

—

NPR's a letdown this morning. The local station's doing its fundraising telethon, which means my enlightenment's limited to "support us to get this over with" and "if you listen to us, you should want to support us."

I get to Mr. Crotcher's house at 4:59 but wait seven minutes before knocking on his door.

"Good morning," he says, letting me into the house. Without waiting a second, he asks, "What did you think of last night?"

I think of Dez but give him an indifferent "I don't know."

"Fascinating," he says, and it makes me feel like a lab rat.

He claps his hands together. "Well, let's get started. This morning we're testing microphones to figure out which ones to use for each instrument. Oh, do you know a female singer? I think a female singer is my album's missing piece. It won't be as country-sounding, mind you, or as simple. I'd also like much more instrumentation for my album. The first time I tracked it in '69, it was simple, but over the years, the lyrics, and I, really, have grown more and more complex and layered. An extra harmony here. A guitar riff there. It's fitting, don't you think? Life starts off simple, but over time, it grows so complex it can't ever be as linear as it used to be. That, my young friend, is one of the reasons why the good old days will never exist."

I realize I like how Mr. Crotcher talks outside of class. He doesn't complain about how things aren't like they used to be, or how he misses days when kids weren't on their phones all the time.

"What if you start the album off simply and add an instrument on each track?" I ask.

"Ah, now there's an option, another analogy of life. However, this brings us back to the idea of life, and I could be wrong about my initial assessment. Does life start with silence and end with silence? Or does it start with chaos and end in order?"

"Well, you can't hear anything when you're conceived," I say.

"Can you not? Why are there studies that claim playing classical music to a baby in the womb increases its IQ?"

"I mean, none of those studies actually prove the increased IQ is a direct result of the music. There are too many—"

"Variables?" Mr. Crotcher interrupts. "Just like the rest of life. So, from the outset, there is chaos, variables everywhere, and it stays that way for the rest of life." He chuckles. "I find it funny that somehow our lives are both monotonous and chaotic, such an impossible combination, but it is our reality, and we try to manipulate our indefinable reality into a definable one. It's the curse of man, desiring all knowledge. Instead of treating life as a gift, and living as gifted people, we waste our time working on our own conclusive encyclopedia that contains answers for why every single thing in the universe works the way it does."

He pauses and takes a deep breath.

"I am old, Adam, and I know many old men who will tell you they know hundreds things for certain because of the time they've spent on the earth. I warn you, do not believe them. They are full of well-intentioned, age-dented, delusional bunk." He smiles. "You should only trust old men who know two or three things for certain. Luckily, you are currently in the company of one, and I am about to let you in on one of my certainties. Are you ready for it?"

I shrug. "Sure."

"It's simple: there is always a variable we cannot account for." Mr. Crotcher turns to the window to watch a runner pass by on the sidewalk. He stays there for a little while as though his bones don't want to move.

I know we're talking about an album, but there's something unsettling about this conversation. Is it because it's so mysterious? Is it because I don't really believe there's ever a point in life where we can't account for all variables? It's not like he's asked me how I feel about something, or given me a lecture on addiction, or porn. Why am I feeling attacked? I take a brief mental vacation and direct a short film starring Dez naked.

Damn. I'm not supposed to be doing that today.

This sets me back a little bit, but it's not a big deal. I just wasn't paying attention.

"So, the beginning of the album is going to be chaotic?" I ask.

Mr. Crotcher snaps back to life and starts collecting microphone stands from a closet.

"Yes. Now that I've given it some thought, I'm certain that the beginning of life is the most chaotic of it all. But we should keep in mind that we are only going to record a musical album, not compete in a debate on which part of life is the most chaotic. There are many musical options available to us that we need to think through. We can't just align ourselves on the side of clever analogy because it makes us feel pompous and intelligent. Though, don't get me wrong; we deserve to be recognized for our stunning looks and peerless brilliance." He nods like he's signaling himself to get to work. "Can you grab that guitar out of the rack, please? The cutaway, not the hollow body."

I have no idea what a cutaway is, so I just walk over to his guitar rack and hover my hand over each of the guitars. He yips in affirmation when I touch the headstock of an acoustic guitar. I pick it up and marvel at the palm-sized hole worn in the wood below the strings.

Over the next hour, we cycle through a plethora of different microphones, testing the tone of each one. He explains the difference between condenser and dynamic mics, and why we need a condenser mic for the guitar—because the guitar has high frequencies and needs a sensitive mic to catch them. He finally picks one called the Mercenary KM69, which is apparently worth a lot of money even though it sounds exactly like all the others we've tested. After a little while, he disappears downstairs and gets two glasses of lemonade. We sit and drink. He looks out the window. I look at all the records on the wall.

"Do you ever feel exhausted, Adam?" he asks.

The question comes out of nowhere so I'm not sure what to say. "I'm sorry?"

"That twisting in your heart; that pull in your brain telling you things aren't what you want them to be. Does it ever tire you? It does me, always." He finally looks at me. "I know I said I wouldn't talk about this, but I feel like I need to, before it's too late. I have news for you, Adam: you *are* addicted to pornography."

Master should run away. Master should leave. He's lying. False! Gollum!

"Tell me if this sounds familiar. Last night, during Addiction Fighters, you compared yourself to everyone in attendance, even Dez, whom you couldn't take your eyes off. You told yourself you were fine, that you weren't addicted to anything, and decided to prove it today. How has that gone for you? Have you succeeded?"

There it is. This is the drop I've been waiting for: You are addicted. You need to be fixed. You aren't good enough. I stand and walk toward the door.

"That first night I came over to your house, you tapped your fork on your plate to a song on the radio. Do you remember that?"

I stop but say nothing.

"I asked you to stop, which, in my recollection, is when you started hating me. Is that true?"

Again, I say nothing.

He continues. "The song on the radio; it was an Amelia Hunt song. It was Gabby's favorite song. At the time, I couldn't handle how happy it made you because it was *her* song. Not yours. Seeing you enjoy it made me mad because how could something so treasured by my Gabby also be loved just as much by you? I'm sorry, Adam. I truly am. I was and continue to be a flawed man, and I hope you can forgive me."

I put my hand on the doorknob.

"If you don't come back, you will be expelled from school, possibly worse. You should have been reported to the authorities, but you weren't. You face a life-and-death choice here, Mr. Hawthorne. Choose wisely. You can leave if you wish, but I'll have to report it. And even if you do leave, I'll see you in my living room at seven-thirty tonight for your first Transparency Forum. There's no more running, Adam. You *will* face yourself." He picks up the Mercenary KM69 and shakes it in my face. "We *will* face ourselves."

I'VE NEVER READ IT

My Formula for Fineness

Amount of things I don't think about > things I do think about

Amount of things I don't think about > things that matter

Thinking about things that don't matter = same result of thinking about things that matter

Therefore,

Amount of things I don't think about = doesn't matter

I'm driving home, but I'm also on the log in the Pacific. The empty expanse of both places has me thinking about things I don't think about.

This is a thing I never think about:

Me sitting alone on the curb at the corner of Acker Street and Marvin Lane crying by guts out.

This is a thing I never think about:

It was midnight. Addy just told me The Woman asked her to move with her to Portland and she'd said yes.

I hugged my knees on that curb and did what my dad always told me was fine for guys to do—rock 'em, sock 'em ugly cry. I was in the midst of such a cry when Addy sat down next to me.

"Ten out of ten," she said, trying to cheer me up with a joke. "The scrunched eyes are a good touch."

I wiped my cheeks on my sweatshirt sleeve and then tried to flatten the scrunches out from underneath my eyes.

We sat silent for a moment.

This is a thing I never think about:

How that moment felt like a good-bye, and the weight that comes when you want to say everything, but can't seem to say anything.

"Adam, I'm not moving because of you. Our parents need us. You with Dad. Me with Mom. They've been there for us, now it's our turn."

This is a thing I do think about:

The problem with being smart and analytical is that people expect more from you. If I'd constantly been lying or drinking or getting in trouble at school, something, maybe Addy wouldn't have left. But I was all straight A's, clean shoes, and big words. I wanted to tell Addy that big words aren't synonymous with a strong heart. That words were only as big as the mouth that said them, and a person seen as only their words is about as true as gold-plating and as revealing as the tip of an iceberg.

This is a thing I don't think about:

I was just as lost as The Woman and Dad, and I was supposed to be in charge of my dad's recovery.

"I can't be Dad's wise and guiding wingman," I said. "I'm not like you, Addy. I can't just—"

"Bull, Adam. You *do* just. You always *do* just."

"Addy, please don't move to Portland."

"Mom needs me, Adam. I can't leave her alone."

"It's not our responsibility to fix our parent's hot cluster of a marriage fail."

This is a thing I never think about:

She stood, sighed, and then pulled me off my butt into a hug. "But it is our responsibility to love them."

What about me? I wanted to say. *I need you. I want you to stay here. I need you.*

The next morning, Addy was gone. So was The Woman. So was my dad.

This is *the* thing I never think about:

I was truly alone.

—

I've given up on not thinking about porn.

I've needed it to get through this horrible day. This day where somehow, in just a few short minutes, Mr. Cratcher made me think about things I don't think about. Where I've been up since ass o'clock. This day where Addy still hasn't responded, even when I called her three times. This day where I'm now sitting in Mr. Crotcher's living room with a bunch of random guys, listening to him talk about how the Transparency Forum works.

The forum is pretty much like the Addiction Fighters meeting, just on a smaller scale. He says it will help us be more "intimate and honest about life."

I'd almost rather be in the Hunger Games.

Almost.

"Of course," he says, taking a sip of water, "the end goal is to get you young men to a place where you could meet without me."

I'm pretty sure that none of us would *ever* do that.

"Anyway, I've taken up a good bit of our time, so let's get to business. Because this is Adam's first forum, let's go around and discuss our stories. Elliot, why don't you go first?"

Elliot sweeps the hair out of his eyes and flashes a brief smile. "So, my mom committed suicide when I was eight. After I told her I hated her."

Whoa. Way to come out of the my-life-sucks gate swinging.

"My dad blamed me for her death and kicked me out of the house, so now I live with my grandmother. I started cutting because I wanted to feel something else besides numbness . . ."

I zone out. I don't mean to, and I don't even know what I'm thinking about, but I know it has to do with me and girls and sex. I just want to do it. I think about Dez on top of me. Moving slow. Moving sexy. Why haven't I had sex yet?

From the way the world depicts high school, you'd think I would've scored by now. I feel a shot of adrenaline rush through me and I feel my hand reaching toward my phone.

". . . all that to say, this group has helped a lot. Trey, your positivity has been a huge help, so thanks for that. Adam, I'm stoked to have you here. I think if we can get past the awkwardness of the first few meetings, it will be great for all of us."

"Do you have any advice for Adam, Elliot?"

I pull back when I hear my name. My eyes were open the whole time, but now they're actually open and I see Elliot in thought. His head tipped the side to get the hair out of his eyes. "Yeah, stop being a fuck-up."

Everyone laughs. The way he says it is so self-reflective even I laugh.

"I'm kidding," he says. "I don't know. I guess, uh, you can fight all this if you want, but if you really want to change, you have to realize you're as fucked up as everyone else. Oh, and realizing that getting better doesn't happen if you run away from things is pretty big, too. You're addicted to porn, right? That's why you're here?"

I lock my jaw. The question sets off my Gollum brain. He's yelling. Messing up words by adding random *ses* to things that don't need them. I try to shut him up as Elliot gives an awkward glance to Mr. Crotcher as if to ask, "Was that not okay to say?"

"Adam?" Mr. Crotcher asks.

No. I'm not. I'm here because someone did something stupid at school and it wasn't me. I'm here because Mr. Crotcher made me be here. I say nothing.

"Al—alright," Elliot says, "well, I just said that to, you know, let you know we're all struggling too."

That's not what he was originally going to say. I see it in his in his eyes as he glances around at the other guys for help. Trey comes to his rescue and starts to share.

Trey is the oldest Knight of Vice, clocking in at nineteen. He didn't have any incredible trauma that inspired his addiction. He just was super popular in high school and liked women and, unlike me, was blessed with the ability to charm. At some point, he realized he was taking advantage of his popularity to have sex with as many girls as he could. After high school, girls weren't as readily available and suddenly he started feeling depressed and empty. He ended up spending most of his time on Craigslist, trying to find strangers to meet up with at least once a day. His parents intervened and told him about Mr. Crotcher's program, and he *willingly* joined. This fact alone solidifies my theory that Trey and I are too different to be good friends.

"I became a consumer," he says. "I still am, but now I believe the fight to be a better person is worth fighting."

Trey rambles on for forever, and at some point he tells me to let go of my judgments because they'll keep me from entering into the fold. To finish his time, he puts a hand on my knee and tells me how glad he is that I'm here.

Then it's Mark's turn. Thank God for Mark. He talks for a minute, maybe a minute and ten seconds. When he ends, we have this moment where he looks at me with weighty eyes and I nod in understanding. Neither of us want to be here.

"I'm probably the happiest you're here," he says.

"You're welcome," I say, and he laughs.

By the time the Transparency Forum peace pipe gets to me, the group time's gone over by fifteen minutes. Mark and I stand to leave. I expect Trey and Elliot to do the same, but they don't. In fact, it looks like their night is just getting started.

"See you guys later," I say.

Mr. Crotcher waves. "Bye, Adam. Bye, Mark. Feel free to stay if you'd like."

I pretend I don't hear him and open the front door. Mark bounds down the stairs.

"Hey, do you want a ride?" I ask. "That's my car right there. I can bring you wherever, no problem."

"Oh," he says. "Um . . . nah, don't worry about it. I've got to wheel my brother home from a friend's house. See ya."

"Alright, bye."

—

Some girl named Britannia is riding a lucky guy I'd prefer to remain nameless. As long as he doesn't have a name, I can replace him with myself. I'm filled with heat, on the edge of everything, and my cell phone rings. It scares the crap out of me, and my mojo turns into a distant memory. Though I'm pissed at the interruption, I'm glad I'm not turned on by fear. No one wants to date a guy who goes hard in a horror movie. I pause the video and check my phone. I don't recognize the number, but I answer anyway, trying not to sound to out of breath.

"Hello?"

"Is this Adam?"

Sweet mercy, it's Dez. Suddenly, I feel embarrassed or guilty. I'm not sure which, and I don't know why I'd feel either.

"Oh, hey," I say.

"What am I interrupting?"

Does she know? Do I play it off? I try a simple, "Huh?"

"It's stupid for people to ask if they're interrupting something because life's a bunch of actions that make up a whole. So, at any point in time, when I call you, I'm going to interrupt something. The question is: is the thing I'm interrupting worth interrupting? So, what am I interrupting?"

"I, uh—nothing really. Just reading."

"Aw, you're literate? How unique of you."

Her playfulness pulls me out of my stupor. "I really just wanted to be set apart from the rest of the pack, you know?"

She laughs. It's a mighty sound.

"I got your number from my sponsor. He had the sign-in sheet from the other night," she says.

I cock my head. "Your sponsor?"

"Yeah, you're supposed to find a sponsor to call in Addiction Fighters. You know, someone who's been through some of the process to help you talk through stuff?"

"Oh," I say.

"Anyway, she told me it wouldn't hurt to find some friends going through the addiction process to talk through stuff with. She also told me she thinks I'm more of a lost teenager than an addict, which is why I'm never calling her again. Anyone who thinks their shit is greater than mine is more lost than I am. So, I'm in the market for a new person to call, and I thought of the Knights of Vice. I figured you were as good a pick as any."

"Gee, thanks."

"So, you aren't an asshole. You care. That's a good start. I need someone who cares. Okay, so I'm just going to dive right in: I've been thinking about being utterly fucked up."

"Okay?" I'm unsure what she wants me to do or if I'm supposed to do anything.

"It's exhausting, you know? It feels like I'm hungry all the time, and everything I eat just pushes me closer to nowhere. I see the reason for the whole higher power thing in the twelve steps, but that confuses me, too. People always say God's the answer, but they never tell me what he's the answer to. What are the questions? How do I figure out the questions? It's like solving for X when the only information you have is that the answer is Y. But even then, if the only two variables we have are X and Y, wouldn't that mean X equals Y? That God is both the question and the answer? How the hell does that work?"

"You know, I'm a genius with formulas and even I don't know how it works. Sorry."

"I was just watching porn," she says, and I wonder if this conversation is legal. Guys and girls aren't supposed to talk about this topic unless it's a random joke here and there.

"Yeah," I say, feeling the words slide out of my mouth before I can identify them. "I was too, kind of."

WHAT?

Why would I say that? You don't say that to a girl as hot as Dez. Or a girl in general.

Or anyone.

"You were 'kind of' watching porn?" she asks dryly. "How do you do that?"

"I was wearing an eye patch?"

She laughs. "Well, I was watching some buff guy with a mustache named Rick do this nameless girl, and I got pissed. In fact, I got so pissed that I opened my window and threw my computer into my pool."

"Seems like a healthy response?" I laugh a little. "Why would you do that?"

"I'll answer by asking another question. A better one. What do you think about the cinematography of porn?"

"The cinematography of porn?" I repeat.

"Exactly, you don't think about it. Here's the thing: how often do you see the faces of the people actually having sex? Like, next to never, right? Mr. Cratcher told me at Addiction Fighters the average age a boy starts watching porn is twelve years old. I'm sure girls aren't too far away from that. Do you know what that means?"

I don't know what that means, and I'm not sure I want to know. This conversation is making me feel incredibly guilty, and there's not even anything to feel guilty about. The only reason I haven't hung up yet is because a girl outside of Addy is talking to me willingly, and even Addy isn't talking to me right now. I can't take this opportunity for granted.

"It means from the age of twelve, we're taught to be consumers instead of people who care. Think about it. There are millions of videos. You go from one to the next, always running away from the last feeling bored. What's worse is I realized I'm playing a part in the destruction of the line between sexuality and sexualization."

"Is that why you threw your computer in the pool?"

"No. I threw my computer into the pool because I had those revelations, kept watching, and finished myself off regardless. That's what pissed me off. I figured out what's wrong with porn, and I didn't even care."

"Should we be talking about this?" I ask, feeling awkwardness rush through my body, making me shift uneasily on my bed.

"Why shouldn't we?"

"Isn't this kind of discussion between guys and girls illegal or something?"

She scoffs. "Typical guy—you're okay with us using our mouths on your junk, but as soon as we use them for betterment of ourselves, or equalization of our genders, you tell us to shut up."

"Whoa, whoa, whoa, not what I was saying."

The phone is silent for a few seconds. I regret saying anything.

"Dez?"

"What were you saying?" she snaps.

"I was just saying guys and girls don't typically talk to each other about this stuff, that's all."

"Well, that's everyone else's problem. Now we're each other's problem. I mean, we're both eff'd to the max, right? So what does it matter?"

"I'm not eff—Yeah, I guess you're right."

Why's Master agree with the stupid woman hobbitses?

Because I think I'm having a moment where literally everything in my life is changing.

Something about her wry honesty hits me perfectly. The way she talks about her flaws. The borderline irrationally snaps at perceived slights. Her strength. This girl is poetry I've never heard before. Is that why I'm so up for agreeing with her? Is it simply just because she's a girl willing to talk to me? I might just be that shallow.

"Adam?" she says.

"Yeah, sorry."

"Ooh, this applies here! 'Happy families are all alike,'" she says. "'Every unhappy family is unhappy in its own way.'"

64

"What's that?"

"The first line of *Anna Karenina* by Leo Tolstoy. It just makes a lot of sense to me. Everyone may be unhappy in their own way, but at least we can all be unhappy together. That way we aren't as alone."

I like her.

I really, really like Dez Coulter.

"Do you like that book?" I ask.

"*Anna Karenina?*"

"Yeah."

"I don't know. I've never read it."

YES, MA'AM

For the first night in two years, I don't fall asleep with porn. Not because I want to quit; I just can't stop thinking about Dez or what she said about being consumers. As I fall asleep, Dez's voice echoes in my ears. Its sharp, sexy, gentle tone is my lullaby.

—

I'm standing on one side of the Deception Pass bridge with my family on the other, but the bridge is gone. Crumbled into the water below. I have *Settlers* cards in my hand, but none of them are ore so I can't build a new bridge. I don't have the resources.

I'm scared.

In seconds, my parents disappear. Then it's just Addy. She smiles then builds a town center, but it's not a tiny wooden token. It's a real town center with real people. A sign on the biggest building says PORTLAND. She goes inside and disappears.

Deception Pass turns into shadow, and it surrounds me like a prison. I can't see more than five feet in front of me.

Sometimes I hear voices, but I never know where they are—if they're in the forest or the water. If I try to chase them, I only feel like I'm getting farther and farther away from where I first was, where my family knew I was. Where someone could find me. Eventually I stop chasing the voices. To survive, I become one with the crush of darkness. I stop thinking about ways out and everything I had before the darkness came. I stop thinking of destinations and only consider the five feet I can see. This five feet is my new Deception Pass and I'm fine with it.

—

I wake up at 4:30 in chills. I stare at the ceiling. Dad comes in a few minutes later.

"You're already awake?" he says. "Don't tell me you're starting to enjoy going over to Mr. Cratcher's house. You're getting soft already."

"Dad, too early for insults."

"Time of day has never stopped you."

"Yeah, well, you're the wizened adult. I'm supposed to be the foolish sixteen-year-old. If you act like me, it throws the earth off its 23.5-degree axis."

"If you keep talking to me like this, I'm going to kick your ass so hard you'll be put on a 23.4-degree axis."

I laugh because it's the first glimpse of Old Dad I've seen since The Woman left. "There we go, that's better," I say. "Apocalypse not now, world saved."

Downstairs we both pour ourselves bowls of Cocoa Puffs. As I'm lifting a spoonful to my mouth, my phone buzzes. I drop my spoon into the bowl, causing milk to splash onto the table. I jam my hand into my pocket.

It's Addy.

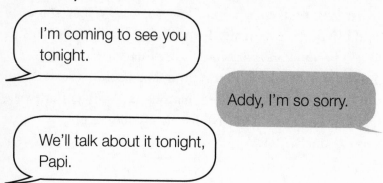

I'm coming to see you tonight.

Addy, I'm so sorry.

We'll talk about it tonight, Papi.

I put my phone back in my pocket. Even though I don't know what it means, just seeing her use the word Papi makes me feel like someone turned on a light. The amount of rightness that fills me makes me realize I can't shut Addy out anymore. I love her too much to lose her. Even if she disappeared thinking it was for the greater good, I can lose everyone else in the world, but not her.

Dad's eyes twitch back and forth between his cereal and the Nicholas Sparks book on the walnut mail table pressed against the corner of the wall.

I let out a small laugh. "You really want to read it, don't you?"

"I really want to."

"Why?"

"So I know what a good manuscript looks like."

"Bucket'a'bull, Dad. You rep Allison Beaker, Charles Mematiane, and sci-fi extraordinaire Colt Cax. You already know what a good MS looks like."

He throws his hands in the air defensively. "Fine, so I still want to figure out how to get your mom back. There are so many men who just give up on love, though. Why can't I be one willing to fight for it? Doesn't the world need that?"

I let out two good, fake throw-up noises and point at my neck. "Sorry. Cluster of Cocoa Puffs stuck in my throat."

"Grow up, kid," he says, shoving my head to the side.

The annoyed smile on his face makes me laugh. I've got to admit, I've liked my dad a lot more since I got suspended from school, and I don't say either part of that sentence a lot.

—

I wait until 5:05 to knock on Mr. Crotcher's door, but after five knocks, he still hasn't answered.

"Hello?" I say, reaching for the doorknob. It's unlocked.

I peek into the living room.

"Mr. Crotcher?"

I walk up the stairs on my tiptoes, trying to keep the old wood from groaning under me. I push the study door open, and Mr. Crotcher is in the corner, sitting at his computer. He isn't moving. Is he dead? I wouldn't be surprised if he was. The guy probably worked with the hottest roving minstrels and bards in the medieval ages.

I walk up to him and poke him in the shoulder.

He snaps awake, taking inventory of his surroundings. I glance at an open notebook by his hands. He's written something, but all I have the chance to read is *"Dear God, why am I"* before he slams the book shut and places it on a shelf above his desk.

He stands and stretches. "Adam, my apologies. I stayed up late last night trying to work out why some microphones weren't recognized by the DAW."

"The DAW, Mr. Crotcher?"

"Yes, it's an acronym for Digital Audio Workstation. The program you mix and record in." He pauses like he's just realized I've been calling him Mr. Crotcher. "What are your thoughts on the group last night?"

I don't want to talk about last night. I actually want Mr. Crotcher to go on another rant about music and how it's like life.

"It was fine."

"Fascinating."

"Why do you say that?" I snap. "You said that yesterday, too."

"Say what?"

"'Fascinating.' It's like I'm a lab experiment or something."

"Maybe you are." He gives me a knowing look. "Would it be a problem if you were?"

"Yeah, I don't want to be fascinating. I'm not just a result in some experiment. My reactions aren't just . . . fascinating."

Mr. Crotcher smiles. "How right you are. So then, answer me this. If you aren't fascinating, what are you?"

This may be the stupidest question I've ever been asked.

"What?" I say, disgusted.

"You are not a fixed outcome or a result. Correct?"

"Right. That's what I'm saying."

"Then what are you?"

"I—I don't know. Why is that even a question?"

"Think about it for a while. When you have an answer, let me know. Now, let's record the first track of our album. Just give me a few minutes to go over the lyrics first. I have some things I want to change."

———

Addy pulls into the driveway, her favorite singer, which also happens to be The Woman's favorite singer, Amelia Hunt, is blasting out her windows. I'm sitting on our stairs waiting for her and the first thing I see is that there's a bunch of stuff in the passenger seat.

She turns off the truck. Amelia Hunt stops singing "Ain't No Man Worth Your Soul" as Addy gets out and walks straight over to me.

"Okay, I'm going to get a little preachy, but you're going to listen to me, *and* you're going to like it, because I'm me. Capiche?"

I nod. I don't feel like finding out what would happen if I said, "No capiche."

"I miss my little brother. I miss him a lot, and I want him to come back. I get that the divorce hurts, Adam. I really do. But you're letting it kill you, and me. I haven't heard an honest feeling from you in two years, and I haven't been pushy because I didn't want . . ."

"I know," I interrupt. I feel more of a need to make sure I never have to go as long as I have without Addy again than to keep her from my feelings. "I'm sorry. I'm so, so, so sorry."

Addy's head snaps back. "Really? That's it? I didn't even get to my ultimatum."

"You don't have to. I've been a bad brother. Person. Just let me try to tell you stuff again."

"Well then," she says, walking back to her truck and grabbing a box and a duffle bag off the passenger seat. "I guess I'm moving in."

"Wait, what do you mean 'moving in'?"

She points to her truck. "I take bag and box, and I move back into my old room. Honey child, I stay with you for an indefinite amount of time."

"You're kidding me."

She smiles. "It was the ultimatum. You agree to be honest with me, and I move back for a bit to help you straighten out. You don't, I leave without saying another word."

The news makes me feel like my veins are flooded with light, but I play it off. "You wouldn't have silently left. You would have said something. You're incapable of just walking away."

She drops her stuff on the ground, gets in her truck, and drives away.

I watch the street, waiting for her truck to pull back around. My phone rings after a good five minutes.

"See?" I say, "you couldn't do it."

"Yo woman is here."

"Dez?" I yell. "Addy, where are you?"

"Yep. Ooh, what's this? She's waving me over to sit with her? Look at me. I've arrived."

I hear Dez's voice over the phone. "Where's Frenchie?"

"On the phone," Addy says.

"Tell him to get over here before I retrieve my computer from the pool."

"Papi," Addy says. "Dez says—"

"Yes, ma'am!"

FOUR LES CLOVER

I walk into Pritchett's and see Addy and Dez sitting over in a corner booth, both balancing french fries on their noses. As I approach, I quickly realize I have to choose a side. Do I sit next to Dez or Addy? If I sit next to Dez, it will be like climbing Mount Everest and putting my flag at the peak. I'll be declaring something I'm not sure I want to declare: I like you.

I'm a foot away.

"Which side will you choose?" Addy asks, drawing even more attention to my predicament.

Dez points at the french fries. "Either way, we have the chosen food of your people ready for you."

I sit next to Dez.

Addy lets out a shout of victory and, much to my frustration, Dez groans.

"Now I have to pay for the food, Adam!" Dez says.

I smile. "You were betting on where I was going to sit?"

Addy nods. "Yep. And my guess was right. Adam, *tu tienes cojones grandes*."

Dez laughs, choking on the ice cube she's chewing on. She slides the fries closer to me. "I like you, so I think you made a great choice."

The three of us talk about everything. The Bothell, Washington renovation. People from Bellevue. Addy's boss. How each of us has a different visceral reaction to rain. Finally, an hour or so later, Dez has to go, so I slide out of the booth to let her out.

"I'll see you guys later?" she says, the booth squeaking as she stands.

"Certainly," Addy says

I point at Addy. "What she said."

Dez smiles. "Bye, Hawthornes."

She disappears out of Pritchett's along with the thousands of forest animals that sing her name.

"You ready to go home?" Addy says. "Now that your love is gone, how could you ever survive one more minute out?"

I roll my eyes. "I'm totally suffocating under the weight of my unrequited love."

"Looks like it."

"No."

"No?"

"No, I'm not ready to go home."

"What are you ready for, then?"

I know Addy deserves my honesty, so why does it feel like I'm latching on to a tooth with a pair of pliers and yanking? Is the hardness a sign I'm not ready? A sign that no one can ever understand me? That people will only ever leave me on curbs at intersections and on trees in Puget Sound? I close my eyes. I can't lose Addy. So whatever the result, I know I need to try, and I decide that I'll carve my words and feelings out with a Swiss Army knife if I have to.

"I'm ready for talking, but I'm going to need another shake. A strong one."

She smiles. "Mint Butterfinger?"

"Stronger."

"Whoa. Oreo Butterfinger?"

"I think so."

We order a second round of shakes, and when my Oreo Butterfinger slides onto the table, I shove the straw in my mouth and take a giant, slow, and agonizing first milkshake gulp. I close my eyes, and take a breath.

"Adam, it's okay. I don't want you to feel like you have to castrate yourself in order for this to work. Let it come natura—."

"Home life has sucked. I've ignored it since you left, but it's sucked. For a while, I tried to get Dad to snap out of it. Making jokes and stuff, but it never worked."

Addy grabs her shake and then settles into the booth. Her eyes are focused on me. Her ears, all mine. The look on her face is one that says, "I've missed your heart" and suddenly I'm brought back to our *actual* vacation to Deception Pass. Where I'm telling Addy everything.

I talk to Addy about my frustrations with Dad and The Woman. What it's been like since she left. I talk to her about how they both hurt me, but I don't talk to her about how she hurt me, why I was suspended, and I definitely don't talk to her about porn. As weird as my relationship with it is right now, I want to keep it safe. It's the one thing I have that's never frustrating. If I'm mad, Addy might not be there, but a million naked girls are. Always.

She doesn't press me for information. She doesn't try to unnaturally shove herself back into my brain. She asks clarifying questions every once in a while; she even orders me a third milkshake. What she does might not seem like much to anyone watching, but, to me, it's everything.

She loves.

And after the last two years, the literal sight of her sitting there soaking in everything I say, feeling my hurt, being with me, is like finding a river running through the middle of the desert. It's like being told things that seem wise, but I can't understand.

—

The next morning, I wake out of another Deception Pass dream. This one feels so heavy that my unusual and unexplainable stint of not looking at porn ends before I go to Mr. Crotcher's.

It's 4:56 on a Sunday morning so no one's on the roads. Unlike yesterday, Mr. Crotcher's waiting for me at the door when I pull into his driveway, so I pretend I'm on the phone. I don't want to go into his house early or on time. Traditions are sacred. My traditions have been off lately, and I'm afraid to find out what would happen if I mess with this one.

We go up to his study, and he sits down in his office chair. "So I've been considering songs, Adam. Some songs on this album have the same title, but the lyrics have changed so much that they're completely different. Some songs I've replaced entirely. I know there's some lost in my journals and books that should probably go on the album, but I'm just too tired to look. Right now, I have nine picked out, but historically, the album has had eleven songs." He opens the DAW and starts clicking around. "I'm considering writing a twelfth, but I'm not sure if I'm the one who should write it." He looks at me, waiting for me to volunteer.

"I'm not going to write anything. I suck at that kind of stuff."

"Ah, but you don't. Despite your fork tapping, one of the reasons I brought you here to help me with this is because I am very aware of your poetic capabilities. I grade your papers."

"Do you make everyone in your programs write songs?"

He smiles. "No. You are the only one who I've subjected to this elegant torture."

"Why me?"

"A songwriter's heart is a forest of glass," he says. "The people we invite into them must know how to walk among the trees."

I laugh. "So you decided the kid who hates you the most was the best choice? The fork thing *was* when I started hating you, by the way."

"I know," he sighs, "and I'm sure I didn't make it better by being persistent with you."

"Is that what you call it?"

"You just remind me of me when I was your age, and I wasted most of my young life. I haven't . . .I don't want to see you do the same."

I don't know what to say, so I don't say anything.

"What if we cowrote a song?" he asks, changing the topic for me.

"Doesn't this album have personal significance to you? Why would you want a co-writer who can only rhyme 'do' with 'I love you'? That's like, the oldest and most overused trick in the lyrical book."

He looks at me with disbelief but then says, "That trick could work considering I want to write a love song."

"A love song?"

"Yes, I've never had one on the album. I have many songs that take honest looks at my failures as a husband. Lots of songs about love, but all of them fixated on how bad I am at it . . ."

He stares out window but snaps back a few seconds later.

"I have no songs that just simply praise Gabby for being loveable. You've heard the type before, the sappy songs people play on anniversaries and wedding days."

He rubs his temples. "It's a flaw of mine that I cannot look at things without seeing dichotomy. Every coin has two sides. I just happen to have a fixation on the worn and beaten one. It was often a sore spot for Gabby. She often said something like, 'You've written a jingle for a Styrofoam manufacturing company, but you can't write a pure romantic song about your wife?'"

He shakes his head. "It is true, there is a shortage of men who write love songs specifically about their wives. Ha. Amazing. Five years after her death, she continues being right."

"What are the album's song titles?" I ask.

"Always different, though I would very much like to return to . . ."

Instead of finishing his sentence like a normal human, he closes his eyes for a second, and then opens them and stares out the window again.

"Mr. Cratcher?"

"Yes, let's record. I apologize."

——

It's nighttime. Addy's doing some telecommute work at the nearest coffee shop, and I'm staring at my computer, itching to surf some videos. After my porn fiesta this morning, I thought I was done feeling guilty about it, but there's something pushing against my gut, making me feel a tiny bit of unease about my normal ritual. It isn't much of a feeling, but it's enough to have stopped me from typing "free porn" into the search bar three times now.

My phone lights up with a number I don't know. I pick it up as fast as I can. "Hello?"

"Adam?"

It's not Dez. It's definitely a guy. That's incredibly frustrating.

"Trey?"

"Hey, man, Elliot and I are going to head over to Pritchett's for a milkshake. Want to come?"

"Yeah, sure."

Good.

Lord.

Has the sky opened up and begun to rain down fire and smoke? Why would I pass up my sea of digital women?

"Alright," Trey says, "we're heading over there now. Meet you there?"

"Yeah, sure. Is Mark coming?"

"No, he said he had stuff to do."

No, he doesn't have "stuff" to do. Well, except drugs, which is definitely the "stuff" he's doing. I only know because "I've got stuff to do" is my code for "I'd rather look at porn." I guess it's not a very original.

"Cool," I say, "I'll see you over there."

I stand and give my computer a confused stare. I feel like we're breaking up or mad at each other, and it makes me feel uneasy. I sigh and then head downstairs, thinking about how pathetic it is that I feel like I'm cheating on an inanimate object.

I poke my head into my dad's office. He's skimming through what he (and the rest of the literary agent world) calls the slush pile. He gets *at least* twenty emails a day written by aspiring/desperate authors who want to escape the suffocating loneliness of unpublished writing.

"Anything good?" I ask.

"You know, sometimes I have to respond to aspiring writers with 'I'm sorry, your stuff just isn't for me,' but I wish I could tell the truth. For example, this guy's dialogue sounds like two toddlers talking about tax fraud. The thing is, if that were actually the scenario, I might ask to see the full manuscript. I just wish people stepped back for a second to look at the shit they dress in flower costumes."

"That's good stuff, Dad. Tell your potential clients, 'I don't represent shit in flower costumes, but some other agent might.' Anyway, I'm going to hang out with Elliot and Trey at Pritchett's. I'll be back later."

He looks at me as though I just told him I'm going to go look at a house with my realtor.

"What?" I ask.

"Nothing," he smiles. "Go. Leave me alone and bring me back an Irish cream and Heath shake."

I hop in Genevieve and NPR comes on. Before I can back out of the driveway, my phone rings.

"Hello?"

"Why are there no black lawn gnomes?"

I suddenly feel stupid-bucket' a' bull-warm, and my hands stick to the steering wheel.

"Hey, Dez."

"Are we that racist of a society to not have diverse gnomes?"

"Maybe diverse people don't care about garden gnomes?"

"You can't know that. You're white."

"You know what? You're right. I'm calling my lawyer."

"For real?"

"Yeah, I totally have a lawyer."

"What an American you are," she says.

"Should I just save your number?"

"You don't have my number saved yet?"

I feel like an ass for saying no.

"Well, gosh, Adam, should I have picked another Knight of Vice?" She sounds genuinely hurt and angry.

"Dez, my not saving your number isn't a reflection on how I feel about you."

"Well, what is a reflection on how you feel about me?"

Is this a trap question? It has to be. Navigate wisely, Adam.

"I'm considering making you a black garden gnome when I get back to school."

"Don't do that for me, Adam. Do that for the world, for society, but if you do do it, you can give it to me. Just make sure it's for society, not me, but still give it to me."

"How's . . . addiction going?" I ask.

"As swimmingly as ever. Now that I've subjected my computer to waterboarding, I'm worried I'm going to pick something else up. Like this beer my dad left here. Like right now. Hold on."

"Dez? Should you be moving onto something else? Isn't there an AA step for that or something?"

I pull into Pritchett's just as Elliot and Trey walk through the door.

"What do you know, Porn Boy? You were sitting there judging everyone at Addiction Fighters the other day. I know the arched eyebrow of the 'at least I'm not that bad' face when I see it."

"Ouch, Dez. You were the one who called me, remember?"

"Yeah, sorry. I'm just frustrated. I want to be fixed. My dad yelled at me for not being driven enough again tonight. It's like a nightly thing, now. Aren't I too young to be this broken?"

The thing Mr. Crotcher said about the beginning years being the most chaotic pops into my head, and I get a little pissed at myself for thinking this hard. I don't understand how I can avoid thinking for two whole years and then be washed away in it in a matter of days.

"I don't think so," I say. "We're all born into chaos, and I don't think it ever goes away. We just get better at learning how to find beauty in it." I say this, but I haven't tried finding beauty in anything but women, especially the naked variety.

"Where's the beauty in a girl who cycles through life-threatening addictions because her parents expected her to be a banking expert by age fifteen? Whatever. Just save my number."

Click.

"Dez?"

Silence.

I add Dez Coulter to my contacts, hop out of Genevieve, and wander into Pritchett's. My typical sitting place is unoccupied. Seeing it empty and knowing I won't sit there makes me sad. I scan the place for Trey and Elliot and see them waving at me from the back of the diner. I wave back and then weave through the sea of green diner booths, making my way toward the bathroom. While I put toil back in toilet, I ignore a strange tug in my chest that I don't recognize. I just know it has nothing to do with my bowels. I also ignore the voices saying, "You're addicted to porn, Adam. Feeding the addiction isn't a good thing" and make a playlist. I decide I'm particularly excited about a video called Four Les Clover.

A LITTLE LESS LIKE
A PIT OF DISPAIR

"My family's from El Salvador, but that doesn't mean I watch *Dora the Explorer*," Trey says.

Elliot shrugs. "I just figured."

"White people always 'just figure,' and it needs to stop." Trey smiles. "But really."

I laugh again. I've been laughing all night, which is kind of awesome. I'd gone to the bathroom as soon as I walked into the diner because I wanted to put off an awkward meeting-Mark rerun. I didn't expect to actually have fun with these guys.

"I agree, Trey," I say. "That's why I've always tried not to think. It's safer that way. No drama, no racism, no constant worrying if you're doing the right thing."

"Listen to this guy," Trey says with dramatic hand gestures. "No, wait. Don't listen to this guy. That's horrible."

We share a laugh, but Elliot looks at me like he's got me figured out. "You actually think that, don't you?"

I pick up my milkshake. "Is it a problem if I do?"

Trey lets out a breath of air, like my statement is the heaviest thing in the world. "Well, I think so. Yeah, actually. It isn't going to get you anywhere. That's for sure."

I don't know if it's the giddiness I feel from a sudden Dez-filled life, or if Pritchett spiked the shakes tonight, but I don't stop talking. It's the point of the conversation where I shouldn't be talking any more.

Talking = thinking.

Relationships = thinking.

Everything I'm doing right now = thinking.

"I guess maybe I used to think that? Well . . . maybe I still do. I don't know."

"Addiction Fighters really got to you, huh?" Trey asks with a victorious smirk.

"Kind of. I guess. I don't know. A lot is getting to me."

On a completely different topic: porn.

I can't stop thinking about it. It feels like my junk has a strange non-physical itch for it.

"This is important, A, but hold on," Elliot says. "Mr. Cratcher's calling."

I point at Elliot's phone. "Mr. Crotcher calls you? How adorable."

Trey lets out a manufactured laugh, the laugh people use when they don't like what you said, but they don't want to make you feel bad. It reminds me that I really need to stop talking. These guys aren't going to understand me, and they can't do anything for me I can't do myself.

Master speaks truth. I sees it coming, I does. They will hurts you. Gollum!

I'm about to get up and leave when Elliot's face turns paler than Moby Dick.

"Yeah," he says, and a few seconds pass before he speaks again. "Yeah, I'm with them. We'll be over in a minute."

We hear Mr. Crotcher hang up, but Elliot doesn't take the phone from his ear. He just sits with a look of terror on his face, staring at the space between our heads.

"Elliot, what's wrong?" Trey asks.

"It's Mark," he says. "He's dead."

—

$$Mark + drugs + too\ many = Mark's\ dead.$$
$$Mark's\ death + me = questioning\ everything + only\ being\ able\ to\ think\ in\ formulas.$$
$$Mark + addiction = death.$$
$$Me + addiction = death.$$
$$Mark = death.$$
$$Mark = me.$$
$$Me = death.$$

—

Cure for not thinking about porn? Have a friend—or whatever Mark was—die while thinking about it. It's four in the morning and, instead of staring at the computer, I'm staring at the ceiling. Helpless.

My dad won't wake me up this morning. He stayed up until three last night waiting for me to come home because I stayed with Elliot and Trey as long as I could. Mark had been in the Knights of Vice for six months. I was/am a mess, and I'd only known him a week. The other two took his death really hard, like uncontrollable sobbing hard.

I think about waking Addy, but she stayed up with my dad and she gets really crabby when she doesn't sleep. I pick up my phone and scroll down to my newest contact.

I call her. Each unanswered ring makes me very aware that I'm on the uncharted seas of Adam Hawthorne's emotion.

"Hi, this is Dez. There are 1440 minutes in a day. Pick another one and try again."

I hang up before I have to leave a message. She's probably sleeping, and I don't want to talk to a machine right now. I throw the phone onto the bed, and suddenly everything in me feels like it's swallowed by the black space of Deception Pass.

The phone rings.

I gasp in relief.

"Hello?"

"To what does my REM sleep owe the pleasure of this call?"

"Mark's death."

A beat of silence reigns.

"Shit."

"The only thing I can think about is that I'm Mark," I say. "I know that's weird. He was addicted to drugs. I'm not addicted to drugs, but I'm—I've figured out I can't stop thinking about porn. Watching it. Needing it. Even if I wanted to, I don't think I could stop. I don't have control over it."

"How'd he die? OD'd?"

"Yeah. His vice killed him, but at the same time, I feel like his vice hurt me, too. It's like . . . we're all volcanoes and we wander around engulfing each other in our disaster."

"We're all natural disasters," she says.

"Yeah, or maybe we're all unnatural disasters hoping to figure out how to be natural."

"How are the other Knights of Vice?"

"Sucky, but I guess everyone's sucky."

"I'm typically not an optimist, but maybe consider some people somewhere in the world are happy? It might make you feel less like a pile of crap. Just a suspicion."

I rub my eyes and look at the soon-to-spawn portal to hell on my nightstand. It's 4:45.

"Dez, I have to go."

"Are you okay? Wait . . . that's an incredibly unintelligent question. Are you miserable?"

"Yeah."

"That means you're normal."

I don't want to hang up. I want to be with Dez Coulter's voice for the rest of the day.

"I'll talk to you tonight," she says, and though I can't make myself smile, my insides seem a little less like a pit of despair.

EVERY SINGLE CATEGORY

I knock on Mr. Cratcher's door. "Hello?"

He answers right away.

"Adam, come in."

I walk inside, and instead of going straight to work, Mr. Crotcher sits down at his computer and clicks on something. Music pipes through his studio monitors, so I sit down and listen, assuming a one-liner filled rant will follow.

The song finishes a few minutes later, and I remain still. It was a good song, but I'm mostly just curious as to what Mr. Crotcher's going to say about it. His eyes are closed, but his mouth's open like he's about to speak.

He shifts in his seat. "'There's a blaze of light in every word, it doesn't matter which you've heard, the holy or the broken hallelujah.'"

I don't say anything.

"Mr. Leonard Cohen, the author of the song, is saying something to you, Adam. There's a blaze of light in every word, both the holy and the broken." He turns his gaze to me. "Have you thought about my question?"

The guy asks me eighty questions every morning. I can't remember which one he's talking about.

"What are you?" he asks, registering the forgetfulness on my face. "If you are not a fixed outcome, or a result, what are you? What is Mark?"

"Dead?" I ask honestly.

"Keep thinking about it. Think about it in terms of Mr. Cohen's song and mathematics. Now, it's time to start recording. We will do it in memory of Mark."

I set up a vocal mic, and Mr. Cratcher clips a mesh screen to the front of it. I'm about to sit and start the DAW when he grabs the mic in his palm, clutching it like he's in pain. He looks out the window again, and before I can ask him if he's okay, he says, "I've changed my mind. Let's record the last song and work toward the beginning of the album."

I scratch my head. "Doesn't that mean we have to decide if we want the album to be crazy at the beginning and simple at the end, or vice versa?"

Mr. Crotcher smiles his all-knowing old man smile. "I'm not sure if that will be my decision."

What on earth does that mean?

"It's your album, Mr. Cratcher. Why wouldn't you make that decision?"

"Many choices come down to life and death," he says, "and everyone has to choose it for themselves."

I throw my fingers over my eyes and let out a low growl.

Mr. Crotcher + words = mind coma.

"A: I don't know what that means, and B: that doesn't answer my question."

"How can you know it doesn't answer your question if you don't know what it means?"

"Gah, okay, can we just . . . record or something?"

"Yes, let's do a few tests to make sure our setup is right."

My phone rings. It's Addy.

I pick it up and walk to the other side of the studio. "Hey, Addy."

"Hey, are you doing okay?"

"I guess. I'm just . . . confused."

"I'm sorry. Listen. I have to run back to Portland to turn in some paperwork I forgot I had to the main office. Do you want to come with me? Get your mind off things? You can bring Dez, or your new dude friends. Maybe Trey will want to come?"

"Elliot and Dez are in school and Trey is working. Do I have to see The Woman?"

"Nope, we don't even have to go to her house."

"Alright, can we go after I'm done with my morning internship of torture?"

"Sure thing."

—

Addy sings along with Amelia Hunt as we drive down the highway, and I do my best to keep from thinking about all the times I came home from school to hear The Woman playing this album in the living room.

"So," I say, trying to keep my brain busy. "How's Brennan. Wait, Brad? Bread?"

"Brent," she says. "He gone. No more Brent."

"Aw, I'm sorry. Why?"

"Because he needed to die."

I reach for the volume knob to turn it down. "For real, Addy, who broke up with who?"

"It's whom. Do we have to get into this now?"

"Aha! See? It isn't fun, is it?"

"I broke up with him."

"Was it messy?"

She nods dramatically. "Totally. No, it wasn't at all. We just weren't into each other. Different personalities, I guess."

"Is that what you told him? Or is that what you're telling me?"

"What do you mean?"

"You get along with everyone, Addy. Personalities don't exist for you. Why did you break up with him?"

She flicks me in the forehead. "Gosh, you're an annoying little twerp. Because I was scared. He started talking about marriage, and making babies, and mortgages, and I just . . . flipped out."

"Because of the divorce."

She rolls her eyes. "Yes, because of the divorce, but that doesn't mean you're off the hook. You can't just, I don't know, do what you've been doing. Me being affected by the divorce isn't an excuse."

"I know."

"Do ya?"

Something I haven't ever said to anyone settles on my tongue. It brings along boatloads of feelings I've been ignoring in hopes they'll go away. I hoped that if I didn't pay attention to them, they'd stop mattering. I try to continue making them not matter, but the feelings push the words off my tongue before I can stop them, which is probably what Addy wants.

"The Woman didn't even say good-bye to me, Addy."

She isn't surprised by this. She just sighs like she's been waiting for it. "I know, Adam. I know."

"She left. No explanation. No, 'I'm sorry.' Nothing. She was supposed to be one of the few people who loved me so hard I could trust her with everything, but she just disappeared."

The next thing I'm about to say, I've thought about since Addy literally left me on the curb. I know she wanted the best for everyone. That it wasn't just a normal abandoning, but intention wasn't enough.

"And you—" My throat closes up. The dark of Deception Pass reminds me that I'm alone. That Addy is gone. My Gollum brain is screaming. "You followed her."

As soon as I say it, I feel a giant gate lift in my chest. "You left me with a dad who only cared about getting her back. You left me, too. Everyone left me for The Woman."

Addy's face goes flat. "I didn't leave you. We talked about it and agreed that Mom needed me and Dad needed you."

"But I needed you. I wasn't strong. I was so lost and hurt, and you wanted me to be this wise guide for Dad, but I needed a wise guide for me and you left."

"Damn it, Adam! You never told me that!" she yells, slamming her fist on the horn. "You just . . . stopped. Everything. Why didn't you say you needed me before I left? Why didn't you say that while we were sitting on the curb? Why did you just agree to me going with Mom if you were just going to get angry at me? If you knew you needed someone to be there?"

"I don't know! I was in middle school. How could I have known that?"

We're silent for a good five miles, but I know it won't last. With her, it never lasts. It's why I love her so much.

"I'm sorry," she says. "I wasn't trying to abandon you. I just . . . thought you were okay. You're always so well-spoken and smart and I thought me leaving was what we'd both decided."

"I mean, I don't know. We're both at fault, I guess. I just needed to say it. Get it out of my head."

"I understand, but I'm still sorry. I just feel like I'm part of the problem, you know? I'm sorry."

I nod. "I know. I forgive you."

"So what's next for us, Adam? What's next for a couple of kids like us? All messed up and nowhere to go."

I laugh. "I don't know about you, but I'm going to date Dez Coulter and make it through my suspension without killing Mr. Cratcher."

"Ooooh, goodie. Honey child, I like her."

"Yeah, I do, too. A lot. A lot. A lot. I like her with all of the 'a lots' available for use in the English language."

"How many 'a lots' equal love?"

"I wish I knew. You know what I do know, though?"

"Nothing," she says. "You're a punk-ass kid who knows nothing."

I point at the highway sign. "There's a Jimmy John's at the next exit."

She swerves into the next lane but gets back into the one we were in only a few seconds later. "Sorry, squirrel in the road."

"Addy, you may find this dramatic, but if you don't feed me, I'm literally going to die."

"You know what else is a cause of literal death?" she asks, changing lanes again and getting on the exit ramp. "Actual death. And if you abuse the word *literally* again, that's what will happen to you."

—

It's one o'clock in the morning.

I'm staring at the computer again. My knee's bouncing like I'm in withdrawal. This echoes what I've been thinking, what everyone's been saying.

I, Adam Hawthorne, am addicted to porn.

I need it to make me think less, to make me feel less, to numb me. After Addy and I got back from Portland, I haven't been able to stop thinking about Mark's death, about how his vice led him around like a dog on a leash.

Everything's an incredible heaviness.

I swing the laptop screen up and type in my favorite porn site URL. My heart's throbbing, my junk metaphysically itching. A page of thumbnails explodes onto the screen, and I feel the adrenaline surge through my veins. Suddenly, all I can think about is her, and her, and her, too.

My phone rings. I'm sure it's Dez. I know it's Dez—she's the only one who would call me this late, but I can't right now. I don't need humans. I need Glitter. Someone who doesn't make me think about anything except how hot she is and raw sex.

The phone stops ringing.

I make a playlist.

—

I feel horrible when I randomly snap out of sleep at 3:00. I look at my computer like he betrayed me. Did he? Why do I feel so miserable? Death still hangs over me, but I don't know if it's because I suddenly see mine on the horizon or if I'm still hurting over Mark's. Maybe it's both. Either way, I want to feel better. One minute awake and I need relief. So I give it to myself.

Relief courtesy of Stacy and Daniela and Avery and Harmony and Lane and Mattie and Linn and Ashley and Lacy and Siphora and Jessica and Unnamed Girl and Bored Housewife and Hot Schoolgirl and Neighbor's Sister and Hesitant Teen Thinking She Was At A Modeling Agency Interview and and and and and and and and and and and and and and and and and

—

It doesn't work.

I feel the same amount of hollow. Possibly even more. This feeling always hangs in the air like cigarette smoke after I finish, but I was always able to write it off and ignore it. Why now? What's wrong?

I need real sex? Maybe I need a different category or something. Something more intense. Harder. So, for the next two hours, I search through Every. Single. Category.

I DIDN'T THINK ANYONE WOULD EVER NOTICE

The game was called Word Hunt.

My mom would listen through an Amelia Hunt song and pick out two words that grabbed her along the way. The first word was called "the starter," and the second was "the tie in." The point of Word Hunt was to make a vocabulary path (dictionaries were allowed) that connected the two words via synonyms. For example, let's say the starter word was *vicarious* and the tie in was *Enumeration*.

Vicarious. Secondary. Extra. Count up. Addition. Add. Figure. Number. Enumeration.

The person who actually connected the words, and had the least amount of connections in five minutes, won.

A few months before The Woman told me she was leaving, Amelia Hunt was playing in the living room. I walked downstairs after doing homework, and she had a whiteboard set up in the living room. On it, she'd written the words *unsatisfied* and *temptation*.

I gathered the family. We played.

"Let me see what you got, Adam?" The Woman had said.

Dad laughed. "Adam's got jack. I saw him over there writing down random words and coming up with synonyms."

"It's definitely not me. I was just thinking up French words the whole time, which really should make me the winner," Addy said.

I smiled. I'd made a ten-word path.

I'd won that game, but I lost at what came after.

I'd realized the words *unsatisfied* and *temptation* weren't ever together in an Amelia Hunt song. I don't know if anyone else ever noticed, but I did. Instead of doing something about it, I just went up to my room and worried. To forget, I typed in "free porn" in the search bar.

I still hate myself for not asking The Woman about it.

Maybe I could've stopped everything before it went up in flames.

Maybe everything was my fault.

Maybe I deserve to be alone in Puget Sound.

—

I've slept one hour and porn-ed away the rest. I pretend to be sleeping when my dad walks into my room.

"Time for Mr. Cratcher's," he says. "I'm sure he needs you as much as you need him right now."

"Define *need*," I say.

"Can you just be a typical teenager for a day? Where on earth did all this metaphysical definition stuff come from?"

I don't want to think about it, but I don't think I could feel any worse if I did. I may have reached a point where it doesn't matter if I think or don't think.

"The Woman. We used to play-argue before you worked at home."

His face goes soft. "I guess that was a stupid question considering she has a philosophy degree. You have that transparency thing tonight, right?"

I let out a groan. I feel like my body's burning in the lava of my unnatural disaster self. "Yeah."

Dad nods and then crosses his arms. "Is it weird that I'm excited for the Addiction Fighters group on Thursday?"

Thursday.

I get to see Dez. The girl I ignored last night. Suddenly, my week has a tiny blip of goodness in it. Sugar in black coffee. A stray crouton in a salad of old spinach.

"Kind of," I say. "You aren't addicted to anything, though."

"Well, technically neither are you, right?"

Did Mr. Crotcher not tell him? Is he really that blind? Does he think I've just been coming upstairs every day for last two years simply so I can read for my philosophical enlightenment? I guess, in his defense, that he thinks I'm there because of what happened at school. Am I that good at hiding? I guess only Mr. Crotcher knows about my playlists and that was because he saw me making them at Pritchett's once.

He continues. "The group is just as important for those addicted to the ideas of things," he says. "Like getting your mother back."

"Yeah."

We fall into silence. That's one thing I don't want to think about right now, being addicted to ideas. I'm already addicted to something physical; I don't need to add anything intangible. I stand and put on my pants in a few frustrated tugs. I have the sudden urge to throw my computer into Dez's pool.

Dad sighs. "I'm sorry about Mark, Adam."

I shrug. "It's alright. I didn't know him that well."

He shrugs, too. "Loss is still loss. Hurt is still hurt. Doesn't matter how big or small."

"Thanks," I say, and we both walk downstairs for our morning Cocoa Puff ritual, and this morning we welcome a semi-permanent guest: Adelaide Hawthorne.

—

My morning with Mr. Crotcher is dismal. I spend most of my time trying to figure out why porn has started to hurt instead of, I don't know, not hurt. My distractedness makes me press a bunch of wrong buttons for most of the test recordings we do. I accidentally reset all of the levels we've meticulously tweaked over the last two days. Eventually, Mr. Cratcher ends up shooing me out of the chair to do everything himself, and I can't blame him.

On my way home, I have the idea that if I call Dez to apologize for not answering the phone, I might not feel as bad.

She answers after the first ring. Does she answer after the first ring for everyone?

"Oh good, you're not dead," she says.

"Sorry," I say. "I just didn't feel like talking to anyone last night."

"So I have a theory about our kind."

"Okay."

"Hurt isolates us—"

I sigh and interrupt her before she gets any further. "If you're mad at me about not answering the phone, just tell me."

"Shh! This will be a paradigm shifting academic paper later on."

I let out a fake sigh of disgust.

"Seriously? Fine. I'll talk to you later the—"

"No! No. I was kidding. Come on. You're supposed to get my sarcasm," I say.

"Whatever. I'll talk to you later."

She hangs up.

I stare at my phone in disbelief, and then a few seconds later, her name appears on my screen.

"Dez . . ." I say before she can take over the conversation.

"What, Adam?"

"Can you just forgive me for not answering?"

She laughs. I'm a little confused as to how she can go from hanging up on me to laughing. "I'm not your wife. You don't always have to answer the phone when I call. Even if I *was* your wife, you wouldn't always have to answer the phone when I called. However, it's a nice idea, you always answering the phone, I mean. Not the wife thing. Wait, that sounds bad. It's not that I wouldn't consider marrying someone of your stock. I just probably *deserve* to marry a substance-abusing clown or a hot dictator. Actually, back to the answering the phone thing, I'd totally want you to answer all the time if I were your wife. If you didn't, I'd be like 'damn it, Adam, answer. I'm your wife.'"

She's silent for a few seconds.

"Okay, I recant all that I just said. I definitely want you to answer the phone when I call you. It's nice to know there's a number that will always lead somewhere."

"Wow," I say.

"Sorry, I've had like ten cups of coffee this morning. If my mind was a sound, it'd be a bumblebee smacking against a pane of glass over and over and over and over and—"

"Dez! Do you forgive me?"

I just want to feel better. I want Dez's acceptance to snap me out of my dismalness.

"Of course you're forgiven, Adam. You didn't answer the phone. So what? It's not that big a deal. I mean, answering the phone, not your forgiveness. I mean, me forgiving you." She grunts. "God, sorry. I'm not making any sense. The reason I had so many cups of coffee this morning was to keep my mind off Mark. So far it's working. The only thing I can think about right now is running on a treadmill at the highest-ass speed it can go."

I laugh, and then my mouth starts moving, but I have no idea what I'm about to say. "I didn't answer because I was looking at porn. It just like, took me over more than usual last night."

What. Is. Happening. To. Me.

"Damn it, Adam! I'm your wife. Answer the phone when you're looking at porn and I call you!"

I laugh, but something about her saying "I'm your wife" makes me want her even more, and the collision of all these things—me actually wanting a girl outside of sex, my honesty, my feelings about Mark—makes my insides feel like a crossword puzzle and I'm scared into speechlessness. Dez must interpret my silence as anger because she apologizes again.

"Sorry, I'm probably not the best person to talk to about hard things at the moment. Really, Adam, I get it. You medicated. You felt hurt so you went to get rid of it. You're forgiven. Oh, just a warning: when the caffeine decides to stop working, expect a call from me in which I proceed to break down over Mark."

I pull into my driveway and take the keys out of the ignition. "I'd *love* that. Those are my favorite."

"Sarcasm noted. I will punish that comment with extra irrationality and over-the-top sobbing."

———

It's Transparency time, and I lean my head against the back of an old chair that smells like ancient butts and musty coffee.

Mr. Crotcher slowly pulls an unlit pipe out of his mouth. It makes him look less like an old man and more like a gentleman explorer. "Tonight, we're going to talk about Mark."

Trey lets out one of those "heaviest thing in the world" sighs.

"Who wants to go first?" Mr. Crotcher asks.

Not me. I'm drowning in my own guilt/embarrassment/darkness. I'd be happy if I didn't say anything for the rest of my life.

"I will. I've felt this way before," Elliot says. "I've had a little more time to deal with the shit death dredges up." He shifts in his seat as though readjusting is going to make him more comfortable talking about a kid dying. "When my mom died, I felt a lot of guilt and darkness. The whole shitstorm changed me. It made me into a depressed variable, to borrow the term from Mr. Cratcher."

So that's the answer to Mr. Crotcher's question: we're variables. We aren't fixed outcomes or results—we're variables. It's a fancy way of saying we can change. I look at Mr. Crotcher to say, "that's what I am," but he gives me a quick glance with a tilted head to say "almost, but not quite."

I curse under my breath.

Elliot continues, his face somehow emotionless. "We—" He points at each of us "—are still here, and we've got to choose how to move past the guilt and darkness. Like Mr. Cratcher says, it's a life and death decision. We can wallow or we can live better."

That homeless feeling that's been plaguing me starts bubbling in my stomach, and it's stronger than ever. It's so strong and overwhelming that I finally think I know what it is. It's the feeling something's innately wrong with me. That the deep parts of me aren't okay. It's like a tornado of blood, hurt, and nerve is raging in my body, and if I keep it inside, it will tear me apart.

"I'm Mark," I say, interrupting Elliot. "That's why I can't stop thinking about this. I'm Mark."

Elliot stops talking and knocks his head to the side to get the hair out of his eyes. He waits for me to say something else.

"He didn't want to be here," I say. "He was frustrated because he was forced to do this. He didn't want to be helped. He just wanted to be addicted because that was his relief. His addiction was his help, but it wasn't working. He was still miserable. After our last meeting, I asked him if he wanted a ride home and he said no. I know why he said no; it's because he'd already decided I wasn't going to change anything for him. I chose the same thing. I felt the same way. I'd made up my mind that you guys were a waste of time.

"I spent all of last night looking at porn to feel better. It used to make me feel great, but this time it made me miserable. I'm scared—I'm scared I'm just going to spiral into nothingness. Where nothing's capable of making me feel good . . ." I trail off and look at Trey. The kid's smiling like an idiot. I just bared my soul and the kid is smiling.

He puts his hand on my knee. "Welcome, for real this time, to the Knights of Vice."

—

I'm sitting on my bed, staring at the ceiling, when my phone rings. I pick it up.

Best choice I've made all day.

"Hello?"

"We need to conquer something," Dez says.

I smile. I think of the line Mr. Crotcher kept quoting. The one about every word being a blaze of light, no matter if it's holy or broken. That's Dez. She's made of blazes of light and she's both broken and holy. I really want to tell her that. Maybe I should.

"So you decided to spare me from the breakdown?"

"No, it's still coming. I may have lied when I said I had only ten cups of coffee. I had like, two industrial-sized pots. I've been peeing all day."

"You've probably raised the water table a bit."

"If there's flooding somewhere in the world, I'm sure it's my fault."

"So, what do we need to conquer?" I ask.

"I don't know. Just something. Like, when I play with Indecent, my dog, he gets mad if I keep him from ever catching the ball, right? I feel like that's what life is like with us. Everyone is fighting everything all the time, but because we're all addicts, we never catch the ball, so we all need to conquer something."

"Compelling pitch. Any ideas?"

"We should run a marathon backward."

"Why run a marathon backward?"

"Because everyone who's running it forward is doing it on purpose."

"So, we run a marathon backward on accident. Okay. When you figure out how to do that, let me know."

"Look, all I'm saying is that we should think about it for a while and come up with some other ideas."

"Yeah, I'm down."

"Do you, Addy, and your Dad want to come over for dinner after Mark's funeral on Saturday?"

Me, Addy, and my dad? Dinner at Dez's house? Thousands of questions pop into my head at once.

"Why my dad?"

"My dad's writing a book and wants to pick his agent-y knowledge."

"Oh, my dad hates it when people try to butter him up."

"No buttering, I swear. Besides, if my parents are occupied, we can do something else without them constantly reminding me to be a different person."

Something else? What does she mean?

"I don't mean sex. So just stop."

"Did I say that out loud?" I ask.

"Yes, your confusion and hope were quite audible."

I laugh. "Sorry, I didn't mean—"

"Don't worry about it. Oh, I'm addicted to alcohol now, FYI. Hope that's cool."

"It's not, but who am I to talk?"

"Yeah, French Porn Boy, stop talking." I hear a smile in her voice.

"I'll see you Thursday, right?"

"Abso-freaking-lutely."

"Dez?"

"Adam?"

"You are made of broken and holy blazes of light."

The phone's silent for a few seconds. Have I scared her? Should I take it back? How do you take back a comment about being made of blazes of light? You are pure darkness? You are smoky tendrils of evil?

"Finally," she eventually says. "I didn't think anyone would ever notice."

WHAT DOES IT MATTER

This morning, to increase my happiness, I eat one Cocoa Puff at a time. I want to savor every burst of flavor alongside my Dez-induced joy before the rest of my day inevitably turns into a chaotic mess of emotions. Dad watches me in awe of my commitment to single cocoa spheres, but as I'm lifting my sixteenth puff to my mouth, my phone rings. I answer and hear sobbing. So much for puff-to-puff happiness.

"Dez?" I ask.

"It hurts so much."

"I know."

We sit in the "I know" for a while. Sometimes I think an "I know" with a side of silence is a better prescription than using positivity to get rid of the sadness.

Finally, Dez says, "I don't understand the point of the hurt. It's like a Dementor. I wish I could be Harry Potter, but not because I want to have magical powers. I just want to punch a Dementor square in the face."

"Do you want me to laugh?"

She sniffles. "Do whatever you want. You're not my wife."

I stay silent, but I really want to laugh.

"I wish I could have told Mark his heart wasn't dead," she says.

"What do you mean?"

"I just know in my darkest times, I just need someone to tell me I'm not dead. It helps knowing that."

"Oh, so like, if someone reminds you that you still have the ability to feel something other than numbness, it helps?"

"Right."

"Well, I have some good news."

"What?"

"We get to hang out tonight. That's good, right?"

"It is. I'll get to feel extra alive. A dose of life for me and for Mark."

What does she mean by "I'll get to feel extra alive"? Is she saying I make her feel that way? Or is she just saying being with a human is a way to honor Mark? I decide on the latter, because the former is less likely.

"Alright, thanks for listening. I've got to go to school."

"I'll see you tonight. Make sure you punch a few Dementors in the face today. To hell with magical patronuses. Wait, what's the plural for patronus? Patroni? Pattis?"

Dez laughs. Good. I wanted to hear her laugh.

"See you tonight, Adam."

—

Because I'm suspended from school and I have nothing else to do, I go with Addy to Portland after my time at Cratcher's so she can visit two of the construction projects she manages.

I don't get out of the truck for a few reasons. 1: I'm not really into being stared at by a bunch of dudes who are really good at using saws, and 2: Addy told me I'd get in trouble if I walk around without a hardhat.

I watch her interact with the crew and the foreman. You can tell that everyone loves her. They literally all stop working and say hello. Half of them hug her like she were their own daughter. She moves in and out of the entire crew, switching back and forth between Spanish and English. She even speaks a little French to a guy with a bucket of drywall mud.

It isn't surprising that almost every guy here looks like they'd hammer-fight someone to the death to keep her safe. Addy has always been good at seeing and hearing other people as if they were magic. As if their hurts and joys were bigger than hers. Where Dez says, "Anyone who thinks their shit is greater than mine is more lost then I am," Addy says, "Everyone's got their shit and it's up to me to make them feel like they're loved, anyway."

That's why Addy went with Mom. Why she expected the same thing from me with Dad.

Addy gets back into the truck and lets out a deep breath. She looks at it. Deep. Like it's a sight she needs to remember. "Okay. This place is locked down. I got them everything they needed yesterday."

"Do you want to come to dinner at Dez's house with me and Dad on Saturday?"

"Oh man," she says. She's silent for a while but then finally says, "I have to work on Saturday. Gosh, I really want to go.

I'd ask for it off, but I did just transfer states to straighten you out. I need to lay off the requests for a while."

"Well, Dez and I will be dating soon enough," I say. "There'll be other times, I'm sure."

"Papi, you sound so sure. So cocky and . . . *confidente*."

"I'm irresistible. What's Papi mean?"

She shrugs. "Meh. Hey, when am I going to meet all of your Knights of Vice friends?"

She could always come to the Addiction Fighters thing tonight, but do I want another family member there? It's hard enough having my dad there. I'm afraid he's going to start joining the welcome dirge any time now.

"Whatever you're thinking about, the thing you don't want me to go to, that sounds perfect. When is it?"

I groan. "At the Bothell Civic Center, tonight at eight."

"I'm irresistible," she says, starting the truck and turning Amelia Hunt's "Ain't No Man Worth Your Soul" up.

I shrug. "Meh."

—

I'm in my room staring at my computer, waiting for dad and Addy to get ready for Addiction Fighters when my cell phone rings. It's Dez.

"Hey," I say, but for once she doesn't respond, but I hear someone else talking.

"Why do you insist on going to this meeting?" a man says.

"Because I need it. I need a place that feels safe."

Dez. Did she butt dial me?

"You should be studying. You should be working. You should be applying to colleges. Instead you're going to this . . . AA thing. Don't you know how that looks?"

"Oh, well sorry for not making you look like perfect rich people to your friends. What a big problem in the scheme of the world. Totally wish I could be different." Dez says this with intense sarcasm. Dripping. Soaking wet.

"I do, too. Your brothers were never like this. They're off working hard while you're here barely making it through school."

"Dad, I've literally got one B since I started high school," Dez says calmly. Dryly. As though this conversation happens every night and she's done having "feeling" about it.

"That was the first B to ever walk through the front doors."

Dez falls silent. I want to stand up for her. I want to fight for her. To tell her that she's enough, but I've been butt dialed and I'm an addict. What good would that be coming from me?

"You're a Coulter. It's time you stop being a disappointment to the family and focus on school. Focus on your future."

"What about who I am right now?"

Mr. Coulter scoffs. "When you go to jail, don't call us. Pay your own bail."

A door slams and a millisecond later, Dez stars sobbing.

"Dez?" I say, but she doesn't hear me.

I hang up and call back.

No answer.

—

Dez stands at the Addiction Fighter's podium. Any sign of the fight with her dad has disappeared. Her cool blue eyes are more piercing than I remember. She's wearing a dress covered with yellow flowers. A black belt wraps around her waist. She looks like summer in the beginning of November. She's making buds of heat bloom in my chest.

"I'm not going to spill my guts this week," she says. "A lot of people have talked about Mark already, so I'm just going to quote the first line of *Alias Grace* by Margaret Atwood." She lifts her chin and gets that nature-filled tone in her voice. "Out of the gravel, there are peonies growing."

How can Mr. Coulter not see this part of her? How can Mr. Coulter call her a disappointment?

She steps off the podium without saying anything else and, for a good three minutes, no one else takes the stand. Half the room gets it, and the other half knows there's something to get. I think about saying the explanation out loud, but I only have it in formula form, and formulas never work as well when spoken.

Death/darkness = gravel.

Peonies = life/light.

Death < light.

Though sometimes,

Death/darkness feels > than life/light.

All of that makes formulaic sense, but how can you believe light is greater than death when death feels greater?

Trey leans into my ear. "I just realized something," he says.

"What?"

"Dez Coulter is so freaking hot."

—

The meeting lets out and, as long as Dez's here, I'm determined to stay longer than Trey. I refuse to leave him alone with Dez. I like her. I've never actually "liked" a girl, and I'm not about to give him room to practice his mojo.

"It was really nice to meet you, Elliot," Addy says as Elliot leaves. A few minutes later, Dad leaves. Even Doug Bunson leaves. Then it's me, Addy, Mr. Crotcher, Trey, and Dez.

We talk about funny things we've seen on the Internet for a few minutes, but the discussion ends when Mr. Crotcher yawns. His boredom makes sense, because the conversation isn't philosophical, and I don't even think he's seen the Internet, let alone the things on it.

"You better get to bed, Adam," he says. "We're starting on the guitar tracks for the next song in the morning."

Dez cocks her head and looks at me. Curious at what Mr. Crotcher means. Trey comes over to hug us.

"Mr. Cratcher's my ride," he says, leaning toward my ear. "Also, your sister, man? I feel like I'm in love."

Suddenly I feel like a middle schooler, ready to throw fists at a friend because the girl I have a crush on registered on his all-females-accepted hotness scale, when in reality he's digging Addy. I realize how tense I am and roll my neck to try and relax. I hug him back, but not without some solid man pats. I like Trey, but I'm not sure if I want a sex addict emotionally involved with my sister, so I just say, "It happens."

He laughs. "It sure does! Alright, see you at the Knights of Vice tomorrow." He turns to Addy. "I know we've just met, but I feel like I need to tell you, you are the most . . ." He pauses. I can't tell if he's just well-practiced or if he's genuine, which might mean he's well-practiced. "Lively and beautiful girl I've ever met. You even speak Spanish!" He turns to me and laughs. "*Eres mi chica de los sueños.*"

Addy just stands there eating it up. I'm not sure if she likes Trey, but I *know* she loves the attention.

"*Gracias,*" she says. "*Eres como . . . la playa.*"

Trey bows a little and then runs to catch up with Mr. Crotcher. Before he gets to the door, though, he stops, turns around, and looks at Addy for second.

"See you, Trey!" Dez yells.

I wave.

He walks out the door, and, Addy, Dez, and I start laughing.

"Did you just tell him he was like the beach?" I ask.

Addy smiles and nods. "Si. He *was* very sweet, though. Alright, I know Dad's going to want to talk about the meeting when we walk through the door, so I need to make a few work calls before we go home." She winks at me. "Give me a few minutes."

Addy walks outside and disappears, and in a beautiful moment provided by Addy Hawthorne, Dez and I are finally alone. Like, actually physically together. Not connected by invisible data and unsightly cell towers.

"You butt dialed me today," I say.

Before she can answer, a janitor pops out of a door at the far end of the lobby, fumbling with a big ring of keys. When he looks up, he sees Dez and me, he says, "Sorry, kids, I've got to lock up."

"Not a problem, sir," Dez says. She turns on her heel, nodding for me to follow her.

We walk over to a bench outside of the civic center and sit.

"What evils did you set your ears upon?"

"The fight with your dad."

She nods.

"Does that happen a lot?"

"Daily," she says softly. "He can't wait to tell me how much of a disappointment I am. It gets him out of bed in the morning."

"You're enough," I say. "You're not a disappointment. You're . . ." I lose track of what I want to say because I realize how much my words fall short. Dez has heard her dad's disappointment for years. How do I, someone she met a few weeks ago, tell her he's wrong and have her believe it?

She takes advantage of the silence and moves on. "Any conquering ideas?" .

"What if we played in a video game tournament?" I ask.

She pulls a flask out of her jacket. "I'm horrible at them, but I can train." She tips the flask back and the *why* of addiction suddenly becomes so real to me as I watch her attempts to bury all the years of hearing "you aren't enough."

"You know what's weird?" she says between sips. "I feel like you and I have been friends for years, but how long have we known each other? A few weeks, tops? And I've only like, actually seen you four times."

"Do I look like you remember?" I ask.

"You're a lot cuter than I remember, but that could just be the alcohol talking."

"How can I help you stop?" I ask her, pointing at the flask. The question surprises both of us.

"Give me something else to hold. Like a magic rock that keeps me from thinking about the lack of buzz going through my brain."

My heart's beating so hard it could be used as renewable energy. I pull the flask out of her hand. She looks at me as though I've slapped her.

I probably shouldn't do this.

I really shouldn't do this.

Yeah. I'm going to do this.

I grab her hand and intertwine my fingers with hers. I wait for the backlash, for her to scream. To protest in some way.

"Or that," she says quietly. "Or you could do that."

"Hand is greater than magic rock," I say, feeling a holy blaze crawl up my arm. "That's my formula for you."

She forms her other hand into a peace sign, turns it sideways, and puts it next to our intertwined hands. "We're greater than flask." She stares at our meshed fingers for a few seconds, then says, "Isn't this illegal?"

I raise an eyebrow. "What?"

"Feeling so much like for someone you've known for such a short time?"

"That's everyone else's problem," I say, and she recognizes her own words immediately.

She smiles. "Now we're each other's problem. I mean, we're both messed up, right? So what does it matter?"

I nod. "What does it matter."

SOMETHING WE CAN CONQUER

"So smooth, little bro," Addy says, pulling into our driveway. "You did good."

"You watched? Wow, that's really creepy."

"Nah," she says, "it's fine. So, are you official?"

"I mean, no? We didn't actually say we were dating. Like, I didn't ask her out. There was just—it wasn't time yet."

I didn't ask Dez out because it didn't seem right at the moment. To bulldoze past the hurt she was dealing with, but she did say, "Now we're each other's problem." So, logically, to be each other's problem, we have to be each other's *first*.

Addy slams her head against the headrest. "Papi! That's like, the first thing you do. If you like it, put a title on it."

"So I've been meaning to talk to you about calling Dez 'Dez,' instead of calling Dez 'It.'"

She laughs. "Like you can talk—you watch porn all the time. You're calling girls 'It' every night."

My stomach sinks at the comment, but not because it hurts. She knows?

How does she know? Was that a passive aggressive comment? No, Addy isn't passive aggressive. Why tonight? Why did this have to come up tonight?

My silence coaxes her into an apology. "I'm sorry. I shouldn't have said that. I forgot we hadn't talked about that yet."

"How long have you known?"

She looks at me, studying my face to see if I actually want to know. Finally, she sighs, then says, "A year ago. When I came down to help you and Dad clean out the garage, I used your phone to check on something and I stumbled onto your comprehensive playlist library. I swear, I saw seasonal playlists, like fall, winter, and spring. I mean, isn't that why you started going to Addiction Fighters and the Knights of Vice thing?"

So my dad thinks I'm going to Addiction Fighters *just* because of what happened at school. Addy thinks I'm going to Addiction Fighters because someone found out I was addicted to porn. A few weeks ago, I would've been ecstatic that no one knew the whole story, but now I feel like because no one knows the whole story, no one knows the whole me. I consider telling Addy the whole of it, but something in me just halts at the idea of being wholly known, so I just say, "No. Not really. I mean, yes, but no."

"Adam, come on. What aren't you saying? You're leaving something out."

Again, I consider letting go of the whole story, but I can't. "No. I'm not."

She sighs. "Okay, regardless of what got you there, porn is still a problem for you."

How does she know I'm leaving something out? How does she always know? I shake my head and focus on only the porn problem, I don't want to think about the Anti-Adam Order and what happened at school.

"So, you've known that I didn't tell you everything when we talked the first night you moved back?"

She laughs and shakes her head. "Adam, you're Adam. You've just vowed to be honest after two years of lying. I knew there were a bunch of things you weren't telling me, like being hurt and mad at me for leaving you with Dad, and this. That's why I wanted to move back. I knew it'd take longer than a day to learn everything, and I wanted to be here for all these juicy revelations. I love you a lot, and I want you to be better."

The statement makes me realize that my words won't be enough for Dez. She needs love, real love, and time.

I think on all the things I want to be. For Dez. For Addy.

Finally I say, "I want me to be better, too."

Addy hugs me and I don't let go.

"Look," she says, "we don't have to talk about how I can help tonight. Go revel in your new not-really-but-sort-of relationship status. Revel all up in it, honey child, because I'm going to bed. I have to work early tomorrow."

"Addy, I—"

I want to tell Addy I love her, but I'm just like Dad. The chord in my voice connected to the real me is rusted over with disuse.

"I—"

No, Master! Come quick, hide. We slips away, a silent way, to keeps us safe.

"I'm really glad you're here," I say.

She smiles. "Me too."

I don't watch porn at all when I get into my room. I don't even have my nightly staring match with my computer. I just walk into my room and lay in bed, thinking about Dez Coulter, my messed-up volcano of a girlfriend. I've never had a girlfriend before I met Dez, and I don't think I ever want another.

My phone rings. I pick it up in less than a second.

"Hello?"

"What if you turn into an addiction? What if I end up using you just like I use everything else?"

My heart sinks.

She continues. "What if you use *me* as an addiction? What if we just turn all of our unnatural disaster on each other? Remember what you said? 'We're all volcanoes and we wander around engulfing each other in our disaster.' If that's true, how can we last?"

"Wow," I say, trying to ease the tension. "I'm pretty sure that was verbatim."

"It is verbatim because I wrote it down. Adam, we *will* burn each other. There's no avoiding it. Do we even want to attempt this?"

I don't know what to say. I break everything down into formulas. She's right. Everything she says is right.

I've considered it before, but now I'm forced to face it.

Can two broken people ever truly care for each other?

"I—I . . . can we just try?"

"No," she says, "I like you too much to lose you. If we do this, I'll kill you. I'm a cycle of death, Adam, and I don't think I'll ever be able to break it."

"But think about Dez in the future," I say, even though I haven't done it myself. "Think about what you want to be."

"I can't!" she yells, the words hot with anger, and I realize I sound just like her dad. "I can't trust future Dez because she's just as much of an addict as I am now. Doesn't anyone fucking get that? My future is my now. My now is my future."

"So, what do we do?" I ask.

She's silent for a while. When she speaks again, her voice is a compilation of heaviness, calm, and resignation. "I don't know. What do we do?"

I let out a deep sigh. A Trey "heaviest thing in the world" sigh. How can something be doomed before it starts? Is trying to change myself for Dez just a different kind of addiction? Shouldn't I change myself for me, and in consequence, Dez? How can I do anything right in chaos? Everything I think I can do ends up being an addiction. Does human = addiction? Maybe, but if I can't find the strength to fight for me, maybe it's worth trying to fight for someone else.

"We fight for each other. So what if I'm too weak to do this for myself? If we can't fight for ourselves, let's fight for each other."

"Hand is greater than magic rock," she says.

"We're greater than magic rock, together."

"So, we kick our addictions for the potential of love? For the potential of us?"

"Why not?"

She's silent for at least thirty seconds until she says, "Out of the gravel, peonies are growing."

"Yeah they are. Big ass ones."

She laughs in the middle of a sniffle. "Okay, future boy-friend, confession time. I'm not as strong as you, but I'll keep singing if you keep writing the words."

"A: You don't know that, and B: You sing?"

"Well, it was an analogy, but yeah, I do. It may be the one thing I do well."

"Then I may have something we can conquer."

I JUST SHHH

It's Saturday morning. I walk into Mr. Cratcher's without knocking, ignoring the fact that I've had the Deception Pass dream in some form every night since the first Addiction Fighters meeting. Like the whole story of my suspension and porn habits, the dreams feel too deep a part of me to share, and I don't even know what sharing them would do. So, I ignore them.

"Hello, Adam," he says. "A little uppity today, aren't we?"

"Dez Coulter sings."

He looks at me, head tilted with curiosity. "In what way?"

"In every way, but right now I'm talking about the vocal way."

"Well, I will leave it to you to get her on board with our album, which needs a title, by the way."

We walk up to the study. "You've had the same album for the last however many years and you haven't named it?"

He walks up the stairs slower today. He must not be sleeping well. Mark's death is taking its toll on young and old.

"I have," he says, "but just like the music and what songs are included, the title has changed over the years."

"What was the first title?"

"I can't remember. I'd have to look it up. I have it all saved somewhere. Journals and files."

In his study, we do a few tests before we record the guitar track. I fiddle with some of the levels and then, on his cue, hit the record button. We get halfway through the song—it's a faster one in a major key called "What Are You, Elias?"—when he just stops.

I stop the recording. "Mr. Cratcher?"

"We—" He stares at the ceiling as though he's trying to come up with a reason for why he stopped. "We need the original copy of the album."

I stop the recording. "What? What do you mean?"

"What I mean . . . what I mean is that there is a part on this song that *has* to be here in its original form and I can't remember how I did it."

"Don't you have it somewhere in your journals or piles of song demos?"

He shakes his head. "It was only on the first album. I changed it after that because I couldn't handle it. But, now, at the end, it needs to come back. We can't finish this song without it."

He carefully puts the guitar in a wall hanger and looks out the window.

I still don't understand what he's saying. "Where's the first copy? I'll go get it."

"It's gone," he says, cold and frosty.

"Okay, but why can't we go get it?"

"Because we can't. It's painfully irretrievable. Lost in the explosion of hearts." He shakes his head. "The album will just have to be unfinished. It's as simple as that. This song will have to be unfinished."

So, I'm witnessing a Mr. Cratcher meltdown. Mr. Cratcher never melts down. Is it because Mark's funeral is tonight, or is it something else?

"Let's move on. We will just record something else."

"So that song's over just like that?"

"Just like that. Now, let's do some tests. The next song I want to do is a little louder and the levels will need to be adjusted."

—

My initial observation of my first funeral ever gave me a new formula.

The Formula of Funerals and Communal Mourning
Death + a lot of people who suddenly feel their own death coming
= tears and uncomfortable silence

I sit next to Dez, who somehow looks like a blaze of light even though she's in a black dress. I glance at Elliot on my right. He looks confident, like he's climbing a smaller mountain than one he's climbed before.

Dez grabs my hand and my world alights for what, once more, feels like the first time.

My dad, who's sitting between Mr. Cratcher and Trey, leans forward to rest his chin on his hands and he sees us. He looks at me, and a wave of relief comes over his face. Relief?

"I'm glad you're coming over tonight," she whispers.

I nod. "Nighttime's the bane of an addict's life."

"Everyone else in the world is doing something better than you and putting it on Instagram."

I smile. "Do you think your dad and mom will like me?"

She scoffs. "Who cares if they do or don't? You're not my boyfriend or anything."

A feeling of confusion rolls through my chest. I know we decided not to date, and I also know that I never officially asked her out, so why am I confused?

"Good point. Maybe I should pretend I'm drunk. Mix things up a bit."

"I've already got that covered," she says, wiping a silent tear from her eye and then winking. "Oh, just a warning, my family's kind of rich."

"Kind of rich?"

"Yeah, like upper-class rich."

"Oh, okay." I shrug.

"No, I mean, like live-in-an-unnecessarily-large-giant-ass-mansion rich."

"Okay." I look back to Mark's dad. He's disintegrating and he's only just started the eulogy. I wish Addy were here.

"I just . . . I don't want to you to be disappointed in me," she whispers, so softly I almost don't hear her.

I turn to her again. "Why would I be disappointed in you?"

"I—I don't know. I just don't want you to be, that's all."

I squeeze her hand. "Well, it's not like I'm your boyfriend, so it doesn't really matter." I say it jokingly, but I'm one hundred percent sure she doesn't take it that way. Mostly because as soon as I say it, she lets go of my hand.

"I was just kidding."

She looks at me, her blaze of light turning into a bonfire of anger.

I raise my hands. "You literally just said the same thing to me, Dez."

She turns to watch Mark's dad. "It's not polite to talk during the eulogy."

—

Dad and I are sitting in the car on the way to Dez's house— or mansion, or whatever—when he finally asks me about her. "So, you and Dez?"

"We aren't dating," I say, still pissed at her for being irrational during a funeral.

"I didn't know you could hold hands and not date."

"Your views on romanticism are ancient and based on non-postmodern principles. Traditions have changed since you've dated."

"Apparently, because I would've never used the adjective *postmodern* to describe dating someone."

"We're not dating," I say again.

"Okay. Why not? You were looking at each other like you're the anchor of each other's souls."

"Nice."

"Thanks, it was in a manuscript I rejected the other day. Now answer the question."

"We can't right now."

"That's not really an answer."

"I don't know what you want me to say."

"I want a reason why you can't date. Come on, you can go all philosophical and I won't say a word about it."

"We just can't right now. It's that easy."

I should probably tell him about being addicted to porn. He probably already knows. Everyone else seems to know, and knowing that would probably help him make sense of why Dez and I can't date, but no kid talks to their dad about that kind of stuff. Besides, I'm sick of thinking about who knows what and trying to conjure reasons to tell people things.

"That's it?"

"You asked," I say.

"I did. I just didn't expect an answer that I could understand because it wasn't actually an answer."

We drive the rest of the way in silence, Dad not wanting to push, me not wanting to hurt. We arrive at the address Dez gave me to find a custom wrought-iron gate blocking us from their house.

"So, they have money?" he says.

"I mean, you don't do too bad yourself."

For some reason, I feel the need to defend her richness. I figure if she's worried enough to warn me of it in the middle of a eulogy, then she's sensitive about it.

"Yeah, but we don't have a spindly iron-and-river-rock front gate." He leans out the window and presses a button. A few seconds later, Dez's voice cracks through the tiny speaker below the keypad. "Welcome to the unnecessarily large mansion where nothing's ever good enough. I'll buzz you in."

The speaker clicks off. While the gate slides behind the river rock wall, my dad looks at me. "You two are literally made for each other."

"I won't tell Addy about your misuse of *literally*."

He laughs. "I'm pretty sure it wasn't a misuse. I'll let you know after dinner and more observation."

The driveway winds in a crescent curve, up to what looks like a hardcore Bass Pro Shop. She wasn't lying. The place is huge. The wooden entry doors look like they belong on The Vatican.

"Holy—" Dad says. "Way to pick 'em, son."

"Dad."

"Yeah, yeah, no dating. Sorry."

We park under an awning that covers the front door. Well, awning is really an understatement. It's more like a concert pavilion held up by redwood tree–sized logs. Dez appears in the doorway. She looks nervous. No, maybe she looks pissed. No, she definitely looks both.

We get out of the car and Dez yells, "Just . . . leave the keys in the ignition. The butl—George, our assistant, will take care of it."

Dad looks at me.

"Yeah, we have a butler, but he's an asshole," she yells. "Just come in."

She leaves the door open and disappears inside.

"She's the one who invited us over, right?" Dad asks.

"Yeah, I think she's really afraid we'll judge her."

"Makes sense."

We get near the doors, and the voice I heard the time she butt dialed me says, "Why didn't you wait for them to come in? You should always wait for guests, you know that."

"Normally, guests don't have to cross a bitter wilderness to get to the front door of a house," Dez says.

"We are not doing this right now," a woman says—her mom, I'm guessing. "Desiree, stop being difficult, and for goodness sake, go greet them at the door. You aren't that uncivilized."

My dad gives me another look right before a man and a woman appear in the door. The man is tall. He fills the gigantic doorframe well. He has a slight beer belly, but it doesn't make him look out of shape. The woman is a mirror image of Dez: gentle, but confident. Childlike, but mature. The only difference between the two is that Mrs. Coulter's face is a little rounder, and her hair is dyed rich white woman blonde.

"Welcome, welcome," she spouts. "It's so nice to have you here. I'm Mrs. Coulter, but please call me Nellanne." She kisses me and my dad on the cheek.

"Hey, there." Mr. Coulter holds out a hand to whoever gets past Nellanne first. "I'm Terry, it's good to meet you."

We make small talk by the door for a little bit. Every once in a while, I catch a glimpse of Dez pacing in what I think is a living room.

How's it going?

Addy texts while Dad and the Coulters talk about some political thing that NPR hasn't told me about yet.

Holy house.

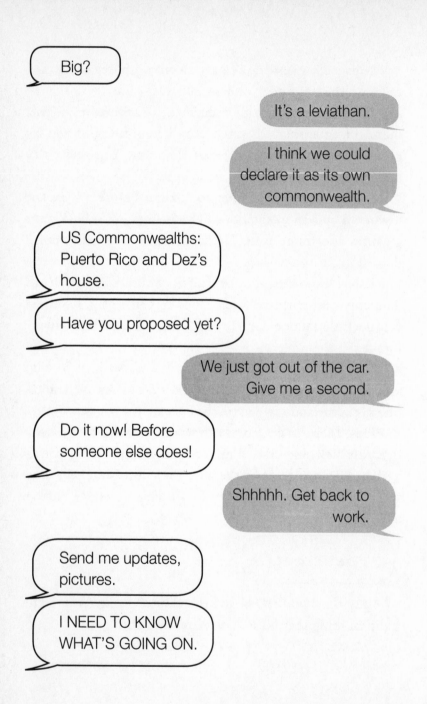

Finally, Mrs. Coulter shoos my dad and Mr. Coulter toward the dining room and excuses herself to see if the cook is ready to serve dinner. I walk up to Dez. She's got a flask in her hand.

"What's wrong?" I ask, touching the bare wrist underneath her sweater sleeve.

"I hate my family," she says. "All they do is push. All they do is say 'your brothers aren't doing that,' or 'are you sure that's the right choice? Seems like you could do better.' I hate it. I want to get out of here."

I nod. "Two more years, right?"

"Yeah, two more years." She tips the flask back. When she's done, I take it from her and grab her hand. Her shoulders drop a little.

She rubs her eyes and then makes a greater than sign with her fingers by our hands. "They expected me to be working some intense banking internship when I turned fifteen. I That's what my brother did, and now he's got some high and swanky job. I just don't like banking, but that doesn't seem to matter. I'm expected to be everything I'm not. If it's not my dad trying to turn me into a financial guru, it's my mom trying to make me into the perfect housewife."

"Well, I expect you to be Dez Coulter."

"Okay, that's really nice and all, but you need to be more aggressive with me. You need to assert yourself if you ever want me to listen to you."

"Dez?"

"What?" she snaps.

"Shut up."

She sighs, says "Fine," and then walks toward the dining room, which looks like the ballroom in *Beauty and the Beast*, except without the dancing brooms or mops.

Disappointing. I thought the rich could have it all.

I follow Dez in right as Mr. Coulter starts telling my dad about Dez's brothers, Rich and Terry Junior. When she hears their names, Dez turns to me and cocks her jaw. Before she has the chance to storm out again, I point at the chair next to mine, trying to pack some seriousness in my eyes. Her jaw resets and slides into a smile. She even laughs. I can't keep up with where she's at emotionally, but Dez = drop-dead, blazing hot in her black jeans and a white sweater, which drops to reveal her left shoulder.

Dinner is served. It's amazing, of course. The only thing that could make it better is if Dez's parents didn't spend most of the time talking about people my dad and I don't know. Finally, halfway through the filet mignon wrapped in bacon, Mr. Coulter says, "So, Greg, I heard you were a literary agent."

Dad's back tenses, but he continues eating like he's never been asked to dinner by someone trying to score an agent before.

Dez gets up from the table and grabs my hand. "I'm going to show Adam the house."

Her dad waves us away. Though he says, "yes, yes, sure," I'm pretty sure he has no idea what Dez said or even cares.

As I stand to leave, Dad looks at me with "please don't leave me alone" eyes. I raise my hands in helplessness as Dez pulls me toward a giant spiral staircase.

She points toward two big, black bulldogs sprawled out on a Persian carpet in the living room. "The one on the left is Indecent, the one who can't stand not getting the ball. The one on the right is Roll Tide. He has very few opinions.

How's porn going?" She lets go of my hand and bounds up the steps.

"The last time I looked at some was the night before we started fighting for each other or whatever. My head's a mess and I'm not sleeping well, but you're worth it."

"You're going to relapse," she says.

I shrug. "You're going to die."

She spins halfway up the stairs, "Why the hell would you say something like that?"

I laugh at the sudden snap. "Why would you tell me I'm going to relapse? It's not like that sort of thing is super encouraging to someone on his first try at getting un-addicted to porn."

"I say it because everyone does. They call this the pink cloud. Your realization that you need to change gives you enough of a buzz that it replaces your addiction buzz. You drop your addiction, but it's only for a time. Then you realize changing is damn impossible, and you go back to your vice with open arms. I'm just warning you about this now so you aren't crushed under the weight of relapsing."

"Dez—"

She holds up a hand. "Just . . . stop."

"What's going on with you?" I ask.

She walks into a room, one about as big as our house. There's nothing on the walls but a poster of the twelve steps. She grabs me by the collar, pulls me in, and shuts the door.

"Ever since you showed up, everything's been so confusing!" she yells. "I was fine with assuming I'd always be an addict. I went to Addiction Fighters to make me feel better about myself. To know my fixed shitty-ness was understood.

It took nothing from me to be there. It felt good to be heard, because I'm sure as hell not going to be heard around here. That was all I wanted out of that place, and then you came and now I actually *want* to be better and everything's messed up. Now I want to actually be better. I want to break my cycles instead of just talking about breaking them, but I don't know what questions to ask or what things to believe. I want to stop consuming everything around me—for you, Adam—and thinking about it is already putting me through withdrawals."

"You didn't have to call me," I say. "You could have called any other person in Addiction Fighters, but you didn't. And now you're yelling at me for wanting to be better like it's my fault. You think I've been gliding in the proverbial air since I met you? I've asked more questions in the last two weeks than I have in my entire life and I hate it. I can't watch porn anymore without feeling horrible. So what used to make me not feel like shit now makes me feel like shit. I'm having depressing dreams. Mark's dead, and it didn't matter that I didn't know the guy, but it's scared the crap out of me."

"I am Mark, Adam. Can't you see that? I'm Mark."

"So am I!" I yell.

We're both silent. She sits down on her bed. My phone buzzes.

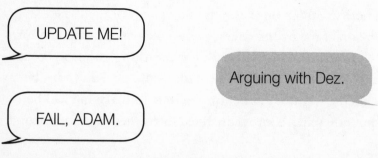

UPDATE ME!

Arguing with Dez.

FAIL, ADAM.

I sit next to Dez.

She grabs my hand. "I read the most confusing first line ever the other day."

"What?" I ask.

"'It was a pleasure to burn.' *Fahrenheit 451* by Ray Bradbury." Her eyes narrow in thought. "Like, who says that? Since when has it ever been a pleasure to burn?"

I think about the feeling that ripples up my arm when our hands come together after being apart. Could that be it?

"I don't know. Maybe you should read the whole book." She falls back on her bed. "I've never read a whole book."

I lie on my back and turn my head toward her. I'm on a bed with an incredibly sexy girl. I've dreamed of being on a bed with a sexy girl forever, and all I can think about is how to make her feel like I see her: a holy and broken hallelujah. I'm not selfless, so why am I not trying to have sex right now? The question makes me wonder if I should try, but then she turns to look at me. Her hair drapes over her cheek. I see blue eyes shining at me like a sunrise. What is it about Dez Coulter that makes me want better things for her? For me? For everyone?

She sighs. "I can't stop wondering. Can two addicts actually love or can they just . . . be addicted to each other?"

"Maybe the answer is yes, even for non-addicts."

She slides closer to me and presses her head into my chest. She folds into me like we've always been that way and it's up to the rest of the world to catch up. There's something about her tenderness that ends all thoughts of sex. Something about the way she presses against me makes me want to keep her safe. I know trying something would be the opposite of keeping her safe, though I can't explain why. Would she be this close to me if she knew why I was suspended? The reason that makes me feel more and more like shit each passing day?

"Adam Hawthorne, don't ever let me wear you down. Don't ever let me stop fighting for us."

"That sounds like dependency to me," I say.

"Just . . . shhh," she says.

So I do. I just shhh.

ON TOP OF ME

Time seems to move quicker than it had before. I don't know if it's because I'm not just spending all my time in my room, or if it's because I now have Dez, or Addy, or Trey and Elliot. I just know everything feels more awake than it ever had before. It's like I was rusty car and someone had to push me down a hill to get me to start. I feel like I'm picking up speed. Moving. Being something that isn't filled corner-to-corner with dark and rust.

The weird thing is, I feel like I've passed my slowness onto Mr. Cratcher. We've been recording for three weeks now, and I feel like going up the stairs takes a few minutes longer. Getting him set up with his guitar is like putting boots on a finch. He just wanders around moving things. Persnickety fidget here and persnickety fidget there. I wonder if it's just a new morning thing or if he's this sluggish at school, too.

One night after Addiction Fighters, the Knights of Vice, plus a few extra, go to Pritchett's. Trey and Elliot sit across from me and Dez, and Addy's in a chair at the end of the table. We're all talking about how, during the sharing time at the meeting, Dez walked to the podium like she was going to speak, but just stared at everyone for at least a minute and then sat down.

Dez shakes her head. "Everyone's always talking about how life's so hectic and overwhelming." The obstinate smile she gets when she's arguing a point playfully, but with the conviction of someone who actually believes it, appears on her lips. "I thought it would be nice to enjoy some silence together, but you didn't even applaud when I walked off the podium. You plead for order and calm, but when it's given to you, you stare at it like you've just walked in on a fat guy you don't know on your toilet."

"You didn't actually say that was happening," Elliot says. "If I walked up to a piano, sat down on the bench, and just stared at you instead of playing, you'd think I was a moron."

Dez opens her mouth to say something, but she realizes she's trapped. "I'd expect you to do whatever you wanted."

Elliot lets out one strong laugh. "BS! Dez, you are always so full of manic pixie BS."

Dez's mouth drops, and she looks so offended that I wonder if she'll ever say anything to Elliot again. "I am *not* a manic pixie."

Elliot and Trey look at each other and then both say. "Right."

"I think it's . . ." I start, but then try to think of a different word for *cute*. Adorable. Sexy. "Avant-garde."

"Oh God, so much BS everywhere," Elliot says, pretending to hurl into a napkin holder.

Trey laughs but then looks at Addy. "You know what isn't BS, Adelaide? Us. Come on. What do you say? Let me take you out. Just once."

Addy shakes her head as the rest of us chuckle at her expense. "Who told bro that my full name is Adelaide? Raise your hand now."

No one raises their hand.

Trey gets an embarrassed smile. "Chica, no one at this table told me. I asked Mr. Cratcher for *all* the information he had on you."

"*Dios mio*," Addy says. "Listen, Trey, if you want me, you've gotta step it up."

"Yeah," I add. "For one, you need to win her brother over first."

Trey waves me away. "Oh, that's easy, man."

Dez raises an eyebrow. "And you've got to win over the brother's girlfriend."

When everyone, including me, turns and looks at Dez, she realizes her mistake.

Dez tries to correct herself, "I mean the brother's . . ."

She can't think of anything else to call herself. It's funny, but, at the same time, I can't keep up with what she thinks we are.

"*Mujer de la noche?*" Addy asks.

Trey laughs. "How do you not see we could be perfect together?"

Dez throws a french fry at him. "Elliot, tell Trey to leave poor Addy alone."

Elliot flicks Trey in the neck. "Hey, man, relax. Dez wants to talk about Dez, not Addy."

Dez grabs the table with a big grin. "Nuh uh! That is not what I said."

I shrug. "That's what I heard." I look at everyone else. "That's what you guys heard, too, right?"

Everyone holds back their laughter long enough to agree. Dez shakes her head in defeat. "I am me, and he is he, and she is she, and you are all assholes."

We laugh, and I realize I've never felt like this: included, like I fit, like I have a place.

Suddenly, as though my heart realized its vulnerability, images of porn crash in on me. In a matter of seconds, all the freedom I was feeling is replaced by my want for porn. My knee starts bouncing. My palms get hot. I get fidgety. I know that I'm not going to survive tonight. Dez takes one look at me and knows exactly what's happening: the pull of withdrawal. The intense incompleteness.

"See?" she whispers. "This is why we aren't dating yet."

"Dez, can you please not make me feel guiltier than I already do?"

"I hate it when couples whisper to each other when they're in a group," Elliot whispers, and everyone laughs.

"That wasn't a joke," he adds. "For real, I hate it."

Trey throws his arm around Elliot as another round of fries is brought to the table. "Hey, man, relax," he says again.

Dez and I look at each other unsettled. Our volcano-ness is spilling over into each other's struggles and we haven't even officially dated yet. I turn away and catch Addy gazing at Trey while he talks to Elliot. Addy catches me catching her, and her only response is a mischievous grin.

—

"You can't make fun of me for not dating when you know exactly why we can't," Dez says.

We're standing outside of Pritchett's. Everyone's left except for Addy, who's waiting for me in her truck.

"Dez, I'm sorry. I just—it sucks not to have something you want because of something that feels so out of your control. I just wonder like, what's it matter what we call it? We'd be pissed if either one of us dated someone else, right? Doesn't that mean we're dating? The whole 'we have no title but I'll be pissed as hell at you if you no-titled with someone else' thing is just as much of a title as dating."

Dez uncrosses her arms and steps closer to me. "We can't be boyfriend and girlfriend yet. We can't date yet. We have to defeat our addictions, remember? Otherwise we'll just burn each other up. We *can* do this. We're awesome."

"That's not an answer to my question."

She collapses into my chest like she's exhausted, so I just hold her.

"You don't think I'm a manic pixie dream girl, do you?"

"I think you march to the beat of your own conga line and it's adorable."

"So, yes, but it's fine, is what you're saying?"

"I think it's hot when you just silently stare at a room full of addicts."

She pulls herself off my chest, her lips pressed into a concerned line. "I just . . . my brothers are the same as my dad; carbon-copy, moneymaker, rich, ignorant types. My mom is the perfect woman and wife who never makes a mistake, but is hollow on the inside. I don't want to be that. I can't be that."

"I really think you're awesome."

She rests into me again. "You're the first one, then. One of my sponsors once said that I was too focused on being different to ever be in a healthy relationship."

"What did you say?"

"Oh, I agreed, one hundred percent."

"So, what does that mean for us, then?"

"I think it means if you look at porn tonight, I'll kick you in the nuts," she says. "How's that for incentive?"

"A: That's not an answer, B: the scariest thing about that is I know you'll actually do it."

"Yeah, I will. I want to date you."

I wonder why she moved on so quickly from my question. I wonder what her quest to be different from her family means for us, but I let it go for now. I probably have some sort of backlash from The Woman affecting my relationships in a similar way. I don't think anyone escapes their families without some sort of bruise.

"So you'll kick me in the nuts to date me?"

She nods. "Yeah. So worth it."

I take a deep breath and then step away from her and spread my legs into a rockstar-ish stance. "Alright, I'm ready. Let's get this over with."

She laughs but then kisses me on the cheek. "If only it were that easy. See you in the morning, Hawthorne."

—

I watched porn for an hour.

I hate myself.

I hate myself.

I. Hate. Myself.

—

The next morning, I sit at the kitchen table with my dad. I shovel spoonfuls of Cocoa Puffs into my mouth, but the act of lifting the spoon, chewing, and fishing more puffs out of the milk seems like a placebo happiness compared to what I felt last night being with everyone. I didn't think Cocoa Puffs could ever lose their shine. I thought their unnatural molecular structure could keep them shining way past their expiration date. I guess all it takes is something brighter to make a shine seem dull. My shine-o-meter rankings are now Addy, Dez, my friends, and then Cocoa Puffs.

Glad that happened.

My phone rings, and it makes Dad look up from his e-reader with his eyebrows all scrunched.

"Hello?"

"Why five?" Dez asks. "There are twenty-four options to choose from. Why five in the morning?"

"Because he's an old man, and though I don't go to school currently, he does."

"Oh, yeah, I suppose I still have to do that later, too. At least it's Friday. Do I have to kick you in the nuts this morning?"

Truth? No truth?

Pros: I tell the truth.

Cons: I avoid hurting her, hurting my balls, and being vulnerable.

"Nope, you don't. You sure you're okay with this?"

"I've never recorded anything. Ever. This is a temporary conquering until we can come up with something better."

"Alright, I'll see you there then."

She doesn't say good-bye. She just hangs up.

"Dez is going to Mr. Cratcher's?" Dad asks.

"Yeah, she's going to sing."

"Huh," he says. "Just make sure you're still focusing on spending time with Mr. Cratcher. I don't want these mornings to turn into the Dez and Adam Show where nothing gets discussed. I think the mornings have been good for you and I'd hate to see those go, you know?"

"Yeah."

"Promise me you'll take advantage of the times you have to have with Mr. Cratcher to focus on yourself?"

"I feel like that's *all* I've been doing, but yes. I will. Hey, we should get a different kind of cereal," I say, standing to grab my keys off the counter.

"Leave it to love to get a man to change cereals," Dad says.

"We're not dating."

"I never implied you were dating. I implied you were in love."

"I guess. I don't really know what that means."

"You're young. You have time to figure it out."

The comment makes me wonder if *he* even knows what being in love means.

As I drive to Mr. Cratcher's, NPR teaches me about the socialist dictator Hugo Chavez. Politics aren't my favorite thing to listen to, but I've been having NPR withdrawals. Their funding telethon ran long because of dicks like me who listen but don't support it.

Dez's car's already sitting in Mr. Cratcher's driveway when I arrive. It's a rust-colored station wagon, and each of the doors are painted a different color.

She leans against her hood, waiting for me. I never knew five in the morning could be so sexy.

"Hi," she says.

I hug her. "Hi. You ready?"

"I've done scarier things than singing with an old man."

I widen my eyes. "Not this old man."

"Is he like Hugo Chavez or something?"

"NPR?"

She nods.

"Sweet mercy, you're perfect."

"You haven't answered my question."

"What does it matter? It's too late. Even if he was Hugo, you already said you'd do it."

"Well, you didn't tell me I'd be singing with a socialist dictator. That's before information, not after information."

I pause before knocking on his door. "Do you have a flask?"

She flutters her eyelashes.

I hold out my hand. "Give it to me."

She rolls her eyes, slides her hand into her coat, and pulls out the shining metal container. "God, you're so annoying."

I take it and dump its contents over the railing.

"That's not fair," she says. "It's not like I can just dump porn over the railing."

I grab my phone from my pocket. "Here."

"What about your mind? I can't dump that?"

"Okay, just . . . it was supposed to be funny."

She takes my phone and stretches her arm over the railing. The phone slides from her fingers.

"I hope there's grass down there," I say.

She holds out her hand again. "Brain, please."

I lay my head in her palm. She leans down like she's going to kiss me but instead she blows into my ear. I shudder then swat Dez away.

"Dez, why would you even do that?" I'm kind of angry, but I'm laughing at the same time.

"Because that was funnier than dropping your phone over the railing."

"Was it?"

"Okay, which is worse: the fact that your phone just shattered into bits and pieces on the concrete below or that you have air in your brain?"

I throw up my hands. "Did you really just destroy my phone? Why—"

She pokes my chest. "Totally kidding."

"You're going to make me insane."

"I haven't yet? Man, I'm losing my edge."

Before we can knock, Mr. Cratcher's head appears in the doorframe. "Good morning, Adam. Oh, good, you coerced Dez to sing on our broken little record?"

"I did indeed," I say. "It wasn't very hard."

"He said 'sing,' and I said 'let's go.'" Dez steps into the house and hugs Mr. Cratcher. "It's weird to see you without the Knights of Vice."

"Well, there's one right there." Mr. Cratcher points at me. "One right here." He points to himself. "And two right there." He points to Dez and then winks at me.

"Ha. Ha. Ha. Aren't you two all buddy-buddy."

"Always," Mr. Cratcher says. "Shall we? I need to teach you today's song before we can record anything. Adam, can you get this young lady some water?"

"I can. Just in the kitchen?"

"Yes, glasses are by the fridge, second cupboard."

I've never been in his kitchen before. This is almost world-changing. I open the cupboard and grab a glass. I hold it to the dispenser on the fridge and a piss leak of water drips out of the spout. I look at the overwhelming amount of magnets, notes, lists, and pictures on his fridge. There's a bunch of Gabby, so while I wait for the glass to fill, I study her features and her smile. I can tell she was a woman who had the eternally beautiful gene, probably like Dez does. Dudes don't get that. We have the hot-then-beer-belly gene. Poor Dez.

Poor Dez? We're not even dating and I'm talking like we're forever.

Forever.

Can addicts have forever?

I shake my head and press the glass back into the stream of water.

My curiosity moves to the edges of the fridge when I finish scanning all the stuff in the middle. In the top left corner, there's a pile of whatnot waiting for me to sift through it. As soon as I touch it, the magnetic disk keeping the pile pinned to the fridge shoots into the sink, giving up on its one task in life. At least half the world's stationary, Christmas postcards, and notes tumble to the ground. I curse under my breath and leave the glass in the dispenser cubby in order to pick things up.

As I gather everything, I find an ancient picture of Mr. Cratcher sitting behind a mixing board in some studio. There's a black guy beside him, wearing the culmination of all that was the sixties: tweed jacket, hair pick rising out of the afro on his head like a skyscraper on a horizon. Behind them, a sign hangs above the door proclaiming Abbey Road Studio: US in a thick and simple script.

Abbey Road? Like, the studio The Beatles recorded in? That Abbey Road?

I take the picture and slide it into my pocket, certain Mr. Cratcher won't notice it's missing. I grab the glass out of the dispenser and run up the stairs.

"I might've knocked some stuff off your fridge," I say, putting the glass down on Mr. Cratcher's desk.

"It is the plight of the fridge hoarder," he says. "I do it frequently. Don't fret about it."

"How do you want to record the vocals today?" I ask, sitting down in the desk chair and opening up the DAW.

"Well,"—he rubs his eyes—"I suppose it wouldn't hurt to do vocal tracks for the first few songs we've tracked. However, let me and Miss Dez practice first. We tested the chemistry of man and microphone; it is even more important to test the vocal chemistry of man and woman. If we sound like brilliance, then we shall record together. If we have a hard time keeping up with each other, we will record our vocals separately, one track at a time."

He pulls the guitar with the hole in it off the wall and grabs the stool out of the recording room—he calls it the isolation room.

"What is the genre we're singing, Mr. Cratcher?" Dez asks. "Rap? Gypsy Funk?"

"I'm afraid my heart music has always been eighties hair metal."

For once, Dez doesn't know if she should come back with wit. She gives me a horrified look, but says, "Oh, cool."

I laugh and give Mr. Cratcher a slow clap. "The beast has been tamed."

Mr. Cratcher gives me another wink, the second of the morning. The first wink was okay, and this one was meh. Any more winks and it will be creepy.

On a completely different non–old man winking topic: porn.

It just hit me like a wave of tingling vibrations. It feels like they won't stop unless I scratch the itch. My knee starts bouncing up and down. I think about the whole drop-the-phone-over-the-railing moment. Dez's right. Though my phone's currently somewhere on Mr. Cratcher's lawn, I can't stop my thoughts, even after the disaster that was last night. I feel incredibly guilty for letting my mind sift through its stored gallery of thumbnails.

"Boys," Dez says, "you're forgetting that my vocal chords are an economy. I'm the only one with the supply, but both of you have the demand."

Mr. Cratcher lets out a thick and hearty laugh. One I've never heard before. "Well said, Miss Dez. Well said. Now, the real question here has nothing to do with music."

Mr. Cratcher pauses and gives us the look of someone who's about to ask about young love: raised eyebrows, a smirk that says "they know nothing" and "I wonder if they'll make it" at the same time.

I cut him off before he can ask. "No."

Mr. Cratcher stares at me. "It isn't normal to be able to answer an unasked question. If one can do that, it means the question is close to the heart. Questions close to the heart are rarely questions, but answers."

"This isn't philosophical, Mr. Cratcher," I say. "We're not dating."

Mr. Cratcher looks to Dez, a knowing suspicion in his eyes. "Is that true, Miss Dez?"

"Yeah," she says. "Not dating."

"Why not?" he asks.

Dez and I decide who's going to answer with a battle of quick head nods and unmoving glances.

"Because we're addicts and addicts can't love," Dez says flatly. "They can only consume. We'll use each other, burn each other, and then lose each other. If normal people can't make it through life without divorce, then the moment we start is also the moment we end."

Start = End.

I think about that formula for a minute and conclude with this: why are my formulas looking more and more like a bucket'a'bull?

This sucks.

Mr. Cratcher sighs. "Miss Dez, have you heard the song 'Hallelujah' written by Mr. Leonard Cohen?"

"No, I haven't."

"Adam, find it and play it for her, please."

I do, and this time I listen closer to the words. One line captures my porn-filled head and it hurts me. It's a beauty-filled hurt though, not a pain-filled one. Is that even possible? Can there be two kinds of pain? A beautiful kind and a hurtful kind?

Love is not a victory march.
It's a cold and it's a broken Hallelujah.

Love is a cold and broken hallelujah. How does that work? Before I can think around that any longer, I hear the line about a blaze of light being in every word. I watch Dez; my blaze of light, knowing everything in me wants her. I've watched enough porn to know what want feels like physically, and though that's present, it's only a little bit of what I feel. The problem is, I can't figure out what *else* I feel. It seems like every time I get close to defining my feelings, she does something new and the definitions die. It doesn't even have to be something huge, just a flick of an eyelash, or the twitch of a muscle in her jaw. Maybe all my feelings are fractions that make up a whole love for Dez Coulter. If that's the case, then it's terrifying, awesome, and confusing all at once.

The song finishes. After a few seconds of Dez staring at her feet, she says, "That's a nice song." She says it so nonplussed that Mr. Cratcher shakes his head in disappointment.

"I ask you the same question I've been asking Adam, Dez. What are you? What is Adam? What are we?"

Dez's jaw clenches. I see the tightness push against the skin under her cheek.

"We're all addicts," she says. "Cohen was just an addict to the Hallelujah."

Mr. Cratcher closes his eyes like the comment hurts. "Just think on it. Both of you, please. Think on it now, in your youth, before you waste your life trying to find the answer like I have."

His plea is so deep and cutting, I think it makes Dez cry. We say nothing else that isn't music- or album-related for the rest of our time together. They finally practice. Dez picks up the song with just one run through.

Her voice = haunting + sunrise + beautiful.

To my surprise, they sound amazing together. Some record exec should be kicking himself for not signing them already. Their voices—his wise and knowing, hers mysterious and young—combine to make my current world less porn-y and more normal.

Dez is quiet as we leave. I walk her to her car, but she doesn't look at me. Before she opens the car door, she says, "That man's an emotional Hugo Chavez."

Without saying another word, she drives off.

I'm struck with how differently we handle hard things. She runs away from them by physically removing herself. I run away from them right where I am. I'm running right now, crafting a scene in which a woman takes her clothes off on top of me.

NOT TO CARE

I'm staring at my computer, leg bouncing in the monoto-nous heat of temptation. I've opened and closed the screen a million times. I already feel guilty for having to fight against this, and I'm struggling to figure out why I shouldn't just finish off the guilt. At least I'd be distracted for a little while.

The front door opens. Addy's home.

I run down the stairs to see her. To get out of my head and away from the computer.

"Hey," I say as she tumbles onto the couch. "How was work today?"

She grunts but doesn't answer right away. "I had to fire four people. One of them felt inclined to tell me that his son would be eating out of the garbage because of me. It's not my fault he hasn't shown up to work on time once since we hired him three months ago."

I slide onto the couch and tuck my knees into my chest. "The guy or his kid?"

"His kid. Totally undependable. How's your day? Did you and Dez make up?"

"I guess."

"I don't know why you two aren't together yet. You already act like an old married couple."

I take a deep breath. "Porn."

She looks up at me. "Come again, Papi?"

"I'm addicted to porn. She's addicted to everything. We want to try and kick our addictions before we can date."

Addy raises an eyebrow. "What will that accomplish?"

I shrug. "Things and stuff."

"You don't even know what it'd accomplish?" she yells. "Ugh, my brother is such a twerp."

"I do know, thank you very much."

"Well, what is it?"

"We don't just want to be each other's newest addiction, you know?"

"Oh, I guess I've never really thought about it that way." She lies back down on the couch. "I gotta hand it to you, Papi, I think you're just complicating a really good thing, but it's your parade, not mine."

"Why do you call me Papi?"

She doesn't answer. She never answers.

"Fine, what would you do if you were me?" I ask.

"Me? Oh, I'd probably kiss a lot and figure out the hard stuff as I went. Tell me, have you ever seen ducks in a row?"

"No."

She lifts up her head. "Have you seen chickens in a single-file line?"

"No . . ."

"Then why the hell are you trying to force the poultry into linear shapes?"

I laugh. "I just came to you for dating advice for the first time in our relationship. Are you really about to let me walk away with 'don't force the poultry into linear shapes'?"

She nods. "Totally."

"I mean, so far it's the best advice I've gotten."

—

At six, an hour before I leave for the Monday night Knights of Vice meeting, my phone rings. I know it's Dez before I answer. Would telling her why I was suspended make me feel better? It would certainly distract me, but maybe telling the girl I'm trying to be a better person for the worst of what I've done isn't the best call because here's the thing:

I did it.

The more I replay the moments in my head, the more it makes me hate myself. My thoughts are an abacus and hate is the beads. Somehow, recently, the sum of me always equals how much I hate myself.

I squash that idea of telling her.

"Hello?"

"Have you ever researched Mr. Cratcher?"

"I don't spend a lot of time Googling elderly men who ravage the minds of youth with philosophical questions about the human existence."

"Do it. Right now."

I flip open my computer, nervous that the simple act of getting online will be enough to break my mind-castle's puny peashooter defenses. I type in "Colin Cratcher" and the results pop onto the screen.

Famed record producer Colin Cratcher under investigation for first-degree murder

Abbey Road producer Colin Cratcher primary suspect in studio murder

New US branch of Abbey Road Studios closed indefinitely due to murder investigations

Abbey Road US assistant producer Elias Harper murdered, producer Colin Cratcher primary suspect

I remember the picture I took from Mr. Cratcher's house this morning and pull it out of my pocket. I stare at it. The black guy standing next to Mr. Cratcher must be Elias.

"Adam?"

"Yeah, here. Sorry. This—this is crazy."

"I've been researching him for the last two hours."

"Do you know what happened?"

"Yeah, so here's what I've got. Abbey Road UK opened Abbey Road US in 1969. The UK execs hired Elias and Mr. Cratcher. Elias got his sister, Gabby, a job at the front desk. Because of the racial climate in the United States, people were pissed Abbey Road hired two black people, so there were a bunch of threats to shut it down. At the time, Mr. Cratcher was addicted to every drug ever and didn't hide it very well, but I can't find any evidence his drug use ever made him violent. Gabby and Mr. Cratcher fell in love around the time Elias and Mr. Cratcher started producing the album you guys have been working on after studio business hours. One morning, the studio head came into work to find Elias . . ." She pauses.

Even though I expect something bad to follow, I'm not prepared for what she actually says.

"... lynched ... by a microphone cable. Because everyone knew Colin and Elias were working together after hours, and that Colin was addicted to drugs, he was the prime suspect.

"The day of the hearing, there were protest groups for both Mr. Cratcher's conviction and release on the courthouse steps. But get this, Gabby was with the group protesting for his release." She pauses, waiting for me to give a reaction. I don't, so she keeps going.

"Mr. Cratcher gave a raw and honest testimony. He said he loved Elias as a brother, and the night he died, they'd both been doing LSD and drinking. Mr. Cratcher said he passed out, and when he woke up, he was in handcuffs. After a nine-hour deliberation by the jury, Mr. Cratcher was declared not guilty.

"A few weeks later, after a ridiculous amount of threats, Mr. Cratcher and Gabby Harper married and disappeared. Currently, the murder of Elias Harper is considered a cold case. A bunch of people believe Mr. Cratcher was framed by a super-active Nashville KKK group because, after his disappearance, a known Nashville KKK leader was overheard saying Mr. Cratcher deserved to die because he was, I quote, 'romantically involved with a . . .'" She pauses to figure out how to say what's next, but her silence fills the blank.

"Got it. Just keep going."

"Abbey Road US was trashed and defaced by people angry with the verdict. The UK execs considered rebuilding, but the name was so tainted by the scandal they didn't want to do any more damage to their brand so they never reopened. The building was bought in 1990, torn down, and rebuilt as another recording studio called Bridge Studios."

When she finishes all I can say is, "Damn."

How else do you respond to a story like that? That makes my story of addiction—heck, even Dez's story of addiction—seem like an episode of *Adventure Time*.

I stare at the picture in my hands. "I don't—I don't even know what to say."

"How is Mr. Cratcher still alive?" Dez asks. "How has he not died of heartache?"

"Can we—can we just not talk about addiction, or porn, or death, or racism for a minute?"

I feel such a heaviness that I, Adam Hawthorne, a man with a penis, want to scream and sob like an infant.

"I feel like I'm being assaulted with adultness, and I'm not ready for it. We're only sixteen."

"Can I just say one more thing?"

I sigh. "Yeah, go ahead."

"The other night at Pritchett's, you said Mr. Cratcher freaked out about not having the original album, right?"

"Yeah, it was more of a meltdown and less of a freak-out."

"I'm guessing the album was either confiscated by the police or left at the studio. What if we tried to get it back for him? What if we drove to Nashville and tried to find it? If we did, we could finish the album for him. That's something worth conquering."

"How would we even do that? The case was closed years ago. All of the stuff they confiscated is probably destroyed or something."

"Does it matter? What if we tried? What if we gathered the Knights of Vice and tried?"

"Our parents would never let that happen. Besides, how would we even pay for it?"

"Adam, do you not remember the Coulter Mansion of American Waste? Money isn't a problem. I can just tell my dad some friends and I want to check out a college in Nashville and he might even charter a private jet for the occasion."

"What on earth does your dad do?"

"Stock swindler."

"By that, do you mean stock trader?"

"I *mean* stock swindler. It doesn't matter what he does. *We* should do this. It would take our minds off everything. It could be like one big stand of justice. The trip where the Knights of Vice defeat their vices. The retrieval of a lost album in the memory of racial equality. Everything about it reeks of battle."

I pick around the idea for a while. It seems super improbable that parents of addicts would let their kids go on a soul-searching trip to Nashville. We live in Washington. Nashville is more than a million steps away. Also, my research shows that when addicts soul-search, they typically decide their souls are easier to manage with the relief of a vice.

"I can't just leave. I have all this suspension crap to do, and being at Mr. Cratcher's every day is just a part of it. If I skip, I can be expelled from school. I want to go back to school, too. I miss being good at something without trying."

"Maybe we can talk to Mr. Cratcher. Get him to let you go as part of the punishment."

I laugh. "Yeah right. I'll let you do that."

I look at the clock. It's almost six-thirty and I haven't eaten or taken a shower. Even though where I'm going is completely populated by dudes, I'd like not to smell myself and think, "Ass of grim reaper."

"Come on, Adam. What if we beat our addictions because of this trip? We could date, actually date for real." She's silent. It's the silence that always comes before she says something that makes me want her more.

"I—I really want to love you, like, a greater-than-kind-of love you."

Good. Ness.

I want that, too, Dez.

Soy bad.

I really realljy wanoijt . . . youbei

"You know I can't say no to that, but I don't—"

"Just think about it, okay? Just think about how to make it happen. At least do that before you say no."

"Okay, I will."

"You promise?"

"Nah, I don't really feel like promising things right now."

"Adam, I'm your wife. Stop being so annoying."

———

Taking a shower proved to be the same amount of challenge as staring at my computer. I kept pushing porn away with thoughts about the trip. I replayed what Dez said about wanting to love me in a greater-than-addiction way over and over in my mind and that helped, too. I say all this like I was a victor in some giant mental fight, but my shower was only two minutes long.

I walk into the kitchen and reach for the Cocoa Puffs. I grab a bowl from the cupboard below. I tip the box toward my bowl, looking over my shoulder to see if my dad's in his office. The familiar patter of Cocoa Puffs falling into a ceramic bowl has changed into a swift *woosh*. I look down and see a bowl full of the gridded rectangles of Life.

"Symbolic, Dad," I say.

A chuckle drifts out of his office. "What better way to start the day with a bowl full of Life? God knows we need it."

I sit down at the table. "I like your use of poetic analogy."

"I've always considered myself a poet."

After a lifetime of only ever eating Cocoa Puffs, I can't tell if my first spoonful of Life is disgusting or revolutionary.

"What would you think about me taking a trip to Nashville?" I ask like I'm asking if he wants to go to Pritchett's later.

He doesn't respond, but I hear the rustle of him getting up from his chair. He walks over the kitchen table and sits down. "Why Nashville?"

Though she doesn't sit up and she can't see me from her spot on the couch, Addy adds, "Yeah, why Nashville?"

"It's such a long story," I say, shoving a spoonful of Life in my mouth. "Do I have to explain it to you?"

"Yes," Dad says, "you have to explain it to me."

"Yes," Addy says, "you have to explain it to me."

I tell them about Mr. Cratcher's meltdown about the unfinished song and finishing the history of the album. I explain what Dez found out about him online, her proposal about the trip and how maybe it would help the Knights of Vice beat addiction, being together. Belonging. After I finish, they both just look at me.

"Dad?" I ask after, like, two minutes of silence.

"I've been a miserable father since the divorce," he says, looking over at Addy and then me. "I was probably one before the divorce. I realize I've never talked about Mom outside of my grand ideas to get her back. I've also never asked either of you about anything that might get my hands dirty, and I'm sorry. All that to say, I know I haven't been around for you, Adam. I also know I don't deserve an answer to what I'm about to ask, but I have to ask the questions, and my consideration of this trip hinges on the way you answer."

Why can't things ever be easy? Why is everything always some giant battle?

"Okay," I say, feeling insanely uncomfortable. I stand up to wash off my spoon and bowl.

"Are you addicted to pornography? And have you told anyone what really happened at school?"

I look at Addy, who's now sitting upright and staring at me over the back of the couch. Her eyes are wide. Did she tell him? God, I'm so sick of talking about this stuff: my feelings, porn, girls, hurt, pain, death, blah, blah, blah.

I'm. So. Damn. Sick.

I grab the keys off the counter, walk out the door, and get into Genevieve. As I pull out of the driveway, images of Dad sitting at the table waiting for an answer haunt me, and I want nothing more than not to care.

CRY

I walk into Mr. Cratcher's living room and sit in the first available seat I see, which just so happens to be next to Mr. Cratcher. I can't help but stare at the guy. After finding out about all the BS he's been through, I hate myself for calling him Mr. Crotcher. Even though I realize I've stopped doing that at some point in time, I still feel like a jerk.

Great.

More guilt.

My phone vibrates. I know it's Addy.

That was incredibly mean, and stupid if you actually want to go to Nashville.

I don't answer.

"Well, everyone," Mr. Cratcher says. There's a strange look on his face I can't figure out. I know Trey and Elliot see it, too, because they keep looking at him as if he's turning into an elk. "Before we start, I want to make sure you guys know why you are together . . ."

Elliot, Trey, and I look at each other.

Our look = WTF?

"Humans are made to be together," Mr. Cratcher says. "Throughout your lives, isolation will be your greatest enemy."

I think of my Deception Pass dreams. Being alone in the Puget Sound. The crushing darkness.

"Despite what culture says, all humans are weak. Men are not exempt from this. Everybody has their own share of pain. You three have already seen death and will certainly see more. To survive the heaviness of the world, you need to experience it with others. If you can do that, you teach each other to see the beauty in chaos. That is why you've come together. Why you drive here every Monday and Friday night. You need each other to live. Don't ever forget that."

The silence in the room is daunting. It's like his statement is a final warning to us.

"Now," he says, "who's going to share first?"

Me. I am. I need to. Otherwise I may turn into a black hole.

"I prided myself on feeling nothing, like, a month or so ago, but right now, it seems like I feel everything. There are so many things to think about, questions to ask, so much hurt, everywhere, all the time. I feel like I'm going to be swallowed whole by everything, not just porn. I don't know how to make any of it stop or where I start. The only times I find relief are in moments when I'm with Dez, and the other night, when we were all together at the diner."

I pause.

"I felt that, too," Elliot says.

"Yeah," Trey adds.

Their confessions shock me. We were all feeling the same thing.

I continue. "There are these moments where, like, I see hope in her face, well, in everyone, like, it's a part of who we are. Even though everyone is as messed up as me, they're a hallelujah. I love those moments, and I want to believe they aren't limited to a few seconds a day. I want those kinds of moments for hours. I just don't know how to get them. I keep trying to figure out how it happened with us at the diner because maybe then I could do it again."

I don't know what else to say, so I just stare at the other guys, hoping someone will say something that will make me stop whining like a toddler.

Adam Hawthorne, toddler, looking for a parent with backpack leash.

Elliot shakes his head like I said something he can't believe. "That was fucking beautiful, brother. You were just a halle-lujah to me."

Trey smiles. "Maybe all it takes is just telling each other the truth, man."

Mr. Cratcher shifts in his seat. A tear slides off his cheek and disappears into the carpet. He looks in pain, but as usual, I can't tell what kind it is.

"Excuse me, boys," he says, lifting himself off the chair with a substantial effort involved.

"I've never thought about it before," Trey says. "Being together is a way of seeing beauty. Man, all this stuff seems like it's over my head, but it kind of lessens the idea of addiction, you know?"

"What do you mean?" I ask.

"It's like, deciding to see a thing as pretty cheapens addiction. Like, if I saw a chick with huge boobs." He holds his hands in front of him to show how huge he's thinking. "I'd normally want to do her, right? Well, if you think about the beauty of her, the . . . whatever you said, the hallelujah, it makes banging seem less like just a thing and more like love."

Both Elliot and I laugh.

"And you want to date my sister?" I say.

"You were almost there, Trey," Elliot says. "Almost."

Trey laughs, too. "Maybe I'll get it eventually if I keep hanging with you guys."

Suddenly, there's a crash somewhere in the house.

Trey, Elliot, and I look at each other.

"Mr. Cratcher!" I stand and run into the kitchen with the guys right behind me.

Through an empty doorframe, by the refrigerator, I see Mr. Cratcher, collapsed on the floor in the bathroom.

No.

Mr. Cratcher = my first blaze of light.

Mr. Cratcher = wisdom and hope.

Mr. Cratcher cannot = death.

Mark already = death.

I don't need any more = death.

Dear God, please let Mr. Cratcher not = death.

—

Elliot, Trey, my dad, Addy, and I sit in the waiting room in Seattle's Overlake Hospital waiting for some word about what's going on.

I called Dez. After I told her what happened, we were silent for ten minutes before she said, "I'm on my way."

He knew. Mr. Cratcher knew. That's why he gave us that speech before we started the Knights of Vice. He felt this coming. I think back to all the times I asked him questions about the album and his response was, "I'm not sure if that will be my decision."

He either knew he was dying or he felt it coming.

Suddenly, I know that whatever the doctor says will ruin us.

The elevator dings. I look and see Dez behind the doors as they slide open. I stand to go to her just as a doctor turns into the waiting room.

"Are you friends and family of Colin Cratcher?" he asks. None of us say yes, but the look of dread that washes over our faces must answer for us.

"Did he ever speak to any of you about his lung cancer?" More silence.

"I suspected as much. Mr. Cratcher was a frequent patient here. We've known about his cancer for at least a year now. Around Halloween, fluid started building in his lungs. We pumped them, and after some observation, released him. Before he left, he told me, 'This will be the last time I'll see you. Thanks for all you've done.' I personally thought he would have shown up in this state much sooner. With all that said, we've drained his lungs again, and he's starting to recover. However, regardless of his recovery, he only has about two weeks left. Three weeks max. You can visit him in a few hours, but I'm sorry to tell you he will not be communicative."

I can tell the doctor's done this before. He has a formula for it. A deep look in my eyes when he says specific words, but not long enough to be uncomfortable. He uses a gentle, but brutal, honesty. His tone is perfectly honed and shaped in rooms filled with awkward silence.

"I'm sorry I have to give you this news. I have to check on my other patients, but if you have any questions, just head over to the nurses' station and have them page me. I'll do the best I can to answer them. Again, I'm very sorry."

The doctor waits a few seconds before walking away, and his absence reveals Dez. She stands with a hand over her mouth. I walk over to her and pull her into me. The hurtful kind of pain explodes, and the only thing either of us can think to do is cry.

GO DO STUFF THAT ISN'T PORN

The Knights of Vice and Dez and Addy all sit in the living room at my house. None of us talk. We just stare at the floor, but we don't want to leave each other. I haven't let go of Dez's hand since we left the hospital three hours ago.

I don't understand how I can go from experiencing no deaths to one and a half of them in a matter of months. As soon as I started thinking, as soon as I started asking questions, it happened. Pain came. Now, even if I wanted to make myself stop asking questions, I don't think I could. I have no idea how I avoided it before. Chaos seems so present now. I feel like I'd have to be a moron not to notice.

The doorbell rings. I hear my dad say thanks, and then he appears with four pizza boxes in hand.

"I'm not sure if you guys are hungry." He puts the boxes on the coffee table. "I was, and I figured pizza never hurt anyone's feelings."

He grabs a few pieces, and the Knights of Vice attempt some pitiful thank-yous as he walks out of the room.

As I watch him leave, I feel an overwhelming urge to answer his questions. The ones he asked a day before. It's as though now that Mr. Cratcher isn't going to be around, I need someone else smarter than me to know what's going on. I need someone else willing to ask questions that piss me off, like "What are you?"

I stand, letting go of Dez's hand. She immediately uses her newfound freedom to grab a slice of pizza.

I follow my dad out of the living room and into his office.

"I've looked at porn since I was twelve, but I wasn't addicted to it until The Woman left."

Dad turns around, giving me every bit of attention he has.

"That's what I've been doing in my room," I say.

God, this is so hard. I feel like the words can't fit through my mouth, like square pegs trying to escape through circular holes. Just like when I first started talking with Addy. Luckily, he already knows why I was suspended, so I don't have to spill that on him, too.

"Hours and hours. I didn't know I was addicted until Mr. Cratcher told me. Until I met Dez. This will be a shock, but I've never had sex. I wanted to, bad. Everything that's happened is because I wanted to have sex more than anything, but I wasn't ever close enough to anyone to get it. I didn't want to be close to anyone. The Woman made me not care about other people. I figured if you could love someone as hard as you loved her and have it not matter, then why care? Why not just use people before they used you?"

He stands silent. Still. As if the act of listening fastens him to the floor.

"As for what really happened at school. I know you know, but I just . . . can't talk about it yet. Not because I want to avoid it or pretend like it didn't happen or because I think it's not a bad thing, because it is. I see that it is now. I like, feel the wrong of it like it's breath on my neck or a punch to the gut. I—I'm so broken, Dad. Like. So broken, and now that I know it, I'm afraid of people realizing I'm *too* broken to be around. That's why I haven't told anyone what I did to make the Anti-Adam Order do what they did. And all of this—suddenly having friends, like real friends, Addy, Dez, Mr. Cratcher, Mark, the list goes into space. All of it just hits me over and over, and it's the most painful and healing thing that's ever happened to me. I still don't know what any of it means. I'm still addicted to porn, but I don't want to be."

He stares at me. I can't read his eyes. Are they cold? Are they angry? Indifferent? He puts the pizza down on his desk, and then, for the first time in my life that I can remember, my dad hugs me. I've never given a thought to my dad hugging me, and I think if I'd thought about it before now, I would have cringed. But now that he has, I will expect him to do so for the rest of my life.

Being honest is one of the hardest things I've ever done. It doesn't come easy like lying or telling half-truths, but it does come with freedom. What was it that Trey said? Not the whole banging a girl with big boobs fiasco, the other thing? Something like: "If we're just honest together, it creates those hallelujah moments."

Suddenly, I have an answer to one question. It isn't a life changing answer, but it's an answer I didn't have before.

What do you do when death's heavy on you?

Go to Nashville, find that album, and then finish a forty-year-old project.

Together.

—

We all sit at Pritchett's. The fries are silently picked at. Milkshakes slurped with sadness. Even Addy is silent. I nod at Dez and she taps against her milkshake glass.

"Hear ye, hear ye," she says.

"What?" Elliot snaps.

She ignores him. "Everything sucks. We all hate ourselves. And now that Mr. Cratcher's about to kick the can, we're in dire need of something awesome to take our minds off the intense magnitude of suckitude."

"Very honest introduction," Addy adds.

Dez raises her hands. "Hey, it's not false information."

"Keep going," I say.

"Where was I?" she asks.

"In dire need of something awesome."

"Right. Therefore, we're in dire need of something awesome. A few incredible facts about Mr. Cratcher have come to light via the interwebs that suggest this possible something awesome."

Dez explains everything she found out about Mr. Cratcher and my picture. She proposes the trip to Nashville and finishing the album and how being together could help us beat our addictions. How it would make Mr. Cratcher happy to see his album finished before he died. When she finishes, Trey and Elliot just look at each other.

"I can be the creepy old chaperone," Addy says. "I have vacation days I need to use before the year's up. I mean, if you guys want me to. I'm not really in on the whole addict camaraderie, but I do like you as people."

Trey looks at her. "I want you to go. Maybe a few days will be good together. You'll realize how that little one-year age difference between us doesn't matter."

Addy laughs. "So apparently Trey's going."

Dez smiles. "I didn't think he'd be hard. Elliot?"

Elliot looks at all of us but points at me. "You're already into this?"

I nod. "Yeah. Dez and I talked about it a little bit already."

He sighs. "Shit, I can't say no if everyone's going."

"So, you'll go?"

He nods. "I mean, if our parents are all chill with it. Yeah."

"Well then, fellow Knights of Vice members, honorary and actual," Dez says. "You're charged with talking to your parents about it tonight. Use any means necessary to get it to work."

Trey nods. "Cool. You know, now that I think about it, this could be really awesome."

"It will be," Dez says.

"Yeah," I say, feeling like we're about to embark on one of those adventures everyone dreams about.

I think about my friends. About this moment. About the future. I'm so overwhelmed with a hallelujah in the middle of a storm that I stand on the booth and raise my milkshake. Most of Pritchett's looks at me, but I ignore them.

"We head east for freedom, fellowship, Mr. Cratcher, and old-man music!"

Dez stands on the booth, glass raised, and then Addy, which of course makes Trey stand, as well.

"I'm not standing on the booth," Elliot says.

I start chanting, "Stand on the booth. Stand on the booth."

"I'm not doing it, so stop."

The rest of us start chanting.

"Guys, if you don't shut the hell up, I'm leaving."

Slowly, everyone in Pritchett's joins in the chant. Addy, Trey, Dez, and I share a laugh but keep going, getting louder and louder.

Finally, he curses a million times but stands. The booth strains under him. He wobbles, trying to get his footing, and he starts to fall over. Pritchett's goes silent. Trey reaches to catch him and grabs his wrist. Elliot rights himself and flips us all off.

"He stood on the booth!" I yell.

Pritchett's applauds.

I raise my milkshake. The others do as well.

"For Mr. Cratcher!"

The Knights of Vice respond. "For Mr. Cratcher!"

—

"Dad, it's not like we're going to millions of nightclubs. I don't even know what a nightclub is. You said a while back that if I was honest with you, you'd think about letting me go on this trip."

My dad sits in his office chair, shaking his head. We've been arguing back and forth about the Nashville trip for thirty minutes now. "I am thinking about it, Adam, and of course you know what a nightclub is. You have one in your room."

"No, I don't."

"You have all the benefits of a nightclub in your room."

I cock my head.

"Porn, Adam. You have porn. Forget it. It was a bad analogy. All I'm saying is, I just don't think it's the best idea. You are sixteen—"

"Addy and Trey aren't. Elliot is seventeen."

"My point is you've only had your license for a few months. What if it snows? Do you know what to do in the snow? What if you get in a wreck? You don't even know how to change a spare tire."

"If it snows, Addy or Trey will drive. If we wreck, Dez will get us there with all her money. If we need to change a tire, Dez has roadside assistance with AAA."

"What if someone gets hurt?"

"No one will get hurt."

"Someone will probably get hurt."

"Addy, then."

"You can't just answer everything with Addy."

"Why not?" she asks, walking through the door and dumping her black backpack on the couch. "I'm totally up for being the answer to everything. It'll be hard for you two to believe, but I don't get the chance to be it often."

My dad sighs. "You're telling me you're up for being the sole chaperone of a bunch of . . . whatever they are?"

Addy leans against the wall, pulling the drawstrings on her Coalweather Construction hoodie so that the hood forms a tight circle around her face. "Trey is an adult. So he's in charge of his own self, but the rest? Yeah, I think they'll be all right. If we run into trouble, we can just come back. If any kids can be trusted with a road trip, I think it's these ones. Regardless of their addiction status. Besides, I really wanna see the Blue Bird Café where Amelia Hunt got her start."

"What about Christmas?" Dad asks. "Are you going to miss Christmas?"

"Addy," I answer. "Kidding. No. We'll be back before Christmas."

My dad opens his mouth like he's going to ask another question, but after a few seconds of silence, I point at him.

"Aha! See? You're out of parental concerns. I've won."

"You've done nothing of the sort. I'll think about it, Adam."

"Dad! You literally have no more questions."

He turns around and starts scrolling through his agent inbox. "I'll think about it. That's all I'll give you for now. Now go do stuff that isn't porn."

LORD OF THE FLIES REENACTMENT

I place a mic stand in front of Dez and lift the microphone up to her lips. "Okay, so I think this is how he did it."

"God," she says. "This album is historical, monumental, riddled with lore and scandal. It's got to be poetic and good and perfect, yet it's going to sound like someone let a bunch of toddlers loose in a music studio."

I sit in front of Mr. Cratcher's computer and prep the DAW for recording. "It won't be that bad. I had enough time with him to figure out some things. His masterpiece will sound like someone let a bunch of teenagers loose in a studio, at the very least."

"That might be worse, because everything we do is on purpose. I mean, don't get me wrong, working on this album will be like the coolest thing I ever do, but still. I feel like someone just handed me the Mona Lisa and a paintbrush and told me to restore it."

"Meh, it'll be fine."

"You do realize you've got to sing with me, right?"

"This album is doomed. How many songs did you record with Mr. Cratcher?"

"Just that one. What was it called?"

"Um." I click around, trying to find how he labeled it. "D&C."

"That doesn't help. That could mean anything."

"Dungeon and cataracts?" I ask. "Death and cancer?"

"Just, shhh." She covers her eyes with her right hand. "Dust and Cradle. It's 'Dust and Cradle.' There's a line in it that goes, 'From hurt to love, from abandon to enough, from dust and cradle we live.'"

"Well, at least we know one song title out of eleven."

"Did you talk to Trey?" she asks. "He said he plays electric guitar. Didn't Mr. Cratcher want every instrument ever on this album? How was he going to make it relevant but also keep its soul? Was he going to allow synths or are they too synthy? Can we take some modern musical liberties with it? Or should we keep it away from reverb? Glitch effects? Accordion? What's the line?"

"Wow. Did you drink coffee recently?"

"No. I'm just a concerned freelance musician trying to do another man's life work justice. No big deal."

"The music will work itself out. It'll sound like it sounds."

"You sound like every band interview ever. What happens when we finish it?"

"Maybe we can find some of his old contacts in Nashville and be musicians for a living."

"Finally, a life plan. My parents will be thrilled."

I clear my throat and play an older version of the song we're about to record. I'm not going to lie—I'm incredibly nervous. I've never considered myself a singer or a musician. I've only ever considered myself a connoisseur of NPR and fine breakfast cereals.

"How about we change that verse," she says. "I don't think saying 'I've been a delinquent, I am a ruler' is the way modern Mr. Cratcher would've written that."

I watch her as she writes down some substitute lyrics on the window with a dry erase marker. Her face catches the morning sun, and the sight makes me want to tell her everything about me. To be known. To banish the darkness of Deception Pass on my own time, not anyone else's.

I want to tell her everything.

I think about talking to my dad. Telling him why I haven't opened up to anyone about school, and then I shake my head, trying to snap myself out my Dez-induced daze.

She lifts an eyebrow. "Involuntary shiver?"

"Huh?"

"When you suddenly get the shakes, but not because you're cold. It's like your body decided it was allergic to itself."

I smile at her statement, and the way her gray military jacket hangs off her shoulders. I walk over to her and put my hands around her waist. I pull her back into my chest, but she turns around. I'm so overwhelmed with her light that I need to kiss her. I lean toward her lips, but she puts a finger on mine.

"Future Boyfriend, we can't be that yet."

My happiness dies. "But what if what we *want* to be and what we *can* be aren't the same thing? What if what we want to be isn't possible?"

She kisses my forehead. "That's something I'd ask, not you. You need to believe it for the both of us."

"That's not fair. What about the times when I can't?"

"You don't have those. Not like I do."

That's not true at all, because I'm currently having one. What if we're in a perpetual state of not yet? What if we're never good enough?

No.

There has to be a better way, and I need to fight for it. I need to fight for Dez. Maybe fighting for her starts with telling her everything. Maybe one of the ways we aren't "that" yet is because she doesn't know all of me. She'll have the chance to leave me, yeah, but maybe the only way to ensure our future of being "that" is by giving her the chance to choose all of me. The dark and the light.

But what if she leaves?

I just got her.

She's the only girl who's ever wanted to date me.

She'll leave.

You're too broken.

You're dirt. Unforgivable.

You aren't worth fighting for.

You're worth a stick of Juicy Fruit. Why would she stick around?

All of this rushes through my head over and over. Echoing on itself, gnawing its way into my nerves, and I know that the spark I have to ignite my honesty needs to catch the fire quick, otherwise it'll die before the words get out.

"Future Boyfriend," she says, taking my hands off her waist. "Justin Timberlake and Beyoncé didn't get giant Twitter followings by standing around like idiots in a music studio. We need to record. I have to get to school—"

I take a deep breath. "I asked girls at my school for sex. I offered money to a few."

She looks at me with soft eyes, prompting me to tell the story. Telling me whatever I say next she'll understand.

"I had this list on the back of my door of all the girls at my school I thought were hot. A list of girl's names I was working through."

I still feel like dirt. I still feel responsible for pouring my unnatural disaster self all over someone else. A bunch of someone elses.

I look at Dez. Waiting for her to tell me we're done. Waiting for her to see me as unlovable, just like my mom did when she didn't even say good-bye. Just like the way Addy's leaving told me my mom was worth more than I was. Her eyes bore into mine, but she says nothing.

"I didn't care about people, Dez. The Woman leaving, Addy, my family. I'd decided that people weren't worth the manual labor of caring I think because I believed that about everyone else, I believed that about myself. I love porn because there's no labor involved outside of moving my hand. Those girls don't hurt me. Anyway, in the span of a week, I'd asked a bunch of girls to have sex with me who were in the same group of friends, who now call themselves The Anti-Adam Order. I offered one twenty bucks to do me in the hallway. She pretended to say yes and started making out with me right in the hall. Then before we went anywhere, she started screaming. Teachers came running. They used that, the fact that I'd offered her money, and the other girls' testimonies about my asking for sex to win the suspension."

I pause. Too afraid to look at her. Too afraid to let our souls touch.

"At the time, I didn't think I deserved that retribution from those girls. Now, the hardest part about remembering is that I was so sure I hadn't done anything wrong. So sure I was the victim because I hadn't forced myself on the other girls; I'd only asked, only offered money. I thought I was in the clear, but I'm so not. I'm the opposite. I'm a smoky tendril of evil. The Anti-Adam Order is legit. They formed because of how much I sucked at being a human."

I laugh and wipe a tear forming in my eye.

"Now I'm part of my own anti-order. I hate myself for all of it. For what I still do."

I've feared this moment since we talked on her bed after Mark's funeral. Is this enough for her to decide I'm too messed up? Can a girl only have so much grace for a guy? Especially one who was trying to pay girls to do him? The Woman didn't have any grace for my dad, and he didn't cheat on her once. I'm pretty much handing Dez a platter full of steaming bucket'a'bull and asking, "Am I still awesome?"

My eyes feel wet. I wipe at them haphazardly and aggressive as though I can catch the tears before she sees them, even though I've been crying through the whole story.

She grabs my hand. "Look at me."

I bring my gaze up. "It's just my eyes sweating. Not crying."

She laughs and then pushes herself onto her tiptoes and kisses my forehead again. I feel like a Pokémon. Like, before that kiss, I was Adam, but now I've evolved into Adameo: body of fire with nine million HP.

"You have nothing to worry about, Future Boyfriend," she says. "I like my men like I like myself: human. I don't know what the Anti-Adam Order is, but I'm not in it, and if we were all honest, we'd all have our own anti-orders. What you did was wrong, yeah, and you'll have to deal with it, but that doesn't make you horrible for infinity. We're all just dirt with legs. All of us. We may think we aren't, but we are. Okay?"

I wipe my eyes again. "Yeah. Yeah. Okay."

"Thanks for telling me."

"No one else knows. I haven't even told Addy yet."

She nods. "You should."

"I've just been so scared. I think . . . so I've been having these dreams about the last vacation my family went on before The Woman left."

I tell her about each one. How, in every one, my family leaves me and I'm alone in darkness so crushing it feels like I can't breathe.

"I've been thinking the dreams were about the moment I realized my family left me. I mean, they are, but I also think they're about how I didn't do anything about it. The deception is the distraction of me blaming the crushing darkness on everyone who left. Some of it is their fault, but I gave myself to isolation without a fight. Maybe the dreams are saying as long as I think the darkness is other people's fault, I'll wait for them to fix it. I'm deceived into thinking I have nothing to do with my own isolation, so I just stew in my hurt and drift further and further away from shore."

She holds my hand and considers the dreams. "It sounds to me like maybe you get off the log and swim back."

I laugh at the simplicity of it, but it makes so much sense. "Yeah. Yeah. Me, too."

"Deception Pass Park," she says. "I've always wanted to go there."

I laugh. "I'm sort of afraid of it now."

She kisses me again. "Maybe we can fix that. Now, let's sing together about the woes of an old man riddled with cancer."

I let out a sigh of relief and sit in the office chair. I might have romantic feelings for Dez, but they're temporarily replaced with how thankful I am for a friend as kind and caring as she is.

I've never respected anyone more than I respect Dez Coulter right now.

—

Dez and I walk into Mr. Cratcher's room, and I'm not sure which one of us isn't letting go of the other. It was the same way when we came four days ago.

"My dad said yes," I say. "All our parents said yes. We won the battle. Mostly thanks to Addy, but still, your Knights of Vice are going to Nashville over Christmas break. We're going to get your album back. We're going to finish it for you. We promise."

"It helped a lot that we could all use the 'our mentor is dying card,'" Dez says. "So, thanks for that."

"I'm going to take our daily morning time and get better at the guitar. I may have snuck into your house the other night so I could listen to the last eight versions of your album and dig through your journals. I also may have stolen the extra house key under the planter."

"I helped," Dez says, smiling. "It may have triggered a new addiction—stealing—but I've managed it by taking paper clips out of my dad's office. I'm not sure how long I'll be happy with that, but the good news is it's a lot cheaper vice than alcohol."

I look up at Dez. "Did we tell him everything?"

She thinks for a minute. "Oh, I keep thinking about your stupid question and I don't know yet."

"I don't either," I add. "And it *is* a stupid question."

The smirk on Dez's face disappears. "Wait." She bends over and whispers something into his ear. "Is that it?" She stares at him for a few seconds, waiting for him to answer.

"It's close? That's good." She turns to me. "Future Boyfriend?"

"Yeah?"

"Did you ever make a guess at his question?"

"I tried 'we're all variables' once and he shook his head."

"Was it a 'no, you're an imbecile' kind of shake? Or was it a 'you're close' kind of shake."

"The latter."

"Hmmm."

"What?"

"I've just decided that I'm going to read *Fahrenheit 451* by Ray Bradbury during our Nashville trip."

"Okay, then."

—

It's the Monday before Thanksgiving, and Addy and I are sitting at the kitchen table eating dinner before we go to Transparency Forum (which has, not surprisingly, grown to include Dez and Addy) when my dad comes through the doors, talking on the phone.

"Really?" he says. "Wow, that's . . . weird. Yeah, I'll sign it. Just send me the papers. Okay. Yeah, that sounds great. Yep. Bye."

I shove a spoonful of Life in my mouth. "Wbho wub thbat?"

"So attractive, Papi," Addy says.

"Hbey, wbhen"—I swallow—"a man needs information, he needs it. Why Papi?"

"When a woman needs a ham sandwich, she needs it," she says. "Am I right?"

We fist bump, and I look back at my dad.

"Mr. Cratcher's lawyer," he says.

Mr. Cratcher must've finally let go. The doctor keeps telling us the next time we see him he'll be gone, but Dez and I go every other day and he's always there, breathing. It isn't much of a life, but it's still life.

"So . . ." I say, waiting for Dad to drop the bomb. I've been preparing for this the last few weeks. I tell myself every morning I've seen the last of him, and that the heaviness will go away eventually.

That somewhere in this chaos there's beauty.

"So, before I say anything else, how long did you look at porn last night?"

I drop my eyes back to my bowl.

"Adam?"

Addy flicks my ear. "Adam?"

"Does anyone else find it awkward that my porn habits are being discussed by the whole family at the dinner table?"

My dad shakes his head.

"Nope," Addy says, "love makes this totally normal. Now answer."

I groan. "For like, two hours."

"Why?" Dad asks.

"Dez hung up on me like she always does when she's pissed about something, but this time it just made me feel horrible."

"So you medicated?"

I sigh. "Yeah. Sure."

"Okay, well, I want you to consider this. I'm not going to force you to do it, but just consider getting rid of your laptop, or at least getting some sort of accountability thing for it. Same deal with your phone. This is one of those life or death decisions Mr. Cratcher was always talking about, and you have to make it for yourself. You affect others now. You know, the Knights of Vice, your girlfriend—"

"We're not dating."

Addy rolls her eyes.

"It doesn't matter if you are or aren't," Dad says. "Think about how porn trains your ability to love others. It's a battle, I know, but it's only a battle if you keep fighting. Your sister and I can only knock on your door so many times. We have work to do. We're willing to help, but in the end, you have to choose what you want."

"I'll pay for the accountability software," Addy says, "that way you have no excuses. Actually, after this conversation, I'm marching you upstairs and we're signing up for it. How about that for some action steps?" She leans toward my ear and whispers, "Boom."

I stare at them both, reminding myself I wanted them to ask me hard things.

"Now," Dad says, pausing to make sure I have nothing to say to Addy. "About Mr. Cratcher. His lawyer, Mr. Stevens, said Mr. Cratcher's will was made out to Gabby even though she passed on. Apparently, Mr. Steven's pushed Mr. Cratcher to change it for the last five years, but Mr. Cratcher and Gabby had no children and neither had family, so Mr. Stevens assumed it still hadn't been updated when he flew into town last night to deal with the estate, but he found a new will."

I nearly choke on my cereal. If he says I've inherited Mr. Cratcher's estate, I may have to fill out a will of my own.

"And there were four inheritors."

"Adam Hawthorne, Elliot Brickman, Trey Lyons, and Dez Coulter?" I ask.

"Yep."

Holy.

Addy laughs, "No way, that's crazy."

"So, we get all his stuff?" I say.

"Maybe. We don't know a ton about how this is going to happen, and Mr. Cratcher isn't dead yet. He still might recover."

He won't recover. He's been in the lion's den way too long to come out whole.

"Mr. Stevens is calling everyone or their parents, so the rest of the Knights of Vice will know about—"

My phone rings.

"Hello?"

"We're inheriting all his stuff?" Dez says.

"Yeah, I guess. Crazy, huh?"

"I call his old man books."

"I don't know how we thought we were going to record the album if this didn't happen. All his recording equipment would've been sold off."

"Our destiny hath been ordered by the almighty to be folk stars."

"I don't think folk stars exist. Sorry, baby."

Did I just say *baby*?

Addy's eyebrows bunch and she looks at me. I just shrug. Why am I suddenly a fountain of pet names, especially one as stock as *baby*? I've never called her anything but Dez and/or objects found in nature. A mountain in the morning sun. A forest of trees in a northern fall.

"Want to go to the house early and look around?"

Okay, so she has no response to essentially being called "a useless human." That's good. Why is *baby* a pet name? If Dez and I ever get to the pet name stage, it's off the list.

"Yeah, I'll head over now."

I stand and put my dinner plate in the sink. "Addy, do you want to come over early with me?"

She shakes her head. "Nope. I've still got to take a shower."

I wave the comment away. "You don't have to take a shower; there's no one to impress."

Addy shrugs. "I don't want to impress anyone. I just smell like garlic toast. See?" She holds her hand out to my nose. I take a whiff and smell nothing, but I fake gag like I just ate something disgusting.

She laughs, drops her plate into the sink, flicks my ears, and runs up the stairs.

—

"This man should've been on a hoarding show. Look at all this."

I turn to the right, but I can't see what Dez is pointing at, which I guess is kind of her point.

"It's just his garage, though," I say. "His house is pretty clean."

"Adam, I can't even see you. It doesn't matter how clean his house is."

I push against a pile—and by pile, I mean mountain—of whatnot. The thing-mountain tips to the side, hits another thing-mountain, and Bothell, Washington, has its first ever avalanche.

"Sorry," I say, waving dust away from my face. "Are you okay?"

"I was just hit in the head with a kazoo signed by Bob . . . Dylan. How does that even happen?"

I poke around in a box of what I thought were vinyl records, only to find folder after folder of tax records.

Vinyl records. Taxes. Honest mistake.

"I'm pretty sure this guy collects Seattle's 2011 tax forms," I say. "Wait. These are just his, from the last fifty years. Holy . . . Mr. Cratcher was making between $100,000 and $300,000 a year for the last twenty years. How is that possible?"

I'm not going to lie. I feel both giddy and guilty when I think of how much he'll leave behind.

"I might know," Dez says. "Come over here."

I walk around boxes, totes, and stacks of newspapers to find Dez staring at a box filled with pictures. No, not pictures, sheets of lyrics matted in picture frames.

She holds a long, skinny frame out to me. Behind the glass are five sheets of paper. Her mouth hangs open in shock, which is kind of sexy. I want her to be surprised more often. I grab the frame and read the sheets of college-lined notepaper. I know these words. I know these words. I skip to the last page.

To the man willing, and forced, to be invisible. Your willingness to enter into my mess has always been the deepest of sleep to me. You are rest, my friend. Your line, "blaze of light in every word," will haunt me forever. However, as always, I wrote everything else. Just in case you decide to forget. As your letter requested, I will not reveal your name or location. However, if you decide to work under a pseudonym, please let me know so I can help you advertise what your beautiful wife calls "an underground songwriting career."

All the best,
Leonard Cohen

"There's a ton more," Dez says, "but none of them use Mr. Cratcher's name. Some use The Chaos Writer, but that's it. I wonder how many music stars know the Abbey Road scandal guy was writing their songs?"

"Okay, can we first talk about the fact that he has a letter from Leonard Cohen talking about how he wrote the line 'blaze of light in every word'?"

"Do we have to? It kind of makes Mr. Cratcher seem like a douche."

I don't know whether to laugh or to defend him. "You probably shouldn't call a guy who's about to give you his estate a douche."

"But he played that song for both of us, knowing he wrote that line."

"It shouldn't matter. The words impacted him, and he wanted to share it with us. It makes those moments where he played the song for us a little different, yeah, but it shouldn't lower Mr. Cratcher to douche status."

"Since when did you become sensitive?" she asks.

"I met this girl who made me care about stuff and my machismo has been declining ever since."

She puts a frame down, grabs my hands, and slides them around the curves of her waist.

"The world doesn't need any more men who don't care," she says. "Or any more men who think that machismo declines because you're vulnerable and keep tabs on how you feel."

I want to tell her I'm kidding about my machismo declining, but I feel her sincerity and decide against it.

Her blue eyes melt me in the middle of a hoarder's garage. I want to kiss her, but I've already tried that and it didn't work, but then again, here she is, putting my hands around her waist and I wasn't allowed to do that before. Confused, I put my feelings somewhere else. I try to feel such a strong hate for porn that I'll never think about it again, although, thinking about not thinking about porn makes me think about porn.

God.

I feel guilt rise in my gut, but I focus on her arms around my neck and the warmth of her waist sending the beautiful kind of pain up my arms.

She pulls herself tighter into my chest. "The world and I need you to be Adam who cares."

"I lo—"

She puts her finger on my lips just like she did when I tried to kiss her in Cratcher's studio a few days ago.

"Not yet. I want it to be true when we say it. If we want to survive, our love can't be a shadow. It's got to be a blaze. I need to know addicts can blaze."

"I know they can. If there's anything I've learned in the last few months, it's that there's a blaze of light in everyone."

"You say that, but blaze equals fire, and fire still consumes. In the end, I still need a high, and I want/don't want it to be you." She makes a greater than sign with her fingers and points it at my chest. "I want the greater-than love. Until we have that, we're just volcanoes. Keep believing in us, Adam."

There it is again. The idea that *I'm* the one who has to believe in us. The idea that just me believing is good enough to carry us through to the other side.

"Hello?" someone yells in the other room. It sounds like Trey. Dez and I let go of each other and go back to looking through the lyrics.

"Hey! We're in the garage!" I yell. "Be warned, this place is an avalanche of loot and plunder."

"Did you guys get the phone call?" Trey asks, being vague in case we didn't. He sticks his head into the garage, "Holy . . ."

"Yeah, welcome to our next, like, million years," Dez says.

"How are we going to decide who gets what without killing each other?" Trey asks.

"I don't need much," Dez says. "I just want to be able to finish the album."

"Let's save that discussion for when Elliot gets here," I say. "No need to start a *Lord of the Flies* reenactment."

MOMENTARY COLLISION OF BEAUTY AND CHAOS

It's December 17th, and Christmas break has struck. I stuff some shirts and the one other pair of jeans I own into a backpack. I look around my room, wondering what else I have that deserves to be brought to Nashville. It's been a month since Dad got the call from Mr. Cratcher's lawyer about his estate, and, in that time, the Knights of Vice have kept meeting. Pritchett's switched to holiday flavors for milkshakes, I only have a month left of suspension, and Mr. Cratcher is still somehow hanging on.

As I'm packing, I notice the Ask List on the back of my door. I'd forgotten it was there. I walk over to it, unpin it, and dump it behind my door. The first thing in my official throw-in-Dez's-pool pile. I grab my computer bag and absentmindedly unplug my laptop cord from the wall.

Wait.

This is a trip where we beat our addictions by being together and focusing on the hallelujah moments. Why would I bring my computer when it's like, half the problem? A month's time of accountability software has definitely helped, but I'm nowhere near fixed. I'm as far from fixed as Michael Phelps is from winning a gold medal in lacrosse. Would Dez get mad at me if I brought it? Maybe she'd run it over with the SUV her mom secretly bought us just for this trip.

SUV + just for this trip = rich white ignorant person mindset = Dez pissed = Trey, Elliot, and me having to beg Dez to use it.

I rub my eyes and pull my computer out of the bag, but I don't put him down. I stare at him, waiting for something to rise within me and choose the right thing. What if we need him for research? What if we need to write stuff down, or put our leads into a spreadsheet? What if all our phones die and this is our only way to communicate? This is a communication decision, not a vice decision. Besides, Addy *did* sign me up for that accountability software. She'll hear about it if I look at anything. It's fine. I slide it in my bag, zip it up, and head downstairs.

I drop my bags by the front door next to Addy's duffel. "Addy?" I yell, but she doesn't answer. I look outside and she's leaning against her truck, talking on her phone. I head over to my dad's office, but he isn't there. I go down the hall and see him moving around in his room. I knock and open the door. He jumps.

"Dad, we're leaving." I look past him. Each of his dresser drawers is open, and I see the handle of a suitcase peeking out from behind his bed. "What are you doing?"

"I'm just cleaning stuff out I'm not wearing anymore," he says. "I was trying to put some clothes away this morning and couldn't get my drawers shut. Donation time."

I shrug. "Sounds fun, I guess."

We walk into the kitchen and he leans against the fridge. "I talked to Trey and Elliot's parents last night."

"Yeah? I didn't know all the parentals were at the cell phone communication friendship level."

"Well, we are now because we all had concerns about this trip."

"So why are you all letting us go?"

"Because . . ." He sighs. "I guess we know you've all had a rough time the past few months. These guys are your friends, and I've wanted you to have friends for a while. As crazy a thing this is, you want to do something with friends and that's a huge thing. And you're all pushing each other to be better, too. You use phrases like 'cell phone communication friendship level,' so you're obviously smart. Addy's going to be there. Trey is almost twenty. I guess we're just willing to take a chance that the trip will help you in some way."

"I know it will. This isn't just some senior-year road trip where our destination is on the corner of Wasted and Laid."

"I know, I know. Still, make sure all of you follow the rules I gave you. If you don't, I'm going to call Mrs. Coulter and have her cut off the funding."

"Like she'd do that," I say. "She's probably happy to have a house that isn't filled with arguments all the time."

"If I have to bribe them by making Mr. Coulter a client, I will."

The Coulters don't really know the full details of the trip. Dez went straight to her mom and told her she wanted to go check out a college in Nashville with some friends. Her mom then relayed the info to Mr. Coulter, who then promptly said no because it wasn't Ivy League. So, because Mrs. Coulter actually has a sliver of a soul left, she bought an SUV and set up lodging in secret. Dez doesn't feel bad about lying, but I sort of do, and if my dad talked to the Coulters at all, he'd realize Dez lied.

"You're making great progress in the seriousness of your threats."

"That may be the best thing you've ever said to me."

We hug. It's cool we do that now. Maybe a lot of other guys don't think it's cool to hug your dad, but it reminds me in some strange way that we're both in this humanity thing together.

"Also, forgot to tell you the principal called and asked how things were going the other day."

"Did you tell her I'm an outstanding citizen, now?"

"No, but I did tell her you're honoring the structure we put in place."

After it became obvious Mr. Cratcher wasn't going to get better, I wrote up pretty much the same proposal Mr. Cratcher gave, but with Addy and Dad as the "mentors." Principal Johnson was chill with it, so I've still been going to the AA meetings and meeting with the Knights of Vice. I've even continued working on his album even though it was a little sad for a while just being in his house alone.

"And?" I ask. Hoping. Praying. Salivating for him to say I can go back to school even though I know there's not a reason I shouldn't.

"She wants to meet with you before the start of the semester, but she thinks the time has done enough for you that you'll start back up after Christmas Break."

I pump my fist. "Awesome. So awesome. Okay, Addy's leaving her truck here, and I'm parking Genevieve at Mr. Cratcher's. We're leaving from there."

"Alright, I'll be sure to call you if I hear any news about him."

News = death.

"Sounds good." I grab my bags and open the door.

"Drive safe, Adam. Please be responsible."

"We will."

—

"Who were you talking too?" I ask Addy as she shoves her phone into her pocket.

She pulls the passenger side sun visor down and uses the mirror to check her hair. "My boss. As soon as I leave, he falls into little bitty pieces."

"You are the wind beneath his wings?"

"And I totally know that I'm his hero."

We pull into Mr. Cratcher's driveway and park next to his lonely, tan Ford Taurus. Trey and Dez are already here. Trey's looking around in our trip SUV—a sparkling blue Subaru Crosstrek Hybrid—and Dez is holding a shoebox full of stickers, putting them all over the trunk lid and bumper. I grab the bags from the backseat.

"What are you doing?" I ask her.

"If I'm being forced to use the blood SUV built on the backs of factory workers just trying to make it by, I'm going turn it into a normal person's car. This way, if one of those factory workers sees us on the road, they won't think it's an SUV bought for a one-time Christmas break road trip."

"Wow," Addy says, running a finger over some of the stickers. "Wake up on the dramatic manic pixie side of the bed this morning?"

Dez glares at her. I know using the SUV makes her feel like she's being like her parents, but it's the best option for travel.

I look at some of the stickers Dez has already put on. Of course, the popular coexist sticker—the one made up of all of the religion symbols—is smack dab in the top center of window frame. Next to that is some band I've never heard of. Next to that is a 26.2 sticker.

"Have you even run a 5k?" I ask.

"Would you two just support me instead of being annoying?" She holds out the box of stickers and I grab a handful.

Addy points at the box. "Give me that 'my other car is a car' sticker."

"Where are you going to put it?" I ask.

"Give me that one, too." She points at one I'd just tossed to the side.

"The one that says 'your mom is watching you'? Are you seriously going to put that one up?"

"Relax, Papi," Addy says and disappears.

"Why does Addy call you Papi?" Dez asks.

"Do you know what it means?"

Dez shrugs. "Ask Trey."

"I could probably just look it up."

"It's a Latino term of endearment for little kids. My older sister still calls me Papi," Trey says, dropping his bags by the back passenger wheel.

I groan, then tip my head back and yell. "Addy, don't call me Papi ever again."

She responds, but I have no idea where she is. "Then what am I going to call you?"

"You could call him Chiquito instead!" Trey says, thinking he's being helpful.

"No! No, you can't." I turn back to Dez. "So, where's the bumper sticker line between normal person and egotistical outdoorsman wanting the world to know he buys Patagonia underwear?"

Dez pauses mid-stickering. "I didn't think of that. I haven't crossed it, have I? How did I not consider the possibility of this being a shrine to consumerism?"

"What on earth are you two talking about?" Trey asks.

"What do these stickers say to you?" I ask.

Trey takes a step back and looks over the smorgasbord of sayings, names, and symbols. "Adventure. Pure adventure, and that the people inside are awesome."

Dez scoffs. "We can't ask the optimist what he thinks. Where's Elliot?"

Trey looks at me with "do something" written all over his face.

"Dez," I say, "why don't we pack the bags so when Elliot shows up, we can just throw his stuff inside and go? You're not your family if you use the car. It's okay."

Dez throws the box of stickers on the ground. "Fine." She walks toward Mr. Cratcher's house and disappears inside, leaving me and Trey to pack the bags.

"She does that a lot, man," Trey says.

"What?"

"The disappearing stuff."

"You can always tell when it's going to happen."

"You can?"

I place my backpack and computer bag against the back seat and then push Trey's bag next to them.

"Yeah, she never uses the word *fine* in any other context. It's always *fine*, and then she walks away or hangs up." I look at him with a smirk and stuff Dez's bag into an empty corner. "At least she's predictable, right?"

He finally realizes I'm not talking out of frustration and pats me on the back with a laugh. "Yeah, man. Totally. You've got that going for you."

When Elliot arrives, he immediately asks if the car was bought used by a hippie, which pisses Dez off even more. He tells her "your manic pixie is showing," which makes it even worse. I add a "Baby on Board" sticker to level out everything, because babies are the great levelers.

Dez doesn't agree.

She throws her hands in the air. "Now it's obvious we have no idea what we're doing."

"Isn't that perfect for us, though?"

She stares at the stickers for at least another minute before saying, "It's perfect, but I'm *not* the mother of that child."

Addy finally comes back and puts her sticker on the bumper of the car. "Here you go, Dez. This will cheer you up."

I look at it. She's combined the two stickers with some clever cuts so they look like one. It says: "My other car is your mom."

Dez laughs and then points at it. "If we did pass the line, that just brought us back." She hugs Addy with a big smile and says, "You're the most amazing person in the world."

"Well, thanks," Addy says, winking at me.

One of the rules instated by the Knights of Vice parentals was that anyone under the age of eighteen can't drive longer than five hours in a row. So, we set up a rotating order that starts with me driving, Dez in the passenger seat, and Elliot between Trey and Addy in the back. Dez was the one smart enough to figure out that if we rotate to the right, she and I will sit next to each other for more than half of the trip.

I pull onto I-90 East, which we'll be on until Iowa. I'm a little nervous about driving five hours on a highway. I've only ever been on a highway about thirty minutes, but I don't tell anyone that. Dez declares the front seat passenger gets to pick the music, and she plugs an aux cable into her phone. A warm folk song comes on. I've never been an avid music listener, so I have no idea who it is, but the music fits the mood: the glowing morning sun beckoning us to drive into it, the warmth of Dez's hand on my knee, the buzz of tires spinning on and on. In this hallelujah moment, I think we all feel like we're more than addicts. When we start replacing words in movie titles with poop (*Indiana Jones and the Poop of Doom*), I feel my age for the first time since Mark died. I'm in love with it all.

Dez leans over to me and whispers, "I could swear I love you."

"You probably do," I whisper back.

She snickers and hits me in the chest.

"I think you're alright," I say, and she just rolls her eyes.

I smile, enjoying this momentary collision of beauty and chaos.

LIKE, RIGHT NOW?

We stop for gas on the border of Washington and Montana, right past Spokane, in a suburb called Liberty Lake. I take Dez's debit card and fill up the SUV while everyone else goes inside to perform the traditional we're-stopped-but-we-don't-necessarily-have-to-go-to-the-bathroom look around the convenience store. I call my dad to tell him where we are and that none of us have spontaneously combusted.

A minute or so later, Elliot comes out with a bag of Bugles and two bottles of Gatorade. I leave him with the pump and run inside because I actually have to pee.

We pull away from the gas station with Trey as the driver and me in the passenger's seat. He sits in the driver's seat like an old woman, back completely rigid. Both hands latched onto the steering wheel like it's about to fall out the window. For an optimist, and for someone who's been driving three years longer than I have, he's very distrusting of other drivers. Every time someone changes lanes by/near him, he rides the opposite edge of the lane and curses. Addy starts calling him *Abuela* (grandmother), which everyone else adopts pretty quick.

Dez passes me a bag of Sour Patch Kids. I pick through them, looking for the yellow ones.

"Who on earth picks out yellow ones?" she asks.

"That is pretty weird, brother," Elliot says.

"It's because I always used to eat everything but the yellow ones," Addy says. "I conditioned him to like the reject flavors. You're all welcome."

I lift up the Sour Patch Kids into Trey's peripheral and his talons slowly release the steering wheel so he can give me an open palm.

"Have you ever considered just using 'bro,' Elliot?" Trey asks.

Elliot puffs a condescending burst of air through his nostrils. "Have you ever considered not being optimistic?"

"That's not even the same thing," Trey says, looking over his shoulder again, and again, and again before getting into the travel lane.

"Please watch as the Abuela attempts to change lanes," Addy says. "View his persistence in checking his blind spot."

"Hey," Trey says, "I care about the lives in this car so much that I check multiple times. Adam doesn't even use a turn signal. You can thank me when we arrive safely."

"Awww," Addy says, "Guys, look at how much he cares. Everyone give him a hug. Come on."

Addy leans forward and so does Dez.

Trey doesn't look at them. "Not while I'm driving. Stop it, not while—girls, stop. *Stop!* Not while I'm driving."

"Mastermind Dez, go over our plan again?" I ask.

"Okay," Dez says excitedly, as though she's been waiting for someone to ask this question. "I thought we'd start by checking the police station that handled the crime scene. If that comes up short, we can head over to where the Abbey Road US studio used to be. There's a new recording studio in there, so they might have an idea of how we could find it."

"What if neither place has it?" Elliot asks.

"Then we do some sleuthing. I brought a bunch of Mr. Cratcher's lyrics and journals, and a letter he wrote to Leonard Cohen where he calls himself both Colin Cratcher and The Chaos Writer. Mr. Cratcher's been writing and co-writing songs since the seventies. I'm sure there's someone in Nashville who knows about him who can help us."

"Wait . . . where's our hotel?" I ask.

Dez rolls her eyes. "It's not a hotel."

"What does that mean?" Trey asks.

"Mom rented us a mansion in Brentwood."

Dez might be pissed that her family is rich, and she might want to have nothing to do with them—I can totally understand why—but the rest of us are definitely not upset with their money. I'd never tell her that, of course. Also, in hindsight, I'd take back the sweet-goodness-we-have-a-mansion-to-sleep-in look that I gave Addy, Trey, and Elliot a second ago and use it when Dez wasn't staring directly at me.

"To hell with all of you and your consumerism," she snaps. "I'm going to sleep in the backyard and only step inside to track dirt onto the sparkling Italian marble floor."

Addy rolls her eyes.

"Why don't you just rent your own hotel room?" Trey asks.

"Shut up, Abuela," she says.

I know that the rest of us would be laughing if we wouldn't be eaten by the tiger in the backseat, but laughing at Dez Coulter when she's attempting to be as different from her family as possible is an honest-to-God Mr. Cratcher life and death decision.

—

Elliot stops on the side of the road around eleven. I'm the only other person awake, and it's only because Dez is sleeping with her head in my lap and I don't want to miss a second of being able to play with her hair while she sleeps.

"We should've stopped to get a hotel in Billings," he says. "I didn't know when that gas station guy said there wasn't much past Billings, Montana, he literally meant nothing."

"Well, we didn't follow I-90 all the way. Google said it was quicker to take this middle-of-no where road than to dip into Wyoming."

"Well, Google should warn people when they're about to enter Middle-fucking-Earth."

"Are you too tired to drive?"

"Yeah, I know I've only done four out of my five hours, but I'm going to fall asleep if I keep going."

"I'm good to go," Dez says, stirring below my hand. As soon as she sits up, I feel the bliss drain out of me. Now I could fall asleep in seconds.

Addy doesn't lean up or open her eyes, but she says, "It's my turn next, I should do it."

Dez shakes her head. "Nah, Addy, I've got it."

"You sure?" Addy asks.

"Yeah." She arches her back in a stretch. I know it's stalker-ish to watch her, but I do. She catches me watching, but smiles. "Did I have a blaze of light moment?"

"Sweet mercy, yes."

She laughs. It sounds like daytime.

"Should we wake up Trey?" I ask. "Keep the rotation going?"

"Nah," Elliot says. "The guy's out cold. I accidentally spilled half my Coke on him about thirty minutes ago and he didn't flinch."

Elliot takes my seat and I get to do my time on the hump.

"Welcome back, Elliot," Addy says.

I sigh in disappointment.

"What?" he asks me.

"You're not as beautiful as Dez."

"Better get used to it, brother. You get this face for the next five hours. Maybe you'll get used to my attractiveness if you let me sleep in your lap." He starts leaning toward my legs.

I push against him. "Get out of here."

"Aw, you guys are adorable. Aren't they adorable, Addy?" Dez says, putting the car in gear and pulling back onto the road.

—

I wake to the sound of a cry. At first I think I'm hearing things because the cry is so muffled it sounds like an extra whine from the car tires, but then Dez brings a hand up to her face. I sit up and check if anyone else is awake before saying anything.

"Are you okay?" I whisper.

She wipes her nose on her sleeve. "No."

"What's wrong?"

"I just want to be better and I want to never go home. I want to be here, in this moment, forever. As soon as we get home, the adventure's over and I have to think about the chaos again."

"A: We haven't even got there yet, and B: We'll have each other."

"Only an addict would say B. We've been over this, Adam."

"That's not what I meant."

"Then what did you mean?"

"I meant, okay, so that is what I meant, but people say that kind of stuff all the time when they're—when they like someone."

"But we aren't people."

"But we're us."

"Exactly." She isn't crying anymore. Now she's a tamer version of her indignant self.

"We don't have to stay the same. We change. Both you and I know that. Doesn't that mean we're in a constant state of being different? If we're always changing, doesn't that mean we can never just be addicts? An object in motion stays in motion?"

"An addict in motion stays an addict."

"I don't believe that," I say. "I can't believe that."

"I can. When all I feel is the push for another buzz, sometimes that's all I believe."

I lean back in my seat and press my head against the window. Am I just another buzz to her? Does she expect me to wear off like all the other buzzes? Will I?

"So what does that make us?"

She clenches her hands tight around the steering wheel. "That's what I've been saying, Adam, like, that's all I've been saying."

How can we have a shelf life? Humans don't have a "consume by" date.

Human ≠ milk.

Human = life.

There has to be a difference somewhere. I know there's a difference somewhere, and I vow to find it before we expire.

On a completely different topic, ever notice how things you shouldn't think about start as thumbnails and then turn into movies? Like porn? Like, right now?

MILLIONS

To keep Elliot awake on the final stretch of the trip—100 miles from Nashville—Dez reads *Fahrenheit 451* aloud. It's not at all what I thought it would be. I had a story about actual modern-day firemen in my head, but this is about a futuristic fireman named Montag who burns books because they were banned. It only took three sentences after reading the first line for us to realize what the first line meant.

"It was a pleasure to burn" = the main character *literally* likes setting things on fire.

Dez must've read the first page at least three times to make sure there wasn't a better meaning. When she couldn't find one, she looked at me, her eyelids halfway over her eyes, and said, "This is why I don't read whole books." She was so pissed she probably would have stopped reading if she hadn't been doing it for Elliot.

It is epically disappointing that "It was a pleasure to burn" was a literal statement. I really wanted it to be a description of how you could feel about something and not about being a pyromaniac.

Dez flips to the back of the book to read the last line. She gives me the same disgusted half open eyes. She's disappointed.

"The last line is 'when we reach the city'?" She stares at me silently for at least thirty seconds before she screams, "What. A. Bloody. Disaster!" Dez rolls down the window, and with a frustrated groan, flings the book at the highway guard rail. The SUV falls silent.

"Well," I say, "that book will *not* be reaching the city."

Dez looks at me, lips flat, but she begins to laugh harder than I've ever seen her. She's contagious, and we spend the next few miles in repeat-the-line-that-made-us-laugh hysteria.

—

The only thing any of us can talk about at the moment is the building in the Nashville skyline that looks like a Batman mask. We've hit downtown Nashville, but it's the tail end of rush hour so we're naming all the buildings in the Nashville skyline and giving them personalities.

"Look at that big glass," Dez says.

"I bet Harvey is proud of his glass," I say.

"He thinks he's God's gift to all the female buildings because of his glass," Elliot adds.

"He spends at least five hours in the morning on his glass," Trey says.

"He dated Google Glass?" Addy adds.

We all shrug and nod.

Fifteen minutes on the other side of Nashville, Dez finally tells us to get off on the next exit. After some right turns, some wrong turns, some playful insults, and some non-playful insults, we're driving into a quiet neighborhood with houses that look like they were built for the emperor of the universe: columns, grand doors, gates, that kind of thing. I've never been to Tennessee before, but apparently Brentwood's a cloister of rich, Top 40 artists from the last fifty years.

Dez stares at her phone and then points to a driveway at the end of the cul-de-sac. "God, this is disgusting." She rolls her eyes at the houses. "Elliot, pull up to the gate, everyone remember this code: 4478."

"2178?" Elliot repeats.

"No, 4478," Dez responds.

"Wait, is it 2478 or 4487?"

"Elliot, really? 4478."

Elliot pulls up to the keypad of the gate. He tries to catch a glimpse of the house, but all any of us can see are trees.

"What's the code again?" he asks.

"Good lord," she snaps, "4.4.7.8. Forty-four, seventy-eight. Four. Followed by another four. Followed by a seven, and then an eight. 4.4.7.8"

Addy starts singing, "Eight six seven five three oh nine," under her breath.

I see Trey wink at Elliot. "Can you repeat that? I'm just going to write it down for him."

Dez's jaw drops in disgust, and everyone who isn't Dez laughs.

"To hell with all of you."

I grab her hand and kiss it. She rolls her eyes and smiles.

I'm pretty sure the driveway is part of the Appalachian Trail. I feel like we've been on it for half the trip. It winds into trees and oblivion. When I start expecting to see the ocean, I finally catch sight of a few house lights between swaying limbs.

We pull up to our vacation mansion. It has columns like a lot of the others do, but it looks a little more rustic. It's as though Dez's mom wanted her to stay in a place that wasn't architecturally different from her house.

"Seeing how this driveway brought us all the way to Florida," Trey says, "let's go to Disney before we unpack."

Elliot blows a puff of air out of his nose. "For real."

We park the car in front of the door and proceed with the just-arrived-to-the-destination traditions of stretching, screaming in relief, and more stretching.

As Trey and I unload the bags, Dez hands me a key.

"Here's the key to the house. I'm taking my stuff to the backyard."

"Are you really going to camp out?" I ask. "It's December. It's like, forty degrees out here."

"I'll be fine."

"Dez . . ."

"Adam . . ."

"Elliot . . ." Trey adds.

"Trey . . ." Elliot says.

"Addy . . ." Addy says, grabbing her bag and walking toward the house.

I throw my hands in the air. "Fine. Do what you want; you're not my wife. But I bet millions you'll be inside before our trip is over."

"You're on, Hawthorne," she yells, walking toward the side of the house. "Millions."

BIRTHDAY PRESENT TO MYSELF

The inside of our vacation mansion looks imported. I think the designer just walked around pointing at places, yelling "Italian marble! Italian leather! South African granite!"

Addy is already in here somewhere, but the place is so big it'd take me years to find her. Trey, Elliot, and I drop our bags at the door and, as all wizened travelers do, run to the fridge.

A vacation fridge is like a prophet. It can tell you if the trip is the chosen one, or if it's just another day. For example, most trips I've been on with my dad had a mini-bar. Therefore, the sign seemed to say the trip would be fun, but there were some checks and balances to make sure the trip's bill didn't get too high. A trip to a place with no fridge meant business. No frippery, souvenirs, or super-sized meals.

As we open the fridge door, I swear beams of heavenly light surround us before we can see inside. Each shelf and drawer is stocked with everything imaginable and unimaginable. The omen is obvious.

We're on the trip of our lives.

"How is TV lobster dinner even possible?" Elliot asks.

I put a hand on his shoulder. "America, Elliot. America."

When the fridge starts beeping at us for having the doors open too long, we scamper off to claim our rooms. Elliot and Trey grab two downstairs, but I find the stairwell, go upstairs, and get one facing the backyard so I can watch Dez. I want to make sure she doesn't freeze to death.

I unpack (dump my bag out onto the floor) and then absentmindedly pull out my laptop to check my email and Twitter even though I was checking on my phone for most of the trip. A few minutes pass and I notice a thick heat filling my cheeks. A mental fog leaves me and I realize I'm staring at two naked lesbians. I stand up so fast my chair tips over. How did I not even know what I was doing? How is it possible to switch off like that?

"Adam?" Addy says from my door. She must see what's on my screen because she says, "Woah, Papi. I guess I'm going to see *that* on your accountability report."

I close the page as my cheeks fill with the heat of shame. This is the first time I've ever been caught.

I look at her. She has a half-cocked "I'm sorry" look on her face.

"It just . . . happened," I say. "I didn't even notice."

"I don't mean to like, be a bitch when I say this, but I honestly don't understand how you can *not* notice."

"You know how when you're out with people somewhere, and there's a small lull in the conversation and, somehow, there's something about that silence that pulls at something inside of you, and before you know it, you're pulling your phone out to check your email or Facebook?"

Addy nods and sits on the bed, holding her hand out for my computer. "Yeah. It's like compulsory. Just a thing you do."

"It's like that."

"Well, I'm going to hold on to your computer, then," she says. "Let me go put it in my room, then I want to call a council."

She gets up and walks out of my room. I notice her phone lying on the comforter when it vibrates. Looks like a text from ex-boyfriend Brent:

> I'll never love again because of you.

I know I shouldn't, but I pick it up, ready to dig into the guy for tormenting my Addy, I accidentally click on the wrong conversation.

> Thanks for bringing up that paperwork.

> No problem.

> The company isn't the same without you.

I check who the conversation is with. It's Addy's boss, Todd Tamlin. Why would he say the company isn't the same if she's still working for them?

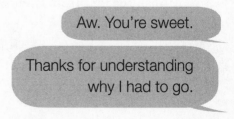

> Aw. You're sweet.

> Thanks for understanding why I had to go.

No problem. Taylor Isbester is a friend of mine.

He owns Isbester Construction based in Bellevue.

Give him a call and tell him to call me for a rec.

If you ever move back, call me. I'll hire you.

Thanks so much, Todd.

I look at the text over and over. This doesn't make sense. Why would her boss be telling . . . Wait. Wait. Wait. Wait.

I read the conversation again. Her boss said the company isn't the same because Addy quit. I don't know where she's going when she "goes to work" or why she's pretending that she's still working, but that's not the point.

She quit her job for me.

She quit her job so she could be with me.

My Addy.

I slide open the text from Brent.

This is Adam, Addy's brother.

> If you ever text my sister
> again, I will find you and
> beat you to pieces.

> Don't blame her for your
> inability to love.

> How you love is your own
> choice and she does a
> damn good job of it.

I block him and delete the text. I know it's something she's wanted to do but hasn't because she's too nice. I hear her footsteps marching toward my room, so I lock the screen and put the phone back on the comforter like I never touched it.

"Papi," she says, appearing in the door. She sees her phone on the bed and quickly comes over to retrieve it. "Come on, I have a proposal for you Knights of Vice people."

I get up and follow her without saying a word. She obviously doesn't want me to know, so I'm not going to bring it up, which is probably a good thing considering I could never repay her for coming back.

She came back.

For me.

—

"Knights of Vice assemble!" Addy yells. "Come to me, my darlings!"

I find the back door—though its size makes it more portal to the universe than back door—and push it open. "Dez, what are you doing?"

I don't see her, but her voice cuts through the darkness. "Setting up my tent?"

"Addy wants to talk to us. If you come to the door, we'll come out to help you after."

"I'm not stepping near that house," she yells.

"Dez, stop being ridiculous," Addy says, walking out onto to the porch. "Just come here."

"No," Dez says.

Addy shakes her head. "Go get the guys and meet me at the Stubborn One's tent."

I run down the hallway, knocking on every door. "Hey guys, get out here."

Trey appears in the hallway and eventually Elliot does, too.

"What's going on?" Elliot asks.

"Addy wants to talk to us. She has some sort of proposal."

Trey doesn't even wait for me to tell him where to go. He just walks toward the living room, leaving Elliot and I to watch him wander aimlessly as he looks for his obsession.

We go outside and stand next to Dez's half set-up tent.

"Wow, Dez," Trey says. "I figured you'd still be figuring out what the shape of the tent was supposed to be."

"Girls can put up tents, too," she snaps. "Besides, this isn't my first rodeo. I lived in this thing for three months in middle school."

"On purpose?" Addy asks.

"I ran away after my dad forgot to take me to soccer practice for the fifth time. Neither of my parents wanted to 'affirm my deviant behavior' so they didn't come for me, which put us in a standoff. I wasn't going to come back until they acknowledged they were being assholes, and they weren't coming to get me until I got accepted to Harvard and pooped gold."

"How did you eat?" I ask.

"I stole family-sized bags of Cheetos from random gas stations on the way home from school. I also slept over at a friend's house a lot."

Trey and Elliot take the rainfly from her and start attaching it.

"Okay, well, while you guys are doing that, I'm going to propose—" Addy says.

Trey throws his fist into the air. "Yes! My charm worked. Chica, I do."

Addy smiles but shakes her head. "Here's my proposal. Well, I guess it's more of a reminder than a proposal. You guys are all here together. I know you've talked a little bit about this, but I think you should really make sure you look at this trip as more than just finding an album. Use it as like, an intervention camp. You know how *The Biggest Loser* contestants go to a ranch to fight against their obesity? Well, this is your *Biggest Loser* ranch, and you can try your hardest to set some good accountability habits while you're here."

She looks at us, watching for any objection. "Therefore, I make the motion that no one's allowed to be alone in their rooms until they're falling over with sleep. Actually, maybe it wouldn't hurt if everyone just slept in the same place. It might help break the habit of going to your vice at night, which I know Adam struggles with. Thoughts?"

Trey nods. "That's a great idea, Addy. She's so smart guys. Sleeping in the same spot will help. I'm sure of it. Let's sleep on the porch! That'd be awesome."

"I mean, we did tell our parents that this trip would help our addictions if they let us go."

Dez looks at me but says nothing.

"I have an idea," Elliot says, looking at both of us. "Give Addy your electronic shit."

"But we have to call our parents every day," I say.

"I mean, I can call Dad," Addy says. "Or we can just leave one phone out on the kitchen counter. We'll notice if it's missing. The guys can give me their laptops and phones. Dez, you've apparently defeated porn so it's up to you what you want to do with your stuff. It might be good just to hand it over anyway. Disconnect for a bit."

Addy saying Dez has "defeated porn" sounds so definite. Has she actually defeated porn, or did she just move on? Now that I think about it, what *is* she hung up on currently? Has she told me? I remember the comment she made the first time she called me. The one about her sponsor saying she was more like a lost teenager than an addict. Is she hiding something? Is she just a lost teenager, or does she really just cycle through things so fast it's impossible to keep up? I haven't seen anything about her that screams addiction right now. I'll have to ask her about it.

"You don't need to hide yours either then," I say to Elliot.

He shrugs. "Just because I'm not addicted to porn doesn't mean I haven't looked at it. It's probably messed up some of my views on relational shit, anyway."

"Gosh, man," I say to Elliot. "I'm glad you have an optimist for a best friend."

Trey nods viciously. "He's a work in progress, Adam."

"He's a work for sure," Addy says.

Elliot shakes his head. "I'm going to tie you all to your beds and make you watch porn." He lets out a chuckle and we all start laughing, but then he stops right in the middle of a bellow and makes his face go emotionless.

Trey shivers. "I hate that. You know I hate it when you do that."

Elliot laughs again and then makes his face go flat.

"Elliot, stop," Trey begs.

"This is hilarious," I say watching the two of them go back and forth.

"I hate this," Trey snaps, so I start copying Elliot.

Trey walks away, slamming the back door of the patio. Elliot gives me a fist bump.

Dez is staring at all of us and frowning.

"Well, I'm not going in the house," she finally says. "So you guys will have to hang out here with me."

"Would you at least hang out on the back porch?" Addy asks. "Meet the guys in the middle here, Dez. Rein your idiosyncrasy in a bit and get on the bandwagon. Don't make a mountain out of a dust pile. I know that's like, your thing, but suspend it for now."

"It's not my *thing*," she snaps, crossing her arms, but I can tell she knows it *is* her thing. It's hard because I know *why* it's her thing and no one else does.

She looks at the sky and sighs in disgust. "I'll meet on the back porch if someone brings me dinner every night."

"Dez," Elliot says, almost disgusted. "Are you really bargaining right now?"

"Fine," she says. "I'll hang out with you on the back porch." And with that, she disappears into her tent.

—

Trey makes us TV dinners and gives Elliot the lobster one. He gives Addy one, too, but hers is on a fancy plate, all arranged and set up like it's a gourmet dinner. He even makes one for Dez, even though she hasn't come out of her tent. We don't want to wait for her to eat, so we head out to the back porch and dig in. Somehow, Trey, Elliot, and I start telling our best "that one time I was such a pathetic addict I did this" stories. They're funny but *not* at the same time. It's not like any of us are above doing pathetic addict things. This conversation seems like swimming with floaties around your arms while making fun of the time you didn't know how to swim.

Addy eventually gives me a look that tells me to cut it out, so when the story pipe comes back to me, I start talking about finishing the album.

"Trey, you're willing to play electric guitar, right?"

"Yeah, man! Absolutely, that'd be kickass. I've always played classic rock so I'm going to have to study up on my folk/Nashville sounds. I got some ideas, though."

"Elliot, do you play anything?" I ask him.

"Eh, not really."

"Yes, he does," Trey says. "Stop being humble."

Elliot flicks his head to the side. "It's kind of embarrassing. I got made fun of all the time about it in middle school."

"Have you noticed you're not in middle school anymore? Just tell him."

I widen my eyes. "Do you play the harp with your toes or something?"

"No . . . I play the cello."

Trey throws up his hands and begins to points in random directions. "He doesn't just play the cello; he dominates the cello. He's the first person at least three Seattle recording studios call when they need a cellist. He's even played on a Death Cab for Cutie record."

"You play for the Cutie's *cabina de muerta*?"

Elliot looks at Addy. "What did you just say? I hate it when you say stuff I can't understand. Why do you do that?"

I look at Trey and he's laughing hysterically.

"Elliot, relax," I say. "Why are you embarrassed by that?"

"Like I said, I got picked on a lot. I mean, look at me. *Emo* is short for 'emotional,' and unlike other posers, I deserve the title. When shit hits me, it transfigures to concrete. Obviously."

"Well, you have to play on the album then," I say. "Mr. Cratcher wanted a cello."

"I'll play if we can give the thing a title. This album is such a mysterious thing, I feel like it should have a name."

Trey nods. "What about: *What Do You Mean Where am I From? America. I'm From America.*"

"*Pancreas Noises?*" I say.

Elliot chuckles. "*Cancer Ward.*"

"*El Cocina de Diablo?*" Addy says.

"*Love, Dark Matter, Jumbo Shrimp, and other Metaphysical Conundrums,*" I say.

"*Music to Pants Your Friends To,*" Trey says in the middle of laughing.

"*Ghosts of Christmas Pastors,*" Elliot says.

We're laughing like someone said *poop* in kindergarten when we finally hear Dez unzip her tent. A few seconds later, she appears on the back porch. She takes a moment to give the house the finger before opening the door to the screened-in area where we're sitting.

In our silence, I notice the comforting roar of the giant propane heater heating the porch and, strangely, it gives me a hallelujah moment by reminding me where I am and who I'm with. Here's to more of those. Here's to hallelujah moments replacing porn.

Dez walks past me, her path aimed toward a nylon camping hammock strung between two of the ceiling supports. She's changed into gray sweatpants and a striped hooded sweatshirt. Even in sweatpants, she looks like she could win awards in every category of attractiveness.

She puts up her hood and falls into the hammock. She grabs the fabric on its edges and pulls it over her so she disappears. I study her shoulder blades as they press against the hammock, moving and flexing as she tries to get comfortable.

"You look like a banana made out of synthetic polymer," I say.

"*You* look like a banana made out of synthetic polymer," she snaps.

She's done being mad, I guess.

"Do you want your food?" Trey asks. "I'll have to heat it again."

"Yeah," she says.

Trey disappears into the kitchen to microwave Dez's previously microwaved dinner. She must hear him come back outside because a lone hand shoots out of the fabric in a very zombie-escaping-out-of-the-ground way.

Trey puts her food in her hand and it disappears into the Hamana (hammock + banana = Hamana). "Thanks," she says, with a sigh. "Everyone, I'm sorry that I'm a bitch sometimes."

Trey, Elliot, and I look at each other. Trey mouths, "What do we say?" Elliot shrugs and they both look at me. I throw up my hands in a "why would I know" kind of way, but in the end, I know the most about the tiger in the Hamana.

"Hey," Addy says, beating me to the punch. "We all have our bad days. Don't worry about it."

"I guess I just got swept up in the trip," she says, not mentioning anything about her family. "I liked being able to forget about being an addict for a little while. I just want to be seventeen instead of like, thirty."

"Seventeen?" I bark. "I thought you were sixteen?"

"Today's my birthday."

I can't believe I know more about Dez's problems than the little human facts of her life. I don't know if I should feel guilty, because she's never told me when her birthday was, but at the same time, I didn't ask.

"It's your birthday?" Trey asks.

"Yeah."

"Well, a birthday party is more fun than sitting around talking about album names! Elliot, Addy, let's go find some birthday things."

Elliot pushes himself off his chair. "Maybe they have flecks-of-gold-fetti birthday cake mix. I'll check."

Addy stands, too. "I can cook up some killer cupcakes if they don't."

Trey pats my shoulder as they walk by. I flash him a thank-you smile.

"Why didn't you tell me it was your birthday?" I ask.

"Because having a birthday in December sucks. Everyone pays attention to Christmas and being done with school. Why bother trying to make a birthday happen? Also, you didn't ask."

I walk over to the hammock and part the fabric. As soon as I see her face, I smile.

"I'm sorry," I say. I roll the hammock down and sit on the edge. "Happy birthday. Is there anything you want?"

She grabs my hand and puts it against her face. The tip of my thumb dips into her TV dinner mashed potatoes.

"To be whole."

"Anything I can actually get you?"

She opens her eyes, and for the first time, I see love staring back at me—not confused attraction or obsessive addiction. I don't know how I know this, but I do. It's like when you know someone is watching you but can't see them.

She gives me the most beautiful and thankful smile in the history of smiles. On a smile scale that starts at Mona Lisa and ends at Jessica Alba, she's the sun.

She leans up and kisses my forehead. "You've already healed five parts of me, I think."

"I won't be able to heal everything. I want to, but I'm as unhealed as you are."

"Five is greater than none, I guess."

"I could swear I love you, Dez Coulter."

"Then you probably do." She grabs my shirt collar and pulls me close to her face. She makes a greater than sign and puts it against my chest.

"I love you, too," she says. "Saying that is my birthday present to myself."

EVERYTHING IS POSSIBLE

The morning comes and the Knights of Vice are all up at eight thirty. Well, everyone except for Addy. She's still out. Like the older sister she is, she tucked all us porch kids in and then went up to her room. She's never been one for roughing it when it comes to sleep. If there's a bed nearby, she *will* occupy it.

Trey, Elliot, and I are trying to figure out how to cook over-easy eggs without breaking the damn yolks while Dez plots our day in the Hamana. I look at her and study the little crease between her eyes while she thinks.

Trey throws another failure-easy egg onto the pile. "I'm not touching another egg."

"Understandable," I say. "Over-easy eggs are impossible."

Elliot points at the plate. "Just grab those and the toast and let's eat. Who gives a shit about the state of a yolk? It will be fine."

"That doesn't make being defeated by unborn chickens any easier to handle," I say.

Trey snickers, grabs a pitcher of orange juice, and walks onto the back porch.

"So, what's the plan for today?" I ask Dez while Trey makes her a plate of food.

"Should we wait for Addy?" Dez asks. "She'll probably want breakfast anyway."

Trey stands up. "I'll go get her."

"You touch her, you die," I say.

He gives me a toothy grin. "You couldn't kill me, man. I'm too scrappy."

"I was thinking we could go out tonight," Dez says.

"For what?" Elliot asks. "To find the album or just hang out?"

Dez looks at Elliot, confusion scrunching her eyebrows. "Oh, Elliot, sorry. I was talking to Adam."

Elliot curses.

I stop chewing.

Did she just . . .

Did she?

"Did you just ask me on a date?" I ask.

Her cheeks flush. "You don't have make it a big deal, I just thought—"

"I'd love to take you on a date. Please, for the love of Harvey's glass, let me take you on a date."

"Okay," she says with a bashful smile. "You get to pick where we go."

Finally, I get to take Dez on a date. Finally. Does this mean we're dating? Does that mean she's accepted it? Does this mean we can forget about this whole kick-our-addictions-first thing?

Addy and Trey come down the stairs. Addy's laughing at something, but I'm not sure what. Trey looks like he was just slapped in the face. I watch her, still feeling overwhelmed and undeserving that she'd quit her job just for me. They grab their breakfasts and take their respective spots on the porch. I stare at her in disbelief until Dez begins her briefing.

"I think we should research today."

"Research?" Elliot asks. "I thought you'd researched everything."

She looks at him with a cold stare. "When Edison decided he wanted to invent the light bulb, do you think his assistant said, 'I thought you researched everything already'?"

"Okay. Edison actually invented stuff. We're just trying to find an old album," he snaps.

Dez waves her fork at him and some egg flies off the tines. "All I'm saying is that we should be as precise as possible. If all five of us are researching, making calls, and finding people who knew Mr. Cratcher, would it hurt?"

Addy shrugs. "Doesn't matter to me. I'm just along for the ride, to make sure things stay kosher, and to make Trey squirm."

Trey shakes his head and then looks at Dez. "I think it's a great idea. I'm willing to be the guy making calls."

"Trey," Dez says, now pointing her fork at him. "You're a true journalist, explorer, and overall conqueror. Adam and Elliot will look through all the news articles on the murder and Abbey Road US. Addy and I will look at news from before the murder and see if we can figure out who he worked with/who would know him."

"Alright," I say. "I'm okay with that as long as I'm next to someone while I'm looking. I don't want porn to be a part of my research."

"Adam, just use your computer," Addy says. "I'll get notification if you start having problems."

"I can just see us debriefing at the end of the day." Dez raises her finger. "I, Adam Hawthorne, have discovered that boobs look like boobs, and that our culture thinks women are disposable sex toys."

"I, Adam Hawthorne," Elliot says, "have discovered that men are supposed to last longer than one minute."

Trey opens his mouth, but I cut him off. "I, Adam Hawthorne, have discovered that all of my friends are dicks."

—

I tip a cup of coffee toward my lips. The last of it drops onto my tongue as Trey walks out of the house. "I just called Marcus Richmond, the director of Abbey Road US."

"Is that the guy who didn't make any statements about the murder?" I ask.

"Yeah, he said he knew nothing about the album except it was named *Hounds of Eden*. When I asked what his opinion was on who killed Elias, he said 'I don't know,' and hung up."

"So maybe Marcus Richmond is the killer," Dez says, writing something down on her clipboard.

I put my empty mug on an end table. "I think what's more important is that we've found out the title of the album: *Hounds of Eden*."

"I think you guys thinking the murder isn't worth solving is straight up white of you. This is a crime of injustice. Does that mean nothing to you?"

"It does," I say. "But we aren't the ones—"

"Then what are we?" she asks. "What can we do? We can't beat our addictions, so why shouldn't we try to conquer this?"

I stare at her for a few seconds. "Why would you say that? We just talked about this as a group last night. It was half your pitch for this trip. Now you're saying we can't?"

"Does it matter?" she asks. "What's the harm in trying to solve a murder case?"

"You two bicker like you've been married for years," Addy says, looking up from her computer. "It's almost cute."

I shrug, but here's the thing: humans need attainable goals, especially humans like us. Like she said a while back, we've got to be able to catch the ball every once in a while. Does she really think that solving a murder case that's been cold for almost fifty years is more attainable than beating our addictions? Heck, getting Beyoncé to be my girlfriend might be more attainable.

She wants to conquer something. I get that. But what happens when she, a seventeen-year-old girl, can't solve a murder case? Isn't that asking for more pain, and in consequence, more addiction? Finding an album is attainable. We can do that.

Solving a murder = bring on the vices.

I want to love and be loved by Dez Coulter. I want us to focus beating our addictions and being dateable past our first date, not fighting crime. I thought she wanted that, too.

"What made you change your mind?" I ask.

"I didn't change my mind."

"Dez—"

"Adam, I don't feel like talking about it."

I sigh. "Just, be careful. Greater than, remember?"

She looks at me as if she knows exactly what I'm thinking, but there's something in her eyes that tells me she's still unconvinced, which makes me unsure why she asked to go on a date or why she said she loved me.

She mouths, "I love you," but her posture is tight with something I'm afraid to ask about.

—

I roll up my button-down sleeves and then shake my head out so my hair returns to its craziness. I take a deep breath and then head downstairs to grab Dez.

It may be a ruse, but there's no stopping it now.

It's first date time.

I smile like an idiot when I see Dez standing by the door, holding out the keys to her SUV.

"Are you ready?" she asks.

"I'm *so* ready. I've been ready for this since I met you."

"Hey, you two," Addy yells, poking her head through the back door. "Be back by eleven, capiche?"

Both Dez and I groan, and then whine, "But Mom!"

"Shut it, capeesh?"

"Got it," I say.

Addy beams. "Have a good first date."

We get in the SUV, and I start driving to our first destination, a little restaurant on the fringes of downtown Nashville.

We pull up to a quiet neighborhood. It doesn't seem like there'd be a restaurant here, so I grab my phone, which Addy allowed me to take out of the house, to check if we're in the right place.

"Are we like, visiting someone for dinner?" Dez asks.

I shake my head. "No, there's supposed to be—ah, there it is. Huh, well that's cool."

A bunch of the little houses have been turned into businesses, and in the first row, there's a teal one with a ramp leading to the front door. A sign on the wall proclaims the name of our destination: THE LOVING PIE COMPANY.

"Oh. My. God," Dez says, turning down the Christmas music on the radio. "You're bringing me to a pie place?" She screams. "You are perfect, Adam Hawthorne! Pie is literally my favorite thing outside of witty conversation."

I park the SUV behind the building and then turn to her before I turn it off.

"Before we get out, you need to tell me something."

She bounces in her seat. "But, Adam . . . pie."

"What is this?" I ask. "What are we?"

She keeps bouncing, unfazed by the question. "You sound like Mr. Cratcher."

"That's not an answer."

"A prospective couple going on a prospective date."

"Why can't this just be a date?"

"Adam, pie!"

"Answer me," I say.

"You know why. Please don't ruin our first date by arguing."

I sigh. "So this *is* our first date?"

She laughs. "Yes, yes. Okay, this is our first date. Now, good lord, pie, Adam!"

I smile. I mean, she did say it.

I'll take it.

We walk into the place. It's a quaint little house. A "specials" board sits against the wall and I lose Dez to it.

"Holy pie!" She says, pointing at the board, smiling. "Strawberry cranberry orange pie, Adam. Adam! Strawberry cranberry orange pie!"

A hostess looks at me. "Two of you?"

"Hostess!" Dez says. "Tiramisu waffle pie."

I nod. "Yes. Two."

The hostess holds her hand out. "Right this way."

She brings us into a small room with a few tables and chairs, but we're the only ones in it. The windows are decorated with red bows and garland. While Dez continues to freak out over the menu, I continue to watch her, loving her more and more for the amount of joy she has simply because of pie. She orders the Frito Chili pie and, I admit, even I freak out when I see, and order, Mac and Cheese pie.

We try to picture the restaurant as the house it once was and figure out we're eating in a bedroom attached to the living room. After that, we recap all of the random facts we've learned about Mr. Cratcher and his life in Nashville.

"The dude was a rock star," I say. "He definitely gave up a lot to move."

"Didn't you say he chose to leave?" she says. "I think, more than anything else, he wanted to love Gabby better. I mean, she chose to support his release in the trial. If that kind of love doesn't deserve the sacrificing of an empire, nothing will."

"Yeah. Give up an empire to gain a kingdom."

"What's the difference between the two?" she asks.

"I don't know. I'd just rather be a king than an emperor. It might just be because I watched *Star Wars* a lot when I was little and hated Emperor Palpatine. I still think he's a dick."

"I think that's accurate," she says. "Both in personality and in looks."

I laugh and grab her hand. She flashes me a smile that makes December feel like July.

"I still want to know what the difference between an empire and a kingdom is," she says.

I look at the sun setting in a marbled orange and pink sky. I don't know if I'm just in a hallelujah moment, but I feel like I'm home. "I guess an empire is a place to fight for, but a kingdom is . . . a home worth fighting for? I don't know."

"I like that," she says.

"Yeah?"

"Yeah, way to BS intelligence."

"We should totally have babies and save the world from the impending stupid apocalypse."

"Of course." She brushes the hair out of her eyes. "That definitely sounds like a purely strategic proposal, not recreational. Sometimes, if you really want to make an impact on the world, you have to pick high-quality mates to keep from creating inept babies."

I nod. "I've never considered myself a high-quality anything."

"Adam, I'd personally trade eighty bear skins for your DNA."

"Only eighty?"

"Did I mention they're polar bear skins?"

We both chuckle and fall into a few seconds of comfortable silence as the waitress brings our savory pies.

"So, how's addiction going?" I ask.

"What do you mean?"

"I just haven't heard much about where you're at right now."

She sighs. "That's because I don't want to talk about it."

"So, what does that mean?"

"That means I don't want to talk about it. Do we have to talk about addiction on a first date? Gosh, Adam, you aren't very good at this."

"Dez, every time you go to Addiction Fighters, you talk about *everything* you're addicted to in front of a giant crowd. Why can't you tell just me?"

She doesn't say anything.

"Dez, tell me what's going on."

"Nothing new."

"Dez."

"Percocet," she whispers. "I'm addicted to pain pills. There, happy?"

Okay, though unexpected, I'm not really surprised by this. It makes sense. It's subtle but effective enough to keep a buzz.

"I'm sorry. I didn't mean to push."

She sighs again, this one deeper than the last. "No, I've been meaning to say something about it."

"Where do you get them from?"

"My mom has chronic back pain. I just take them from her."

"Sounds easy enough."

"Yeah. It is. Can I—can I tell you a secret?"

I push my chair next to hers and pull her into me. "Anything."

She runs a hand through her hair and swallows. "I—I haven't been telling the total truth. About my addictions, I mean. I'm just . . . really afraid someone knowing the truth will rub me raw."

"Remember that time I didn't want to tell you about trying to give girls money to have sex with me?"

"Yeah, I know. That's what made me consider telling you. The fact you trusted me enough to tell me, yet I haven't told you this, has been eating at me." She takes a deep breath. "I know I've said I'm addicted to everything and that I cycle through things. I know that you think I'm addicted to the addiction, but I'm only addicted to everything else because I'm trying to avoid Percocets. I'm afraid of them. It started when I was twelve, when I first started noticing that I didn't want to be like my family, which in turn turned their wrath on me. I was addicted to them, pretty intensely. By the time I was fourteen, I'd gotten bored with them, and a friend said I should move onto something harder. I did and I almost died.

"I got scared for a while and didn't do any drugs. I tried changing, but my parents didn't. I was still always a disappointment. Still never enough. So I went back, and when I got bored with Percocets, I didn't have the guts to go harder, so I'm trying everything else. Looking for something that will keep me from ending up like Mark. Percocets are a gateway drug, and Mark is evidence of what happens when you stand in the gate for too long. They're always available. No one notices. Everything else—smoking, drinking, and such—is so obvious. No matter how hard I try to stay away, I eventually come back to them because I love having a vice that can fit in my pocket."

I kiss her on the forehead, just like she did to me when I told her about getting suspended, about taking advantage of someone who needed me to protect them. "Which pocket?"

Her jaw tightens. "Right."

I slide my hand into her pocket and find two pills sitting in the deepest corner. I take them out, wrap them in a napkin, and put it on the table for the waitress to take next time she comes around.

"You equal greater than that."

"I know."

"I don't think you do."

"Yeah, probably not."

"Dez, you're so much greater than that. You're enough."

"Adam—"

"You're enough."

I say it for myself as much as I say it for her. A tear rolls down her cheek. She closes her eyes and starts to stand.

Not this time.

I won't let her run away. I won't run away. *We will face ourselves.*

I grab her wrist and pull her into my arms. She breaks down. Right there in the bedroom of The Loving Pie Company.

"I don't want this to be my life," she says.

"We can change," I say.

She shakes her head, but she doesn't say anything. She just cries into my chest. I look at her, and for the first time I don't see her as sexy, confident, stubborn, different, and untamable Dez. I see her for what she really is: an innocent girl who's lost in the chaos and trying to find her way back home.

Just like me.

—

To make up for making her cry on our first date, I let her choose where we go next. She picks the giant atriums and indoor gardens of the Gaylord Opryland Resort. Because we're so close to Christmas, everything is decorated accordingly. Garland has been wrapped around posts and handrails. Shimmering lights coat both fake and real trees. We wander around the indoor manmade rivers and pathways for hours, talking and laughing like normal people do.

As it gets dark outside, the atriums fills with people, all here to see the massive display of Christmas lights hanging from the metal trusses and walkways supporting the expanse of glass ceiling. Globes, presents, and stars all hang in the air like they were placed without any struggle. However, I'd imagine that setting up the massive light displays are the one event the hotel workers try to avoid at all costs. Putting up lights with my dad is hard enough, and we only have one strand of lights that we hang off the gutters. Christmas cheer comes at a cost, but there's nothing else in the world like Christmas cheer, which makes it priceless.

The hugeness, mystery, and winter wonderland–ness all combine and make us feel oddly adventurous, and we begin to take random little turns, looking for something new to explore. After I buy her eggnog ice cream, she disappears to find the bathroom and, while I wait for her, I end up wandering up a set of stairs to stand next to a waterfall. All of it. The cheer. The Christmas. The girl. The Addy. The friends. The place I get to go back to.

I feel in love.

Calm. Peaceful. Like I'm nothing but a boy. Like The Woman never left. Like I've never been addicted to porn. Like the Puget Sound dreams have never happened. Like I'm not a volcano. I'm watching drops of water slam into the river below when someone taps me on the shoulder. I turn around and see Dez.

She wraps her arms around my shoulder and, with no ceremony, she pulls me into her and kisses me. Her lips could be as rough as sandpaper, but right now, they feel like the softest thing in the world. I hold onto her waist, pulling her as close as physically possible without being Siamese twins. In this moment, I think I feel everything, but I feel her so specifically I can't define how. I don't know how that works, but that's how everything works with her.

She pulls away, but just barely. Her forehead still rests against mine, and I can feel her breath on my lips.

"I'm surprised you were okay with kissing me in such a cliché place. Especially one surrounded by such an American display of Christmas deco," I say, breaking the silence. "I figured you'd try it in a gas station bathroom or something."

She laughs, and then gives me that smoldering, definition-scattering smirk. "I thought about it."

"I'm sure you did."

"I want to believe in change," she says. "I know it's not fair that I expect you to do all the believing in us. I just don't

247

know if I can believe anything other than addiction. But, if I don't try, I won't know, right?"

"Nope, you won't."

She looks around and then nods. "Alright, well, if we're going to have our first kiss in the middle of a cliché, we might as well make the best of it."

"Certainly, Mademoiselle."

I slide my fingers up her neck and into her hair. She presses her palms into my back. We make out—no, we have a hallelujah moment beside an indoor waterfall. A place almost as beautiful as the natural world, but without the volcanoes.

I guess everything is possible.

BRIDGE STUDIOS

The next morning, we're eating bacon-wrapped Pop-Tarts, talking about what the name *Hounds of Eden* means, when Dez suddenly sits up in the Hamana.

"Guys," she says, giving us all a giant smile.

I remember our clichéd waterfall kiss. I remember that she trusted me enough to tell me her Percocet-addiction secret. Part of me is insanely happy about it, another part is scared shitless, and another part is worried for her. Each feeling is so distinct and new, and they're battling for priority. I put three extra pieces of bacon on my Pop-Tart to ease my mental tension.

"I'm so excited for today," she says. "What if we don't just find an album? What if we find something that clears Mr. Cratcher's name? What if we do it all before he dies?"

I feel the same fear I felt yesterday when we talked about this. I don't know if it's because we had such a good time last night, but it's even more unsettling today.

"That's a lot of what ifs," I say.

"Yeah, but I bet there's something out there, right?" Trey adds.

Dez's face tightens. "Well if the optimist is on my side, I should probably lower my expectations. Let's just go find Mr. Cratcher's house."

Thank you, Trey. Thank you so, so, so, so much.

—

We drive through downtown Nashville and take an exit that dumps us into a suburb called Historic Edgefield. As we sit at the bottom of the exit ramp, waiting for the light to turn green, Dez points at the neighborhood sign gleaming in the sun across the road.

"Turn right here. It should be the third house on the left."

Addy turns, and a few seconds later, we pull up to a normal, non-Brentwood house. It has a small concrete stoop and faded green seventies shutters next to the two front windows.

"Everyone have their clipboards?" Dez asks.

Dez bought all of us clipboards at the drug store because she thinks the clipboards will make us look like professional journalists instead of nosy kids.

"This is crazy guys," Addy says.

Dez makes a *tsk* noise at her. "We'll leave you home if you suddenly want to be all adult-ish."

Addy laughs. "I never said I didn't want to do it. I just said it was crazy."

"So, who's going to talk?" Elliot asks.

"Adam should take this first one," Dez says. "Addy, keep the car running in case we need to run."

"I feel like a chauffeur," she says. "You make out with my brother one time and suddenly I'm just the driver."

Trey snaps his fingers. "Ooh, man!"

Dez grins. "Imagine what will happen next time we make out."

Elliot scoffs. "Teen pregnancy?"

Dez's cheeks explode with red and we all laugh.

Elliot stops mid-laugh. "Teen pregnancy isn't funny."

Trey shivers and gets out of the car. Dez follows.

"No teen pregnancy," I say to Addy when we're the last two in the car. "I promise."

Her eyes look at me through the rearview mirror. "I trust you, Papi. Now go get your information."

We walk up to the house door, and after ten knocks or so, it's obvious our adventure isn't being filmed in a Hollywood studio. After driving two thousand miles, four teenagers stand on the stoop of their dying mentor's old house only to have no one answer.

This is as anticlimactic as it can get.

Dez crosses her arms. "Let's just look around, see if a door is open."

"We can't break and enter," I say. "We're on a journey for justice and resolution, not criminalism."

"That's not even a word."

"We'll just have to come back. It's not a problem."

"Hey!" someone yells.

We turn around. Standing on the porch of the house directly across from Mr. Cratcher's is a man maybe a little older than my dad, leaning against his railing and watching us like . . . like we're about to look around and see if a door is open.

"What are you kids doing?" he asks.

"We're an independent research team," I yell, certain he won't expect that kind of answer from a group of teenagers, one of which looks like he's about to destroy something in emo-laden spiky bracelet rage.

"My colleagues and I are trying to gather some data on a cold case."

The man scratches his beard. "What case?"

"The murder of Elias Harper," Dez says.

The man stares at us for a few seconds. Trey fiddles with his clipboard to make sure our inquirer sees it.

"Wasn't that in the seventies?" he finally asks.

"Yes, sir," I say.

A few more seconds of awkward silence pass before the guy nods toward his house. "Come in. I might be able to help."

—

We sit around the stranger's table. He kindly offers us some soda, but Elliot is the only one of us who accepts.

"So, why do you want information on Elias Harper?" he asks.

"We're journalistic hobbyists," Dez says. "We use our school breaks to research cold cases."

"We've gathered enough evidence to get cases reopened," Trey adds.

I try not to let my face show it, but I feel like his comment pushes our cover a little too far. Luckily, the man doesn't dig any deeper.

"Well," he says, "it's cool to see kids applying themselves to stuff that isn't dangerous or to drugs."

We look at each other. Dez has to bite her lip to keep from laughing.

"I don't know any details about it," he says, "but my dad might. He lived here when it all happened."

Trey slaps the table. "Fantastic!"

"As long as you don't tell him you talked to me," the man says, "I can put you in touch with him, but I can't guarantee anything. He doesn't talk about anything unless money is involved."

"Where does he work?" Elliot asks.

"At some recording studio. At least, I think he still works there. I haven't talked to him in years."

"Why?" Dez asks.

Awkward. Why would anyone ask that?

The guy doesn't blink at the question. "He's an ass. Simple as that. Do you want his number or not?"

"We'd love his number," I say.

—

We sit in the SUV in front of Mr. Cratcher's old house while Dez calls The Ass. Considering his reputation, we figured the guy would stay on the phone longer for a female.

"Hey—" she starts, but covers the receiver. "What's his last name? We never got The Ass's last name."

Addy looks out the window at the mailbox. "Woodrow."

"Is this Mr. Woodrow? Awesome. My name is Mindy Hastings, and I'm looking to record an album. A friend of mine recommended you."

I raise my hands in confusion. She waves me away.

What the crap is she doing?

"There are five of us." She rubs her eyes. "Sorry, I didn't catch that. Did you ask who recommended you?"

Trey slams his head on the back of my seat like we've been defeated.

"Okay," she says, laughing. "Confession. I figured you'd take me more seriously if I said someone recommended me. This town is like one giant party. If you aren't invited, you're screwed."

I can hear the guy laughing through the speaker. I pretend to give her a slow clap, but she just shrugs at her own ability to BS.

"Yeah. Our band name is . . . Knights of Vice. No, not nights with an n. Knights, like medieval dragon-slaying badasses. Haha, right. Well, we'd like to come in and see the place. . . . Yeah, and I'm sure Carrie Underwood wanted to see the place before she coughed up that much money, too. Can we drop by and get a tour today? Great, how about one? Cool. One last question: when I was reading reviews on your studio, I kept seeing these alternate spellings for the studio name."

Her mouth drops.

"Haha, yeah." She turns in her seat to look at all of us. "It's pretty hard to mess up Bridge Studios."

WHIPPED PUPPY DOGS

"What if The Ass is the killer?" Dez asks. "What if he was/ is a head honcho in the KKK and he lived across from Mr. Cratcher, and that's how Mr. Cratcher and Gabby were found out?"

"That's totally possible," Trey says, "but, I think the cops would've thought about that. I'm sure they interviewed his neighbors."

"But maybe the investigation was so focused on Mr. Cratcher, they were lax on their other suspects?"

"I don't know, guys," Elliot says. "I came here to find a missing album, not solve a murder."

She frowns. "I'm just saying it's kind of a crazy coincidence that Mr. Cratcher's neighbor now works in the studio where Abbey Road US used to be."

"I think Elliot's right," Addy says. "You guys need to focus on getting Mr. Cratcher's album so you can finish it when we get back. I don't feel like tracking down a murderer. I've seen enough movies."

"We don't have enough time to do a criminal investigation," I add, thankful that the majority of the group is on my side. "I don't want to miss going back to school because I've been murdered by The Ass. Besides, we need to make sure we're attempting to accomplish attainable things."

"What if he has the album, though?" Dez asks. "What if the killer has the album because it's incriminating evidence?"

"If the killer wound up with the album, he/she probably already destroyed it," Elliot says.

Silence.

Addy grabs the steering wheel. "Soooo, Bridge Studios?"

"Yeah," Dez says, tapping the address into her phone. "Let's do this."

"Okay," I ask. "Why didn't you just tell The Ass that you wanted information about Colin Cratcher?"

"Uh, because his own son hasn't talked to him in years. You think he's just gonna chitchat with a girl who doesn't want to give him any money?"

"Fair point."

"The only way to get this guy to talk is to trick him into doing it. We need . . . ugh. I need to, don't I?"

"Need to what?"

She takes a deep breath and then pulls the glove box open. "I hate this I hate this I hate this I hate this," she mutters as she sifts through a bunch of napkins. Finally, she pulls out a stack of hundred dollar bills like she's touching dirty underwear.

"Holy . . ." Trey says.

"I feel like a one-percent-rich-ignorant-dull-hacksaw that just throws money around because he can for even touching this," Dez says, "but bigger things are at stake and money talks."

"Dez, that's like, a bank stack of hundreds," Addy says. "And you were keeping them in the glove box."

"I'm aware of that." Dez says.

"That's the dumbest thing I've ever seen," Addy says.

"Like, dumb cool or dumb dumb?" Trey asks.

"Come on!" Dez says before Addy can answer. "Step on it. Follow that car!"

We pull out of the neighborhood, all silent and really confused.

Finally, Elliot says, "I don't fucking understand your kind of people."

And we all break into laughter.

—

The Ass doesn't look like an ass. He's wearing a gray cardigan over a V-neck shirt. He's in his late-sixties, but he looks as stylish as Dez. He's all ours as soon as Dez holds up her stack of Franklins and asks, "Do you have to pay for a tour?"

The building looks like what I've always pictured a real studio would look like. A small front desk with a hallway that leads to the sound engineers room. Inside, there's a giant mixing board against the wall, right below a huge window that looks into the isolation room, which is filled with microphones and amps. Somehow the floor in their isolation room is void of the rat's nest of cables that typically marks our home recording sessions. Mr. Cratcher never organized the cables. He just let them cross and intersect until they become one big stringy mass of black wire.

During the studio tour, I provide some good misdirection by talking about what kind of microphones we'd like to use on our "album." I make myself seem like a persnickety sound geek, but I realize very quickly I don't know enough to back up my pretentiousness. Addy realizes I'm about to talk myself into a hole before Dez does and nudges her in the ribs. Dez jumps in and saves me from my ignorance.

"I was doing some research on this place before we came over. Looks like it was a pretty intense crime scene in the seventies, huh?"

I don't know why I expect The Ass to hulk out and tear us to pieces over this question, but I do. The thought that our bodies might be shoved under a floorboard in Bridge Studios is pretty much all I have in my head.

The Ass doesn't flinch. "Wasn't pretty."

"Do you think about it all when you're sitting behind the mixing board?" Dez asks. "I know I would. I would've torn down the building and burned all its contents." Dez acts as if she has a sudden realization. She flays her fingers and pretends to shiver. "Dear God, please tell me this is a different building."

He laughs. "The building was torn down. This place is entirely new and state-of-the-art."

Wow, she's brilliant. It took me forever to figure out her plan. I smile at her, and she winks.

"Can I talk to you for a second, Mr. Woodrow?" I ask.

He looks at me like I just asked him to make out, but we step out of the isolation room and he closes the door.

"Mindy's the money behind this operation. You saw her flash that stack. That's not even the half of it," I say. "Her dad's a wealthy stock trader. We have our band practices in her house and it's huge."

"So?" he says.

"So, Mindy's pretty superstitious. As soon as she figured out there was a murder here, we practically had to tie her to the roof of our SUV with bungee cords to get her to come. Now, I know she's prepared to drop as much money as she needs to get the best quality recordings possible. She flat out told us before we came there's *no* budget."

The Ass's eyes light up. I got him. We've got him.

"I'm just warning you, if you want her to drop that money here like I do, you have to show her there isn't even a cable left from the old studio. Now that she knows you know something about what happened here, she's going to slay you with questions. Just give her the answers and you'll be a richer man for it. We good?"

He runs a hand through his hair. "Why are the rich, hot ones always the weirdest ones?"

Anger rolls through me when he calls Dez hot and weird. Only I can do that. Well . . . and Addy, Trey, and Elliot. Finally, he brings his hand down from his hair and rubs his eyes. "Whatever, kid, let's just get the show over with so we can make an album."

We walk back into the isolation room and I nod to Dez. Her smirk appears for a millisecond. She knows I caught on.

"What did you guys just talk about?" she asks.

"I just wanted to check the mixing board," I say.

"So, is there anything left of the old studio in this one?" she asks.

The Ass crosses his arms. "No, everything was sold off after the trial."

"You aren't just saying that to get my money, are you? Where did it all go?"

He shrugs. "I wasn't around then. After the case was closed, the cops dealt with the personal stuff. Like I just said, anything that wasn't ruined or stolen, Abbey Road sold. That was a long time ago, definitely before Bridge bought the building. I promise you, Mindy, there's no trace of the old building here. None."

"Not even under the floorboards?" she asks.

"No, the foundation was ripped up. Everything about this building is brand new."

"None of the guys that currently work here worked at the old building, did they?"

The Ass casts a disgusted look at me. I just shrug and give him an "I told you so" face.

"No, we're all new staff. The guy who was acquitted of the murder doesn't even live in Nashville anymore."

"Oh. My. God," Dez says, making herself sound like the biggest diva on the east coast. "So he's still on the loose? How do you know he isn't in Nashville?"

"I lived across the street from him. He disappeared as soon as the trial was over."

Dez takes three dramatic steps back. "You knew him?"

"No, no, no, I didn't know him. I mean, I said hi to him every morning. Seemed like a nice guy. Didn't think he'd ever kill anybody."

Dez throws her hands up and pretends to storm toward the door.

"Mindy," I say, grabbing her wrist. "Just chill, okay?"

"I can't. Are you hearing this? This place is probably as haunted as an abandoned insane asylum."

"So what if it's haunted?" Addy says catching on. "We can use that to our advantage. Put a sticker on the album that says we recorded in a haunted studio."

"Look, Mindy," The Ass says, scrambling to cover over Addy's statement. "I've worked here since we opened. I haven't seen a single ghost, spook, or anything supernatural. This place isn't haunted."

"Wha—what happened to the guy's stuff? He worked here, right?"

The Ass is getting super pissed. His jaw is as tight as an overblown balloon.

"He took it all with him when he moved," he says. "There was nothing left in his house. I looked after he left."

"I need to make sure," she says, waving the stack of Franklins at him. "Who can I talk to so I can make sure?"

He throws his hands up in the air. "Look, if you're not going to believe it, then just get out of here."

"Do you want my money?" she asks.

"Mason Crowell," he says. "Mason Crowell was the police chief then. He handled the murder. He interviewed me as a suspect at least three times. Go talk to him, figure your stuff out, and come back when you're ready to record your album."

Dez drops her shoulders and puts her hands on her hips. "You know what? I can't work with an old man with an attitude. Forget this. Come on, band." She snaps at us and we follow her out like we're whipped puppy dogs.

WHY DOES IT MATTER IF I FIGHT IT?

Dez doesn't buy herself lunch. We cover her because, after her Oscar-worthy performance as Mindy, the least she deserves is a free sandwich. We sit down to eat, and I scarf down my foot-long chipotle turkey sub in four minutes and then, because we decided it's not going to cause mass addiction chaos to have Addy give us or phones back when we're out and about, aka not in the house, go outside and call dad.

When the others finish, we drive around Nashville for a little bit then end up going back to the mansion to work on figuring out what to do next. I pick my teeth with a pine toothpick, but only because Elliot got the last mahogany one. Dez has my laptop in the Hamana, and though I can't see her, I hear *tap tap tap tap tap*. Elliot is reading a *Reader's Digest* about trout fishing and is making a bunch of "huh" noises.

Trey brings our dirty dinner dishes into the kitchen and washes them next to Addy. I watch them through the window. Addy smiles at him like I smile at Dez. He makes her laugh, and in turn she makes him laugh. They clean the dishes, pots, and pans together. Since Addy's unofficially joined the KOV, he's been different. Good different. Like Addy's existence has made him grow out of his un-thoughtful horniness. They finish the dishes, and thinking that none of the porch dwellers are watching, Trey turns to her and goes in for a kiss. I wait for Addy to reject him, ready for the entertainment at his expense, but she lets him. Heck, she puts her arms on his shoulders and kisses him back.

My jaw drops.

She's liked him all along.

Elliot notices my incredulousness and follows my line of sight. Then Dez notices us noticing. She turns, sees them, and goes to say something, but I bring a finger up to my mouth and shush her. As strange as it is, I want Addy to enjoy it. I want her not to feel pressure, silly, awkward, or anything besides happiness. After what she did for me, the way she loves me, I want whatever her and Trey have to last. I don't want anything to scare her into running away. No more running away for the Hawthornes.

Addy and Trey break apart, all smiles. He grabs the phone and comes back onto the porch. I watch Dez and Elliot to make sure they go back to their business, and even though they're conspicuously smiling, they do. Addy comes out a minute or so later.

"What's with the face, Trey?" Addy asks. I look at him. His forehead's wrinkled.

Elliot, Dez, and I could make a bunch of make out jokes right now. I, for one, have millions, but I don't, so the other two don't.

"There are three Mason Crowells in Nashville," Trey says. "I'm sure we can find the right one, though. Should we just call them all?"

"Yeah," Elliot says. "Use Adam's 'team of researchers' excuse and tell him we're looking to do an interview."

"We could pretend like we're doing an interview on racism in Nashville. I feel like cops are always looking for ways to get on the other side of racism."

"Abuela Treybo with the win," Addy says, plopping down on the rocking chair and pulling a random book off the table next to her.

"Do it," Dez says. "That's brilliant. It's like, using systemic racism to battle racism. I love it so much."

"Alright, I'll be right back," Trey says. "I have to call my parents first."

I catch Addy's eyes and give her a brother-like nod. Red spreads across her cheeks, but she smiles and goes back to her book.

Dez disappears back into the Hamana. "So, do we want to go check out more of downtown Nashville tonight? We don't have much else to do so we might as well, right? Or we could go get more pie. Mmmmmm, pie."

"I kind of just want another day to relax," Elliot says. "How about we paint the town some color tomorrow? We can just chill and play games tonight."

"Trey hates board games," I say. "Remember the time we tried playing Apples to Apples? He shoved everything off the table after the second hand and we ended up going to Pritchett's."

"Maybe we should just make Trey play games for tonight's entertainment," Dez says. "That sounds more entertaining than anything else."

Elliot snickers and then sticks his toothpick into the mesh screen behind his head. "Yeah, well, while you guys think about that, I'm going to take a nap."

I hold up my hand like I'm in class.

"What?" he asks.

"It's just a nap, right? You aren't going to go do your thing? Because if you want to feel something that badly, I can just punch you in the balls and save you the trouble."

"It's a for-real nap. Cross my heart and hope to die."

"Why couldn't you have just pinky swore or something?" I ask.

"Not as funny."

Once Elliot's gone, I walk over to the Hamana and part the fabric. To my surprise, Dez is sleeping.

I miss being home with her. It's nice being on a trip, but it feels too sensational to be normal. With her around, monotony is an adventure. We could go to Pritchett's every day, sit in our normal booth, order the same milkshakes, and she can make it feel different and awesome every time. I lean down and kiss her. My lips touch hers and my entire body ripples with warmth.

"It didn't work," she says, eyes still closed.

So she's not sleeping. I lay down next to her, wrapping my arm around her waist. "What?"

"Not engulfing each other with our unnatural disaster-ness."

She's nervous. She told me her secret and now she's scared of our closeness. I get that. I felt exposed after I told her about the reason for my suspension.

I grab her hand, hoping it will ease her worry.

"What happens when we erupt?" she asks.

"Nothing."

"Nothing? That's not possible. Name one natural disaster that hasn't destroyed something, even if it was a small destruction."

"Hurricanes that don't make landfall."

"I bet all kinds of fish and birds die in them."

"Can you just, not think about us in terms of impending doom?"

She spins around to face me. Her body adds to the burning of mine. We're like a bonfire in a hammock. A bonfammock.

"I know you think we can be more than addicts. I'm trying to believe that, but the reality is I'm letting myself consume you: kissing, going on dates. What happens when I'm ready to move on?"

"You could just be, you know, doing normal dating things." I lower my voice, knowing that even though Addy probably isn't paying attention, she's still on the porch. "Dez, we just watched Trey and Addy make out. I bet Trey isn't freaking out or worrying if he's consuming her."

"Well, maybe he should be. We're addicts; we move to keep things whole."

"No," I say, "Dez, that's not true. It's only true because you think it is. You're not even trying to think anything else. They're just letting it happen, why can't we?"

"How can I think anything else? This is me. Don't you see the cycle?"

"I do see it, but we're—"

"Variables." She kisses me and then leans her forehead against mine. "I wish I had your strength."

"Says the girl who created a separate identity to get information from a multi-million-dollar studio exec."

"It's not the same. That was just a manipulation technique I learned from my family. In the Coulter Mansion of American Waste, no one can survive without learning how to manipulate and twist. Another cycle. How will we ever be greater than our addictions?"

I'm getting sick of arguing about this. The more I argue about it, the more I wonder if Dez is right. I've never let myself believe we can't change, but I think somewhere in the dark corners of my mind, I'm afraid I'll realize it's true. I don't want to find out that I'm like a ghost trying to touch another ghost.

Adam = live human.

Adam ≠ ghost.

"Because we just are," I say, hoping she'll let it go.

"No, Adam, I'm serious. How can you be holy and broken at the same time? I need to know before I believe it."

I let out a gigantic groan. I feel it rumble up from my chest and into my throat. "Right now, I feel a burn that comes from being here with you, touching you, kissing you. But, at the same time, I know I'll eventually have to get up and leave you, and that's a beautiful pain. You don't believe we can be anything but consumers of each other. You believe you're an addict before you're Dez and that kills me. That's the hurtful kind of pain. Somehow, there are two pains, good and bad, and I feel them both at the same time. I know it's annoying to think about, but what if there are some things in the world that are just indefinable? Like, the existence of two contradictory things. We can't know how they fit, but they do, and maybe it's not up to us to know how."

"I'm sorry," she says.

"For what?"

"For hurting you."

I kiss her and close my eyes. "You're forgiven. I'm sorry for all the times I've hurt you, too."

"Just don't stop burning."

I hear Mr. Cratcher saying, *I'm not sure if that will be my decision.* I almost say it to her, but I decide taking a nap next to my blaze-of-light girlfriend, Dez Coulter, is a better idea.

——

We're in the middle of a game of poker. We're casting our bets with organic peanuts. Dez has bet me a make out session if I win, but if I lose, I have to sleep in the tent in my boxers without a sleeping bag.

The pressure to win's tremendous.

This proposal has turned Trey and Elliot into monsters—and Addy into their instigator. I don't think any of us have ever been this competitive in our lives, but right now, we feel like we're in the Olympics. I put my cards down: three eights, one five of diamonds, and one queen of hearts.

Trey lets out a charismatic "Yes!" and puts down a full house.

I curse.

Addy laughs and claps.

"I'll give you best two out of three," Dez says with a smirk.

"Dez! We just got Adam in his boxers fair and square!" Trey yells. "You aren't making it easy for us to beat this kid."

She purses her lips and shrugs.

It's. So. Sexy.

"Maybe I want him to win."

Dez deals another hand, and as soon as Elliot picks up his cards, he says, "I'm all in."

Dez looks at me, one eyebrow raised. She's egging me on. I know it.

Addy taps my cards. "Let's see your poker muscles. Don't let him push you around like a rag doll, honey child."

I stare at my pile of peanuts then at my cards. I have an ace and a five.

I stand. "Author Waller R. Newell once said, 'We don't need to reinvent manliness,' but gentleman, Dez, Addy, I think Waller R. Newell is a bucket'a'bull. If manliness stays static, it gets buried in the dust of progressive humanity." I pause to let the words sink in, but I know the only one who cares about what I'm saying is Dez, which is the point.

Dez lets out a deep breath and then starts fanning herself. "Is anyone else hot in here? Outside of Adam, I mean?"

"Therefore, in reinvented manliness, I take my hoard of peanuts and declare, I am all in." I push my peanuts to the middle of the table. "Oh," I look at Elliot. "I also declare, suck it."

I throw my cards down.

—

Addy's up in her room, and Trey and Elliot are out cold on their mattresses, but I peek through the Hamana fabric anyway just to make sure we're alone. Dez's hand slides under my shirt. A snap of wind alters the roar of the propane heater. There's no way I'm sleeping in the tent in my boxers.

"I'm so glad you lost," she whispers, pulling her head back to look at me.

"I'm not. That manliness speech deserved better."

"That manliness speech is why I'm making out with you right now. Your quote usage was awesome. I should give you some of the first and last lines I've always wanted to use but can't find a context for."

"Like what?" I ask.

"Like, 'I am dead, but it's not so bad. I've learned to live with it.' That's the first line from *Warm Bodies* by Issac Marion. I've had an even harder time with the first line of *Voyager* by Diana Gabaldon, 'When I was small, I never wanted to step in puddles.'"

"Those *are* pretty context-less unless you know zombies who are afraid of water."

She nods. "Oh, thanks for flushing my pill stash."

Zombies to pill stash. That's a conversational jump I'd never thought I'd make. I thought she was just going to ignore the fact that the night we got back from our date, I took all the pills out of her tent and gave them to the bowels of Nashville.

"You finally noticed?"

"Yeah."

"You don't have any more, right?"

"Nope."

"You promise? We have to be honest with each other if we don't want to kill each other with our volcano-ness."

She looks right into my eyes. Unmoving. Unblinking. "I promise, Adam."

"You doing all right?"

"Yeah, I'm not in withdrawal. I'd just gotten back into them. Like, the two you found in my pocket were the first ones in about a year."

"Why did you bring them when we're supposed to be breaking our vice habits?"

"Why did you bring your computer when we're supposed to be breaking our vice habits?"

"Good question."

"I'm back to flasking now."

I rub my temples. Fighting porn is exhausting enough. Dating someone who needs as much encouragement and help as me = exhausting^2.

"Can we not think about that right now? You still owe me five more minutes."

She stares into the fabric hanging above us. "You're actually keeping count?"

"I'm not trying to avoid you. I'm just staying true to your allotted time, being a gentleman and all that junk."

"How strange of you."

"Shouldn't I get points for the small things, like counting?"

"There aren't many small things with you," she says.

I smile. "I find it ironic you're telling *me* that, but I guess we both have complexes against small things."

"Are you about to do what I think you're going to do? Because if you do, I won't ever let you leave this hammock."

"I mean, I was always obsessed with big things."

She flips on top of me. "I'm warning you."

"That's why, 'When I was small, I never wanted to step in puddles.' I went straight for the ocean."

"Adam Hawthorne."

"Yeah?"

"Either marry me or kiss me."

I don't have a ring.

So I kiss her.

—

We make out until she falls asleep. By all accounts, I'm tired. People don't talk about the calories you must burn in that intense of a make out session. I feel like I should boost my electrolytes with a Gatorade or carb up with a plate of pasta. I might if it weren't four in the morning.

I tried falling asleep with Dez in the hammock, but it squeezed my shoulders so tight it made me feel like I was in a garbage compactor. So now I lay awake in my porch mattress, staring at Elliot drooling on himself, thinking about Dez Coulter. I want her. I want all of her in a way I can and can't describe and it's making me twitch and turn. My heart races at the thought of her naked under me. I turn in my mattress for the one hundred and eighth time. I look at the Hamana. Should I? Should I not? I see the silhouette of her body, her beautiful curves, and—and I love her.

And I love her.

I go through the steps in my mind. We find an empty room. I take off her shirt, and then her pants. It will be my first time, so I'm guessing it will be awkward. I try figuring out what happens after I get her pants off, but the No

Pants stage is as foreign to me as feudal Japan and Ethiopian food. Sure, I've seen the act a million times, but that means nothing. Doctors aren't doctors just because they've watched hours and hours of surgery videos on YouTube.

I take a deep breath and throw off my covers. I swing one leg out, but a question begins to echo over and over in my gut: how will having sex with Dez be any different than porn?

I stare at the ground for a moment, trying to find an answer.

I can't.

Could we have sex without feeding addiction? Without consuming each other?

I'd like to think so, but that doesn't mean I actually could. I cross my arms. My lack of action = cold wind making parts that need to be big, small.

I love her.

But right now my love equals consumption.

Just like she said it would.

I curse under my breath. Dez is right. We consume. It's what we are. She doesn't need someone to consume her body. Too many guys are willing to do that. She needs someone to love her.

Does love = walking away?

Can love ever = consumption?

Can sex ever = love for a porn addict?

Can sex ever = love for any addict?

Is there such a thing as broken and holy consumption?

Question after question.

Gust of cold wind after gust of cold wind.

I can never love her greater than. I'll always want to consume her. A voice comes back into my head that's been absent for the last two months.

Sees the problem now, does he, Masters? People only hurtses people. Gollum!

A tear falls down my cheek. I wipe it away, because I'm sure it will fall on the porch with the crash of history's loudest heartbreak. I can't see how this is true, but I feel it. I know what Dez is talking about now.

Adam and Dez = expiration date, and all we can do is enjoy the burn while it lasts.

I stand, walk into the house, and grab a phone off the counter not caring who's it is. I start making a video playlist. If I'm always going to be an addict, why does it matter if I fight it?

IF WE'RE ASLEEP, WE WON'T FEEL THE TRAIN AS MUCH

The log rolls out from under me. I fall into the water of the Puget Sound. I don't move. One second, I watch the sun as it lowers to hide behind the Deception Pass Bridge into the water, the next there is no sun and I'm sinking upwards. Up is just as dark as down. Dark is below and beside. Every inch dark as the next.

It's cold, but I don't care.

The darkness is here, but I don't care.

I am alone, but I don't care.

—

It's two days later, and we're no closer than we were when we started. Trey set up an interview with retired Nashville police chief Mason Crowell, but the soonest he could meet was tomorrow at lunch. You'd think a retired guy would have all the time in the world, but I guess that's a stupid assumption.

I've been making a lot of those lately.

I've been spending every moment I can next to Dez. Now that I know it's only a matter of time before we erupt, I don't want to waste a second with her. She's noticed something is off. This morning she asked if something was wrong. I just told her I looked at porn a few nights ago—wasn't a lie. Her response was to kiss me and tell me to keep fighting, which I found *incredibly* ironic.

This is all a bucket'a'bull. Even Nicholas Sparks couldn't make this up. Actually, he probably has, and that makes me feel worse.

Addy pulls me aside after lunch while the other KOV members chill on the porch.

"What's going on, Papi?" she says, her face tight with seriousness.

"Nothing," I say.

"Buuuull. Remember, you promised to be honest with me."

Again, ironic, considering the amount of secrets she's kept from me that I've found out by accident: quitting her job, liking Trey.

"Dez and I are . . ." I sigh. "I don't know. It just doesn't seem like it can last."

"Sure it can," she says.

I turn toward the porch. "It isn't that simple, Addy."

She grabs my wrist and pulls me back. "Hey, look at me." I do.

"You will not let the divorce affect this. You and Dez are great together."

It's not the divorce. It's the porn. It's always been the damn porn.

"I know," I say.

"Take it from someone who's already let the divorce kill one relationship. It's no fun, and it's useless. You and Dez aren't our parents."

"It isn't about the divorce."

Addy crosses her arms. "Then what is it about?"

"Addiction."

She rolls her eyes, but she wouldn't if she understood how it felt to be controlled by something. "Papi, don't let Dez's knack for turning small things into giant things affect you. You two just need to date. Be young. You two act like you're thirty the way you talk about all this."

"How? How do I 'just date' when I'm so messed up?"

She opens her mouth to answer, but one doesn't come out.

"It's not a switch, Addy."

"Yeah, but neither is the rest of life," she says. "You can't just let one thing about yourself ruin everything else. That's the biggest part of healing. Moving on despite the hurt."

"I don't know how," I snap. "I don't know how to do that."

Addy's silent. The girl who quit her job for me is crushed under my weight. New guilt pours into my veins. I want porn.

"I'm sorry," I say. "I'm messed up. There's no changing that."

Addy hugs me. "I'm not trying to demean how intense addiction is or what you're feeling, but you're not that special, Adam. We all have our messes. You're not alone in that."

I know she won't let me walk away in a bad place, so I just let her have the final word.

—

Elliot invents a game with Mexican Coke bottle caps that's kind of like a combination of Mancala and marbles. We play it for most of the day instead of going anywhere. It's not like we have anything better to do. We're going to see a movie later tonight, so none of us want to drive out to Nashville yet, and going to the police station would be a waste of time considering we have a meeting with the police chief who was at the crime scene.

After dinner, I pull Dez out of the Hamana and we take a walk around the cul-de-sac. I hold onto her hand tightly, knowing, someday, I'll have to let go. We pass a house that looks similar to ours, the same rustic barn wood steps and thick log patio railings, and see an older woman standing on her porch watching the sun.

"Beautiful!" she yells. We respond with a simultaneous "yeah!" as she walks back into her house.

We head back to the mansion, gather the Knights of Vice, and head out to see the new Cohen Brothers movie. Afterward, we wander around Nashville, and then drive out to The Loving Pie Company. This time we sit in the living room instead of the bedroom.

We get home at two in the morning. Everyone else heads out to the porch to go to bed, but I don't. Instead, I grab the phone off the counter and go up to bathroom. The weird thing is: I don't watch anything. I'm not even thinking of watching anything. I just stare at the blank screen. An hour later, I make my way downstairs.

Tonight, instead of deciding whether or not to sleep with Dez, I feel a different desire. I peel back the fabric, climb in behind her, and pull her as close as possible.

I just want to be together.

"It's about time," she says.

I kiss her on the neck. She grabs my hand and pushes her back into my chest. With the holiest of sighs, she falls asleep and, after an hour or so of shoulder reconfiguration, so do I.

—

In the middle of the night, I feel her get out of the hammock. I'm in a sleep daze that makes everything seem like a dream. She comes back a few minutes later.

"You okay?" I ask her.

"Yeah, I'm in a sweaty dandelion."

I'm pretty sure that's not what she said. I force my eyes open. "What."

"Bathroom, Adam. Bathroom."

I smile and lay my cheek against her back when she crawls back in.

"I built a catapult," I say. Wait. No. That can't be what I said. She pulls my hand over her waist. "I love you, too."

—

As I stare at Mason Crowell, I note two things:

1. I didn't expect him to be black.

2. For being a retired police chief, he doesn't look very old.

Mason Crowell's looks ≠ age.

Mason Crowell's looks = sculpted and ripped black guy.

He wears a baseball cap declaring his obsession/affiliation with the Tennessee Titans, and I'm pretty sure I see a Tennessee Titans "T" inked onto his arm when he takes his jacket off.

"So, what do you kids want to know?"

"Well, uh," Trey says, "we want to just ask you a few questions about the Elias Harper murder."

His face stiffens. He's probably never wanted to talk about this, especially to a bunch of kids.

"You said you were doing a report on police racism."

I look at Addy. She makes an "oh boy" face: gritted teeth, wide eyes.

"Well, it's kind of based around the Harper murder," Trey says. Something tells me Mr. Crowell would stand up and leave if we weren't in his house.

Dez notices Mr. Crowell's distrust and explains everything from the beginning. She talks about how being murdered because you're a different *shade* of human is like killing a celebrity because they're a different *kind* of human. It's a clever analogy that grabs Mr. Crowell, and instead of listening because he has no choice, he listens because he wants to. A few minutes later, she gets him to relax enough and she explains what we're looking for, and why we're looking for it. She gives the information we've already gathered in such detail it's like she has it stored away on an Excel spreadsheet in her brain.

After she's finished, he walks over to his counter and pours leftover coffee into a blender with a scoop of protein powder, milk, and ice and then blends it for a few seconds. "I've never discussed the details of this murder with anyone," he says, pouring the smoothie into a pint glass.

We cast each other some disappointed looks, but Addy just nods like she's sure something good is coming.

"Mostly because there were never any details to discuss. Racism was obvious during that time. There were probably hundreds of people targeting Elias, Colin, and Gabby. Just like there were hundreds of people targeting me for being Nashville's first black police chief." He sits at the table and, though the guy is jacked, he sits like he's weak. It's like he's Samson, and this conversation is his Delilah.

"The precinct kept none of the evidence, I'm sorry. Do you have any other questions?"

My head is filled with overlapping curses. When I run out of swear words, I start combining them.

"Do you think Colin Cratcher killed Elias?" Elliot asks.

"No. No, I don't. I'm *sure* he didn't."

"Why?"

"The same reason the jury was sure." Mr. Crowell takes a giant sip of his caffeinated muscle juice.

"What reason?" Dez asks.

"The song played in the courtroom. He called it evidence. It was called 'What Are You, Elias?' It was Colin's response to the people threatening Elias and Gabby. The three of them had sung on the track together. Colin broke down as soon as the song came on."

"A song cleared him?" I ask, incredulous.

"No. Technically, the song wasn't evidence at all. Colin was the evidence. He couldn't make it a minute without looking back at Gabby for assurance. The man was a wreck."

"But he was high, right?" Dez asks. "He didn't remember that night."

Mr. Crowell shakes his head. "Yes, but it wasn't Colin. Everyone in that courtroom knew that at the end."

I don't feel like making eye contact with anyone. To make eye contact would mean taking on more disappointment.

"You know," Mr. Crowell says. "I may have a copy of that song. I've done my best to forget that day, but I have a blurry memory of Colin giving me a demo after the trial."

"Isn't that something you should remember?" Dez snaps.

He casts her a cold look, and her sharpness wilts. "No, that day reminded me that, though I was a professional agent against injustice, I couldn't end it. I may have been the one with jurisdiction and a gun, but it takes a world to win a battle against anything worth fighting. That was the toughest case of my life. Through my entire career, my day was good if I didn't have to deal with another case like that." He sighs, rolls his neck, and then glances at the clock hanging above the kitchen sink. "I need to go. If you give me a few days to deal with my feelings on this matter, I'll look around to see if I have a copy of Colin's song."

—

"That meeting wasn't nothing, guys," Trey says as we pull into our cul-de-sac. "He may have a song for us. We can't just be disappointed. We did this for adventure, remember? To be together. To fight our addictions with those moments. Wallowing is dangerous for us."

Addy pulls onto the highway and nods. "Yeah, Abuela is right. If you guys can't enjoy this trip for other reasons, we better leave. Having four depressed addicts in one house will be a disaster I won't be able to contain."

They're right. The decline of Adam Hawthorne is happening, and I don't know how to stop it. If I can't figure it out soon, I might go all the way back to the beginning when I was okay with not caring and not asking questions. It sounds so . . . normal.

That night, we play more of Elliot's bottle cap game, which we're now calling Capola, while pretending to be happy. When it's time to go to bed, I don't get into my mattress. I stay with Dez in the Hamana. We don't talk at all, which is when I know we both feel the rumble of our expiration date barreling toward us. Instead of trying to figure out a way to break out of the rope holding us onto the tracks, we hold hands and sleep.

Maybe if we're asleep, we won't feel the train as much.

FINE

Two days later, I'm the biggest unnatural disaster I've ever been. I stay with Dez at night so I don't watch porn, but that doesn't stop me from thinking about it all day, or from feeling the itch every single damn second of every damn hour. Porn's suddenly a phoenix rising out of the ashes. It keeps telling me I won't be fine until I consume it, and it does its best to remind me of that every minute, and it's exhausting.

All I want to do is be someone else. I don't want to consume but, right now, it seems like that's all I can ever do. Knowing Dez will be in my disaster.

What have I done?

Suddenly the Anti-Adam Order feels more right than ever. I deserve the Order. I deserve retaliation, because that guy . . .

That's guy is me. It's not past Adam. It's not someone I used to know.

It's.

Me.

That night, after watching Trey and Addy successfully like each other—sit next to each other, have normal discussion, be normal people in a normal relationship—I grab Dez and take another walk around the cul-de-sac. I want to attempt normal with her, and the act of walking makes her forget about some of her walls.

"I've always dreamed of being a psychology professor," she says with a shy smile. "I'd totally do addictions counseling on the side, too."

"You'd be awesome at that," I say. "With some experience first."

"Maybe I'm just fascinated with my own brain, but I'm amazed people can help others dig to the roots of addiction. People literally get how God fits into synapses and neurons. Call me a nerd, but studying nervous ticks sounds like an amazing job."

As she talks about all of this, a Trey-like gusto fills in her words and motions. Her voice is hopeful, and her free hand waves back and forth, emphasizing random words. This is her. This is Dez. Underneath her layers of fear, she's innocent, a dreamer, hopeful, and all of those adjectives are sexy on her.

She rambles on about religion and the brain for a few more minutes, but as if passion crept past her without her permission, she pauses mid-sentence. The brief glimpse of a free Dez disappears, and she makes sure to throw herself under the addict bus to make up for feeling something other than dismalness.

"But I'm never going to change, so I guess it doesn't matter what I want."

She sighs and gives me a half smile like what she said was funny, but I can only look at her and wish that she were free of herself. Is that version of Dez possible? Is the current Dez, Dez? Is it possible that the real you is the person you make fun of and belittle when they come around?

We get to the end of the thermometer-shaped road and start making our way back. We're halfway to our house when someone yells out behind us. "Hey, there!"

We turn around to see the old woman we saw watching the sunset a few nights ago walking toward us. "Are you the kids staying in the house at the end of the cul-de-sac?"

"Yes, ma'am," I say flatly, even though I don't feel like talking or being polite. "I'm Adam Hawthorne, this is Dez Coulter. There are three more with us, but they're at the house."

"Go grab them!" she says.

I finally see her face. I know I've seen her before, but I don't know where.

"I'm going to have all of you all over for coffee and dessert. I won't take no for an answer."

Dez laughs. "We won't give no for answer then."

—

The woman's house looks exactly like ours. Exactly.

Addy realizes this before I do and asks, "Do you own the house we're staying in?"

"Yes," she says. "I had both houses built in the mid-eighties. My mother used to live there, but she passed on, bless her heart. Come, please sit." She taps her palm on the kitchen island where six black bar stools wait underneath the lip of a speckled black marble counter top.

"So, whose mother was the one who made the arrangements?" she asks.

"Mine, ma'am," Dez says.

"Please call me Miss Hunt."

Miss Hunt. That face.

I look at Addy to make sure I'm not imagining this. Her eyes tell me everything.

The woman in front of us is Amelia Hunt.

Memory after memory of The Woman crash on me, but that last game of Word Hunt taints all of them. Unsatisfied. Temptation. Me knowing. Doing nothing. I feel like getting up and running out of the house, but I don't.

"Thanks for having us over, Miss Hunt," Trey says. "Your home's beautiful."

Addy leans into his ear and whispers something. Trey looks over Miss Hunt over and then grabs Addy's hand.

Normal.

Why can't Dez and I be normal?

"Oh, thank you," she says, "but it's nearly the same as yours. The only difference is that there's a railing in each of my bathrooms because my joints are miserable things. Would anyone like coffee?"

Dez mouths "I love her" to me.

Miss Hunt shuffles around in the kitchen in furry white slippers. She's opening cupboards as though this is the first time in years she's had people in her house. She pulls a red canister of coffee into arms as well as a small bowl filled with sugar. "Are y'all related? What brings such young people all the way from Seattle by themselves?"

"We're not related. Well, these two are," Trey points to Addy and me. "We're all friends and part of an addiction group, and this is like our trip of rebirth."

I wince. I'm not sure if telling the woman who's renting you her house that you're part of an addiction group is a good idea.

Miss Hunt tips her glasses down and flicks her eyes back and forth between the girls. "Are any of these boys giving you problems?"

"They are all outstanding gentlemen," Addy says, smiling.

Dez chuckles and takes a different, less encouraging path. "Well, for me, one of them is, but it's nothing I can't handle."

That's a lie, but whatever.

"Which one of them is the boyfriend?" Miss Hunt asks. Dez points to me.

"You respect her, young man. Over there in a house with no parents around. If you know what's good for you, you'll respect her, you hear?"

Trey and Elliot have a chuckle at my expense, but when Miss Hunt catches them laughing, she stares them down.

"Yes, ma'am," I say, and Dez elbows me in the ribs as a joke. I look at her with what I thought was a smile, but when she sees me, she tilts her head in confusion.

"So, why are you here?" Miss Hunt asks. "How is your 'rebirth' going?"

We have nothing to lose by telling her what we're doing, or at least trying to do. We needed something from everyone else. Miss Hunt? She's just a person, and, despite how much I don't want to be here, a nice one at that. I nod to Trey, and he explains everything to her: Mr. Cratcher. His cancer. Coming here to find the album so we can finish his remake for him. He gives her an overview of the Knights of Vice, and how we're trying, but definitely failing, to support each other to be better people. Miss Hunt stops her busybody fidgeting and listens to him with deep eyes. Her look's one that makes me wonder if she knew all of this before Trey explained it.

While I eat the most delicious tiramisu I've ever had, Trey explains the stalled state of our album search. After he's finished, she takes a deep breath.

"Colin is still alive?"

"Yes, as far as we know," I say. "We haven't gotten any calls yet."

She takes a sip of her coffee and holds the tiny white china mug in front of her face so it hides her mouth.

"Wait here," she says. "I'll be right back." She starts walking but turns. "Did he ever have a songwriting company?" she asks.

"The Chaos Writer," Dez says.

Miss Hunt seems like a person who'd be ashamed if she knew we heard her call Mr. Cratcher a "sly bastard" under her breath while walking away. That's why none of us say anything about it when she comes back with a white three-ring binder.

"I was a friend of Colin's," she says. I glance at Addy and see she's biting her lip. It's killing her not to fangirl.

"I met him in '66. Right when I signed with Columbia records. We wrote songs together for three years." She slides the binder toward us. "He was a genius with words. He made them honest and beautiful, light and dark. He had a way of taking two opposites and bringing them together. I even sang a few tracks on the album you've come here for.

"Right before Elias was murdered, Colin came over my house and told me a bunch of people were threatening to kill him for dating Gabby. A few days after the trial, Colin sent me a letter thanking me for my friendship and that was the last I'd heard of him. Then, in 1984, a songwriter named Leonard Cohen released a song called 'Hallelujah.' There was a line in it that sounded too familiar to be a coincidence, and it was because I'd already sung it on Colin's album. Goodness, if only I could remember what the album was called."

"*Hounds of Eden?*" Elliot asks.

"Oh, yes." She smiles. "Such a good title. I sang for three songs on it. If I remember right, the first one was called 'Heart like a Wasteland.' Oh, and the second was 'Beast of Nashville.'" Her face grows somber. "The third, 'What Are You, Elias?'"

Dez and I stare at each other at the mention of the last song. For some reason, when Mr. Crowell mentioned it, I didn't think twice about the title. Suddenly, I want to find the album more than I did before, but not because I need to conquer something. I want to find out the answer to his stupid question.

I want to know what I am.

"It's a pity he never finished that album," Miss Hunt continues. "He would have made it. He could have played with the biggest of them. Bob Dylan, Fleetwood Mac, Colin Cratcher."

Dez flips through the binder filled with hand-penned lyrics. Each page has two signatures in the top left corner: Amelia Hunt and Colin Cratcher.

Miss Hunt leans against the counter with an air of nostalgia in her eyes and wishful smiles. "When I heard the line 'there's a blaze of light in every word' in Mr. Cohen's song, I had suspicions that Colin was at it again. I contacted The Chaos Writer, but he never responded. Rightfully so." She laughs. "If he'd have taken me as a client, I would have known instantly who he was and he wanted to be invisible."

We're all on the edge of our seats, and no one wants to ask the question that's sitting on the tips of our tongues. We're all afraid of the answer. Dez decides to be the strong one, which is more ironic proof that she can be strong when she wants to be.

"Do you have a copy of the album?" she asks, almost whispering. She grabs my hand. I hold it tight, like I'm waiting to catch her when she trips.

"Colin's? No, no, he didn't let those tracks out of his sight. Back then, everything was analog, you know. It was all records and 8-tracks. Data was clunky and took up space."

"Do you know if anyone else has the album?" Trey asks, the optimist to the rescue.

"If Colin doesn't have it, no one has it. He took back all of the trial evidence before he moved. He didn't leave anything behind. Colin Cratcher wanted to completely disappear. He wanted a new life with Gabby. I'm sure it's in his possession somewhere. He never got rid of anything."

To say I'm frustrated is an understatement. We came all this way—Seattle to Nashville—just to figure out Mr. Cratcher was lying. I start to blame his lie for the state of Dez and me. Maybe if we hadn't come out here, we would've survived each other. Even though I know that's not true—whatever's happening with us would've happened eventually, but it feels better to blame someone else other than myself for once.

"He told me he didn't have it," I say. "He said it was gone. Why would he lie?"

"I imagine he didn't want to bring up that old hurt. That time in his life was extremely painful. When you are a collector of years and aches, there are some old bones you just want to keep buried." Miss Hunt says.

"Can you remember the names of the other songs?" Dez pleads.

She's grasping at anything now. I can tell she wants to cry. She keeps swallowing. Her blinks are like, three seconds long.

"Can you please remember the rest of the album?"

"I'm sorry, I can't," Miss Hunt says. "But please call me when you start working on it again. I'd love to sing on it."

Dez stands and walks toward the door. "Fine."

JUST A CONSUMER

It's been a day since Miss Hunt told us Mr. Cratcher "probably" has the album. Two since Mr. Crowell told us he'd look for the song. Christmas is in three days, and we're supposed to be going home in two. That was the deal.

We don't play Capola.

We don't talk.

We don't do anything.

We're eating breakfast on the patio in silence, each person's frustration and hurt rubbing off on the other. Addy walks onto the porch, fresh from sleep. She takes a good, silent look at all of us and then sighs.

"Okay, everyone, I hate to be that girl, but think it's time to leave."

Trey nods. "I agree. It's not defeat if we keep fighting, but I think in order to fight, we have to leave."

"We can't leave yet. We have two more days," Dez says. "Besides, if Mr. Crowell finds the song, we have to be here."

"No, we don't," I say. "We have technology. He can just email it to us."

"It's going to be on an 8-track or something, Adam. He can't just email it to us."

I rub my temples. "Then he can mail it to us. I want to get out of here. I feel like shit."

"I'm sure we can work something out with him, Dez," Addy says, taking a new tone: a firm, unmoving, non-joking tone. She sounds like The Woman. "We've got his phone number. It'll be alright."

"Yeah," Elliot says. "I've been feeling my triggers. It's time to go. I've come way to far to be pulled back."

"Guys, Addy," Dez moans, "we can't go yet. We haven't even gotten one song. We can't just give up. We still have an album to find. There's still a killer on the loose."

"I'd rather give up than wallow in our collective filth," Elliot says. "We've just been sitting here staring at each other getting depressed. We can do that anywhere."

"Everyone feels bad," Addy says. "I think it won't be a big deal if we cut it off at the chase now."

"Dad could tell I was off," I say. "When I called him this morning, he told me to start thinking about coming home."

Dez shrugs. "Parents don't understand this kind of stuff."

That's it? It's that simple for her? Outside of that, she's still hell bent on finding a murderer? After the millions of warnings we've all given her? After all our conversations? She still doesn't listen. She doesn't even try. I look at her, but before I can say anything, Addy crosses her arms.

"Dez, we should head home today. As the unofficial chaperone, I won't take no for an answer."

Dez stares at flame coming out of the propane heater. "I'm not going to go. I don't want to go home. You guys can just leave me here."

"Dez, seriously?" Elliot asks.

"Elliot, seriously. You guys have good things to go home to. I go home, everything goes back to the way it was. I want the album. I'm going to stay."

"So, I'm not a good thing to go home to?" I ask.

"Adam, cut it," Addy says.

Dez rolls her eyes. "That's not what I mean."

I shake my head. "It's not like I'd be surprised if it was."

"Adam," Addy warns again.

"What the hell does that mean?" Dez asks. "What's gotten into you? You've been a bitch-fest for the last few days."

Addy knows she's lost control, so she doesn't step in.

"That's because you were right and I finally realized it."

"What are you talking about?" Dez asks.

"The expiration date. Not being able to love. All that bucket'a'bull."

Her anger melts, her eyes close, and she folds into a slump in the Hamana. She's hurt, but what else did she expect?

"Adam . . ." Dez starts.

Elliot stands. "I'm going to go pack."

Trey follows him. I should go with them. They feel an eruption coming and are smart enough to get out of its path. Addy, however, just stands there, watching us.

"Dez, I finally agree with you. Isn't that what you wanted?"

"No, it isn't."

"What do you mean, 'no'?" I feel my patience drain out of me and seep into the ground. She never even tried to believe anything else. She just said I wasn't a good thing to go back to. After all this, I'm still good enough to fight for. To change for.

"Dez," I say, "I can't even look at you without hearing you saying good-bye to me. You're doing it right now. You're choosing exactly what you want. Finding a murderer over me because you're done with me. We've consumed each other, and now it feels like we're just scraping the plate."

She sits up in the Hamana. "I want the old Adam back, the one that believed we could last."

"Why?" I ask. "What good did he do? Sure, he made everything feel more romantic, but that was just gold plating, right? We never actually had a chance."

"He made me believe that we could believe we had a chance."

"Yeah, well, you never stuck around to see if we could have a chance, so."

"What the hell does that mean?"

"You always leave when things don't match with your opinion. Does the word *fine* sound familiar? Since I've met you, you haven't even tried to be something else. You don't let yourself get dirty, and when you do, it's a clean kind of dirty. A dirty that's manageable and not risky. As long as you can come out on top, as long as you don't have to do something that pushes you out of your comfort zone or gives *you* the responsibility of doing actual changing, you're okay with yourself. You haven't even tried to believe anything other than what you believe. You've made up your mind, and everyone else has to bend to your every damn whim. The porch. Sleeping in a tent. Bumper stickering the SUV. Semi-dating me. Everything is a *thing* with you, Dez. No wonder why nothing can last for you. Nothing is good enough. You're exactly like you're parents."

As soon as I say the last line, I regret it. But I know it's true. She's never let us just be. She never lets anything just be.

"How is this my fault?" she asks, getting out of the Hamana. "How the hell is this my fault?"

"If you would have just . . . thought for one second we could have survived. If you could have just helped me fight, just let go of the need for perfection, we wouldn't be here right now."

"Oh, God," she says, snarling. "You're the one who's decided to give up. I told you I wanted to believe we could be something. You're the one who's saying we're over."

"But you never believed we could actually be different! You believed in the idea from a distance, always waiting for it to go to hell. You never let us be normal. Everything was always this giant problem. Well, here you go, Dez. You believed this explosion into existence. Addicts can never be greater than love; we just consume."

She covers her eyes, but I still see her tears falling down her cheeks.

I get out of the Hamana and walk toward the back door. "I'm going to pack."

"Fuck you, Adam Hawthorne. Fuck you and me."

I catch her eyes, her watery, beautiful eyes, and the last thing I say to her is, "Fine."

—

An hour later, Addy's in the driver's seat, talking on the phone with the Coulters about leaving Dez there, and I'm watching the exhaust steaming in the cold in the rearview mirror. I look around the car for the cable that plugs Elliot's iPod into the stereo. I sift through the napkins in the glove box and then open the center console. There's a pile of Dez's CDs leaning against the console wall. I slide them back, and instead of finding an audio cable, I find a transparent orange bottle of pills. I pull them out and flip the bottle over. Nellanne Coulter is written on the front. Underneath her name: Percocet.

I slam my fist on the dashboard a million times. A new rage fills me. One that's pushing at my lips. Pushing me out of the SUV.

"Hey!" Addy yells, "Cut it out."

I pull on the door handle, and Addy goes to grab my arm.

"Adam Darren Hawthorne," she yells, "you need to calm down."

I jump out of the SUV and go around to the back of the patio. Dez is still sitting in the Hamana, crying.

"You lied to me. You told me that there weren't any more."

She cries harder but doesn't answer.

"God, Dez. See? This is exactly my point. You don't talk about shit. You just throw your fears on other people so you don't have to deal with them yourself. You're educated enough to make it sound like you're being honest, but in the end, you don't want to come out of hiding. The reason you can't believe in us is because you don't want to. You'd rather be safe than sorry. You'd rather feel like some giant issue was standing in the way of us than try to be normal. Well I'm sick of being the only one willing to risk myself."

"Adam, please stop!" She springs out of the Hammock. "Please. Just please stop. I can explain."

"I don't want an explanation! I want you."

She kisses me. My heart breaks all over again, but I kiss her back, knowing once this is over, it's over. I can't do this anymore. I can't want. I can't dream. I can't ask questions. I can't care.

Should have never explored outside the cave when darkness hides open graves. Gollum!

You're right. And now I hurt so damn much.

Follow me, Masters. I shows you the way, I does.

Dez takes her lips off mine, but she doesn't let go of me. I break her grasp, swallow, and turn my back to her.

"Adam . . ."

I can't care. I can't care. To survive in this world, I can't care.

"Adam, please don't leave me."

I walk toward the SUV. I slide back into the driver's seat, buckle my seatbelt, and start the car.

"Are you done with your hissy toddler fit, now?" Addy asks.

"Guess you shouldn't have quit your job," I say. "What did you even do when you said you were busy when you weren't working? Why did you lie to me?"

Addy turns in her seat. Lost as to what to say.

"What were you doing, Addy?" I ask.

She looks out the window. "I was in Portland. Being with Mom because she thought me leaving her to help you meant I hated her. Just like you did."

"Well, you should've just stayed there."

"How dare you. How dare you say that?"

"What good did it do?" I say. "What does it matter if you're here or not? Things are just always going to suck."

Get rid of all of them, masters. It's best.

Addy stares at me, and then she gets out of the car and goes around the house to the back porch.

"Dude, what the hell, man?" Trey says. "Why would you say that? What's wrong with you?"

"It's none of your business, Trey."

"It is when you treat my girlfriend like crap."

I turn in my seat. "I don't want to hear anything about your girlfriend, so just shut the hell up."

Hurt washes over Trey's face, and before he can say anything. Elliot swings the trunk open and throws his bags haphazardly onto ours.

Addy gets back into the SUV, but she doesn't look at me. "The Coulters said to let her stay and that's what she wants to do. I can't make her come, so if anyone else has any other ideas, speak them. Otherwise, we have to leave her here. I'm not letting any of you stay another minute."

No one says anything.

"Alright," she says, wiping a tear from her cheek. "We're leaving then."

Elliot climbs into the backseat and says, "So much for teaching each other how to see beauty in the chaos."

Luckily, those are the last words spoken in the SUV, which smells like Dez Coulter.

I don't care.

—

Everyone wants Top 40 on the radio on the way back. I'm sure they're all doing it to piss me off. I don't care. I've tried caring the last three months, and I feel worse now than when I started. Here are my conclusions from my brief experiment in thinking:

Care = pain.

Love = non-existence.

Thinking = the painful kind of pain.

The only reason we're aware of the beautiful kind of pain is because we like to think there's an alternative to the painful kind. For once, something has one definition.

Pain = the painful kind.

Porn = cycle of pain that makes you numb.

Porn > pain.

So, what if I'm just a consumer?

GREATER THAN

Home doesn't feel like home. Home feels like Nashville and I hate them both. I don't want to go to my room. I don't want to eat. All I want to do is not exist.

Addy went into her room when we got home and slammed the door in my face.

I don't care.

I'm surfing channels with my pillow behind my back, comforter draped over my legs, when dad comes through the kitchen archway. His jaw tenses firm with concern as he sits next to me. He keeps opening his mouth like he's going to speak but can't find the strength yet.

He sighs. "Have you talked to your sister yet?"

I scoff. "No."

"You're starting school soon. Don't you think—"

"No."

He rubs his temples. "Alright, well I need to tell you this. It can't wait any longer."

He pauses. I expect him to go on another rant about how I can't turn to porn, and how fighting addiction can help you feel whole again, but I've never felt whole, even when

I tried. It's impossible. If you can't ever truly love someone, or yourself, then how can you feel whole? When a puzzle is missing a piece, you can't say it's finished.

Dad takes a deep breath. "So, I called your mom after our second Addiction Fighters meeting."

He's called her every Saturday for the last year. This isn't news.

"I told her I was done calling."

That = news.

"I said I was going to stop trying to get her back. I finally said good-bye."

At least Addiction Fighters worked for one of us; my dad has finally decided to kick Nicholas Sparks in his romantic bucket'a'bull balls.

"Right before you left for Nashville, she called me and we decided to meet to get some closure. So, while you were in Nashville, I went to Portland."

I know where this is going. I stand up and walk into the kitchen, looking for the keys to my car.

Dad blocks the door. "Adam, you can't run away from this. You can't run away from life anymore. I'm not going to let you."

I remember when I said that about Addy, when I wanted that for her and Trey. When I said it to Dez.

"Just say what you're going to say so I can leave."

"Adam . . ."

"Dad, just say it."

His face tightens. "I promised myself I wouldn't try to get her to come back, and I didn't. I stuck to my guns. However, we hashed out a lot of things and discovered a lot of miscommunication and hurt we never worked through. Anyway, it was a really good few days, and she's going to move back to Seattle. She's not going to live with us, but we're going to try again."

So fighting to be a better person worked for everyone else but me? Elliot, Trey, Addy, dad, everyone else got better. Everyone else moved forward and I'm still here. Just like before. Just like when The Woman left.

I scoff. "How long do you think that will last before she gets bored with you and decides the dick next door's more entertaining?"

"Wow. How did that trip ruin you so much?" he asks. "You were growing, Adam. I shouldn't have let you go. What am I supposed to do with you? How do I even help you right now? You know what? You're grounded."

"From what? What do I have that you can possibly ground me from?"

"This house."

"Oh, so you're kicking me out?"

"You're using this place to hide. Get out. Come back tomorrow night."

"Where do you want me to stay? Should I just freeze to death in my car to make it easier for everyone?"

"Maybe," he says, stepping up to me, looking me dead in the eye. "Or call one of your friends and ask for refuge from your dad."

I go upstairs, pack an overnight bag, and walk out the door. I get in Genevieve, turn on NPR, and drive. It's not until I'm halfway there that I realize I'm driving to Mr. Cratcher's house. I pull into his driveway, but I don't turn off the car.

I just sit there for an hour, listening to NPR's strange late night mix of bad rock and classical music and doing everything I can to forget how I feel about Dez Coulter, Trey, Elliot, Addy, my dad, Mr. Cratcher. All the people I let in.

I want everyone who can hurt me gone.

I throw Genevieve into reverse and head toward Overlake Hospital.

—

"Is Mr. Cratcher still in room 322?" I ask the nurse sitting behind a giant circular nurse's station.

"Yes, but visiting hours are over. I'm sorry."

"It's fine."

I pretend like I'm walking toward the elevator, but I slide into a nook with two vending machines pressed against the back wall and wait. It's a long and silent ten minutes before the nurse is called somewhere by a patient, but when she is, I sneak out of the alcove, around the desk, and down the hallway until I reach room 322.

I walk in. He's still there. Alive by breathing, not by life.

I pull up a chair to the side of his bed. "We're done. Dez and I are done. It was only a matter of time, I guess. Out of all the things you warned me about, I wish you would have told me we were doomed from the start."

I think about him and Gabby. They weren't doomed. Was it because she wasn't addicted to anything? Was it because she didn't have a vice? How is it that Trey, a sex addict, can have a normal relationship with my sister? One that's helped him get stronger instead of worse?

"How did you and Gabby do it? How did you not just mess each other up? God, please just wake up and tell me."

I lean back in my chair and stare at the ceiling. "I can't stop thinking about her. I can't stop thinking we could have done something different. What if I could've beat porn? What if she could've beat . . . everything? So many questions and . . ." I pause. Try to figure out what I'm feeling. What I'm thinking. "I wasn't going to ask any questions when I got back, but I can't stop. I have more and more each day. I feel like I'm going to explode."

Then I realize something about Mr. Cratcher. He changed the album so often because he wanted to forget the pain that came with it. That's why he worked on it for forty years. He didn't want to face the pain.

"You chose to face it in the end," I say. "You knew you were dying and you didn't want to leave the album unfinished or that hurt unresolved. Every day we worked on it, you hurt. That's why you lied about having the album. That's why you redid tracks an ungodly amount of times. That's why you spent so long picking microphones. You were fighting to let it go. You wanted to face your last unexplored hurt head on, and you had me there because you didn't want to face it alone."

I am Mr. Cratcher.

I am Mark.

I am Dez.

I am Trey.

I am my dad.

I am Elliot.

I am Addy.

I am my mom.

I cry. I hurt. I really, really hurt.

I can't face this alone.

—

I drive back to Mr. Cratcher's house at two-thirty in the morning. I still have the key I "stole" from under his flower planter. I walk inside and see Trey and Elliot asleep on the living room floor and couch, just like I knew they would be.

Neither of them wanted to be alone, either.

I stand above them, petrified. I haven't apologized to them for being an ass. I haven't even tried talking to them.

"Adam?" Trey asks.

And just like that, I start bawling. He rushes over to me and hugs me, like I never pushed him away. Elliot doesn't touch me, but I feel him there. He even says so after a little while. I let myself feel the failure of the road trip, my disappointment in myself, the hurt of my mom leaving me without a word and Addy following her. I let every hurt I've pushed away in an attempt to be safe roll through me. And, though it sucks, I don't feel alone and that's not nothing. When my tears calm down, I tell the guys the truth about me. That I repeatedly asked girls for sex at my school. That I've always wanted to be whole. They don't do anything but listen, and after I finish, they just hug me. And I realize something.

I need these guys, and they need me. A person's hurt can't be divvied up, but it can be experienced together, and maybe that's what I need to survive.

When Trey and Elliot fall asleep, I walk up to Mr. Cratcher's study. It's the first time I've been in here since Dez and I last worked on the album. I plug my phone into a charger on the top of his desk, sit down, and check all the drawers to distract myself from thinking for a minute. One drawer is filled with office supplies. Another's packed with worn black spines of composition notebooks. The rest are filled with cords and recording equipment I'd do better eating than trying to figure out what they do.

Above the computer, the speckled corner of a notebook sticks out behind a pair of black studio monitors. The notebook he closed the morning I caught him sleeping. I slide a bible off of it, then pull it off the shelf and open it to the most recently filled page.

God, would you make me so utterly broken that I am beyond repair? It's not my spirit I'm discussing here, it's the cancer. I know the spirit that makes up Colin Cratcher is gloriously incomplete, but I don't know why the physical thing that makes up Colin Cratcher can't be the same. If it is the same, then I can't see it. However, isn't my inability to see light in the physical part of me what makes me gloriously incomplete? If so, how then do I live? Do I accept that both my spirit and flesh are one with you in the same way? When you said, 'it is good,' did you mean my flesh as well as my spirit? You must have, yet I don't feel 'good.'

God, I'm the only one to benefit from my death. I don't feel ready to leave my students. Some have yet to grasp that ferrous metals have nothing to do with the Ferris wheel, and leaving them in such a pathetic state feels sinful.

I also mourn leaving the Knights of Vice. I have yet to get through to them that all humans are addicts because none of us want pain and will go to great lengths to get relief. Leaving them without this knowledge also feels sinful, yet I know that when you call a man to come, you call. David may have asked, 'Death, where is your sting?' but he didn't know what it felt like to have your lungs drained of fluid. He only knew we all had to face it eventually and that you were on the other side. May I soon ask David's question and mean it. I ask for enough time to finish my album. To let that pain go. I ask that Gabby and Elias greet me when I arrive, and possibly Beethoven, if it isn't too much trouble.

Your servant,
Colin Cratcher

How could he believe that being human equals being an addict? If that were the case, wouldn't Addiction Fighters have to take place in a baseball stadium? If we're all addicts, how have there been successful marriages?

As I lean back in his chair, I realize Mr. Cratcher asked me "what are you?" not just to be mystical and drive me insane.

He asked the question because it mattered. He knew that if I couldn't answer it, I might spend a lifetime believing I'm something I wasn't and that I'd never know what I'm truly capable of.

—

It's four in the morning when my phone rings. I snap up in my chair and swivel toward my phone.

"Hello?"

"Check your email."

"Dez?"

There's loud music in the background. Her voice is washed out in all the noise.

I hear a bunch of ruffling, and then someone say, "Here."

"Dez?"

"Oh, Adam," she says, pain between every letter and space. She doesn't sound like herself. "I've done it."

I stand like it will help me hear her better.

"Dez, what are you talking about?"

"I can finally use this one."

"You aren't making sense. What's going on?"

Someone laughs. More ruffling.

"*Alasdair Grey, From Lanark: A Life in Four Books.*"

"I don't understand."

"The last line."

Click.

I call her over and over. And for every button I press to get Dez back, there's an unanswered ring that's greater than.

GOOD-BYE

My phone's not connecting to Mr. Cratcher's network, so I turn on his computer. Protools, the DAW, is the first thing that opens once the screen turns on. I minimize it and Google "Lanark: A Life in Four Books PDF." At first I find nothing, but after putting "last line of" in front of my previous search phrase, it brings up a Google book copy. I scroll all the way to the bottom and see "pages 556 to 577 are not shown in this preview."

I curse. I could buy it on my Dad's e-reader, but that would mean I have to go home.

Home = seeing my dad.

I turn off my wifi, then sign into my dad's Amazon account and buy the e-version.

While it's downloading, I open my email. At the top of my inbox is "Fwd: What Are You, Elias?"

My breath catches. She found it.

Dez, I found Mr. Cratcher's song. I had it digitized for you. I haven't listened to it, so I apologize if the quality is sub-par. I hope you and your friends find what you are looking for.

Sincerely,
Mr. Crowell

I hover the mouse over the attachment at the bottom. I consider waking Elliot and Trey, or even texting Addy, but decide against it. I'll share it with them later. Right now, I want this for me. I need this for me. I click on the attachment and a play button appears on the screen. Before I can prepare myself, the song bursts through the studio monitors with a vintage crackle.

They call you names. We call them lost.
They call me traitor; I count it as holy loss.
Traitors just another name for sinner
A name we could all be called.

The wind alone doesn't make a windy day.
It needs trees to move, and a noise to make.
If we believe one man to be the greatest shame
The shared pain of the heart is life to forsake

What are you, Elias?
What am I, brother?

I've written a world's worth of words
In the depths of man's equal dark days
But there's no one word to describe you
There's just blood, flesh, and grace.

What are you, Elias?
What am I, brother?

We are a divine mathematician's variables,
Formed human, in constant change.

We are a changing song of glory,
Made up of a holy and broken blaze.

I finally have the answer.

I'm a variable of broken and holy light, and now that I know, there's only one thing about me that's changed. I've gone from desperately looking for the answer, to desperately wishing I knew what it meant.

I walk past Trey and Elliot, rolling my steps heel to toe to make them extra silent. It's five a.m. so I don't have to be incredibly quiet. If there's one thing I learned on our failure of a road trip, it's that the two of them could sleep through the apocalypse.

I get in the car and pull up *From Lanark*. I see the last line and my stomach sinks. Dread hits me like a punch. I start Genevieve and speed my way to the Coulter mansion on I-405.

I-405 = Dez.

Dez = ?

? = worry. Lots of worry.

Strangely, worrying about her makes me feel lighter. That might mean we've erupted, and somehow, I still love her.

I pull up to the Coulter mansion gate at 5:37 and take a deep breath. I press the blank button at the top of the keypad at least ten times before a groggy hello comes out of the speaker.

"This is Adam Hawthorne. I need to speak with Mr. and Mrs. Coulter. It's urgent."

"I don't think they are awake yet. Why don't you come back around nine?"

"No, I need to talk to them now. Something might be wrong with Dez."

The mysterious person—I'm guessing it's Mrs. Coulter's personal assistant—doesn't respond. She just opens the gate. I alternate between knocking and ringing the doorbell. I hate myself for coming here, but I can't just sit around hoping Dez is okay. Since she called, I've felt like the world is on the verge of collapse. It may be dramatic, but I can't describe it any other way.

A blur appears in the frosted windows on the doors. I have the brief thought that they might not even care, but they can't just not care. They just might not care in the right places or at the right times. The door on the right pulls back slightly so that all I can see is the top half of Mr. Coulter's face.

"Adam?" he asks.

"Hey, Mr. Coulter, I just . . . uh. I just wanted to know if you've heard from Dez?"

That's all it takes for the door to swing all the way open.

"We've been trying to get in contact with her since she texted us last night," he says, bringing me into the kitchen.

"She texted you? What time? What did she say?"

Mr. Coulter gets a glass and fills it with water then hands it to me. "It was jumbled, like she was drunk, but she said she was sorry and muttered some man's name."

Mrs. Coulter comes around the corner of living room. "Terry?"

She sees me in the kitchen and looks down at herself with horror, as though someone seeing her in her pajamas is on a list of extra dirty sins.

"I'll be right back," she says.

I pull out my phone to pull up *From Lanark*.

"You said she was fine when you left her, correct?" he asks.

"Yeah."

Mr. and Mrs. Coulter know she stayed. Addy talked to them about it before we left. However, I'm not sure if they know *why*. Addy and Dez wouldn't have told them about us breaking up, and I didn't mention it when I returned the SUV.

I hand him my phone.

"Adam," Mr. Coulter says, "what is it?"

"The man she quoted. This is his book. The last line's just 'Good-bye.'"

MELTDOWN

I'm speeding back to Mr. Cratcher's house when I get a text from Mr. Coulter.

> Nashville cops called.
> Tickets bought. Meet us
> at airport in thirty minutes.

I run into the house. "Elliot, Trey!"

They stir, but they don't respond, which is good now that I've given it a little thought. I don't know what waking them up would do. Mr. Coulter only bought three tickets, so if they woke up, they'd just freak out and probably keep me from getting to the airport on time. Besides, I don't want to have to explain what I've done to Dez.

I go upstairs and run over to Mr. Cratcher's computer where I left my overnight bag. I bend over to get it and accidentally put my hand on the keyboard. I must hit a keyboard shortcut, because Protools, which is minimized on the bottom of the screen, pops up to a "open file" screen. I go to close it, but I see a file called, "To The Knights of Vice." I only ever open the files from their own folder on the desktop, never search in the program itself, so this is the first time I've seen this. I click on it. The screen opens to a song with five tracks. Each one named after a member of the Knights of Vice. The last track is called "Everyone."

I un-mute the track called "Adam" and a line starts moving across the screen.

"Adam."

Just the sound of his voice makes me feel hope.

"Today, you and Miss Coulter honored me with your company, and after you left, I felt led to leave you this message. I must warn you, it will be long-winded. When you are looking at the end of your life, everything you have aches to be shared more than before. This fact alone will give me the propensity to have more words than normal."

He must have recorded this the day Dez and I came to record together. It also was the day he collapsed in his bathroom.

"It is not a typical adage to say that young love is true. Most cases of it are self-serving at best and purely physical at worst. However, you and Miss Coulter have a palpable connection. The same kind I felt with my dear Gabby. I say all this because your comments about why you are not dating put a deep fear in me. Therefore, since I am on my deathbed, I am making some last requests of you, which I expect you to honor.

"Adam, you and Miss Coulter are allowed to break up because you decide you are different people who do not work well as a couple. You are allowed to break up because one of you can't see themselves marrying the other. In special cases, I'd even allow your breakup if you were simply being downright rotten to each other. However, I forbid you from breaking up because you assume addicts cannot purely love. Though that assumption is correct, it is not exclusive to addicts. The experience of an addict has its differences, all humans are both broken and holy, and we all have the opportunity to waste our lives looking for wholeness.

"In the search of something that makes sense, we make our lives incredibly complicated by expanding everything under the sun until it is more confusing than it actually is. Life can be much simpler if we just let the sun be the sun, the moon be the moon, the trees be the trees, because that's simply what they are, what they were made to be. You'd be a fool if you looked at the sky and said it was a car. In the same way, you cannot say a human is perfect. You need to let humans be humans. Let the indefinable be indefinable.

"Adam, the thing about our sun is that, even though it is made of complex atoms and shares in our groan of un-wholeness, it is ever burning, casting light when it rises and when it sets. We are no different. We cannot be whole on earth, but we can be variables of broken and holy light. We might not be able to love wholly, but we can love truly if we face our pain together.

"Do not squirm through life believing you will only ever be an addict, I beg of you. You are only an addict if you believe yourself one. The addicts, I use this word cautiously, who find freedom are the ones who realize they were never addicts in the first place, just humans in dire need of rightness. Now, please distribute the other tracks accordingly to the Knights of Vice. This will be good practice for you, considering you must do so with my entire estate. Be sure to listen to the track titled 'Everyone' together. Tell Dez every day that she's stronger than she thinks. Love her and the Knights of Vice as best as you can, and know that will be good enough. I must go. It's been an honor to have blazed on this earth with you."

I listen to it again. I almost listen to it a third time, but instead, I just mail the track to myself and run down the stairs with a frick-ton of hope.

I call Addy. It rings over and over, and just when I think I'll have to leave a message, she picks up.

Of course she picks up.

My Addy.

"Adam?"

"Dez is in trouble. I think she's going to kill herself. I'm flying to Nashville with her parents to find her."

"Oh my God, can I do anything?"

"No, I don't think so."

"I should have never left her there," she says. "I—"

"Addy, I'm sorry."

"What?"

"I'm sorry for saying what I did. For arguing with you, for telling you that moving to Bothell did nothing."

The thing is, Addy did everything. She showed me what it looked like to love by loving me in a way I couldn't understand. She showed the answer to Mr. Cratcher's question. She's just as messed up by the divorce as I am, but she still chose to love me, everyone, in selfless ways. She was, and is, a variable of broken and holy light.

That's what I am, Mr. Cratcher. That's what we all are.

"You coming back here changed my life," I say. "And that's the truth. I want to be you when I grow up."

"Papi," she says, "you're forgiven. I love you a lot. Now get off the phone and get to Dez. I'll handle everything here."

"I—I love you, too."

I hang up the phone, and then drive 95 MPH down I-5 toward the girl I can love enough.

I park at the airport, and while running toward the gate with Mr. and Mrs. Coulter, I send Dez a text:

> I'm coming. Please wait for me. Please, Dez.

—

When we land, Mr. Coulter calls the cops for an update, and they tell him there's one cruiser out looking for her and that they'll let him know if they find her. We catch a cab to the rental house. As soon as Mr. and Mrs. Coulter walk inside, they start calling her name.

"She won't be in here," I say, and they look at me like I'm a psychic.

"She refused to sleep in the house. She only ever slept in the Hamana on the patio."

"Hamana?" Mr. Coulter asks.

"Banana plus hammock."

We walk onto the patio. The hammock's empty, and the big heater's turned off. I run to her tent, but she's not there either. We search the house just in case, but we don't find anything.

"Where else would she be?" they ask, but I have no idea.

We drive over to Miss Hunt's house, and even though we tell her Dez's missing, she invites us over for dinner. In her defense, she said she'd make some phone calls first. We stop by Bridge Studios. The Ass is here, sitting behind a desk. He rubs his temples as if the sight of me alone is enough to bring on a migraine. He says he hasn't seen "Mindy," and he looks very thankful about it.

Outside of Bridge, I look up the "What Are You, Elias?" email and copy Mr. Crowell's number onto the back of my hand with a pen from Mrs. Coulter's purse. His phone rings twice, then he answers.

"Good evening, whom am I speaking with?" he asks.

"Mr. Crowell, it's Adam Hawthorne. Dez's friend?"

"How can I help you, Adam? Did you get the recording?"

"Yeah, I did, and I still haven't recovered from it. Listen, I was wondering if you knew where Dez was? I think she's in trouble."

His voice goes from business casual to business formal. "When was the last time you talked with her?"

"Last night."

"Was she showing signs of duress? What was the discussion like?"

"She sounded off. There was loud music in the background and people were talking around her."

"Did she say anything?"

"Yeah, she said, 'Check your email' and 'Oh, Adam. I've done it now.' And she gave me the last line of a book."

"What was the line?"

"'Good-bye.'"

"Have you alerted local authorities?"

"Yes, and there's a cruiser looking for her."

"Come over to my house immediately. I'll make some calls and get some more hands on this as soon as possible."

"Okay, thank you so much, Mr. Crowell."

"One last question: has she ever shown any suicidal tendencies?"

"Um, no. Well, I don't know. She has a history of substance abuse, but she never abused it in a suicidal way. At least that I know of."

"Did anything happen to her that would cause her to turn to abuse again?"

I swallow and close my eyes.

This is my fault. Our eruption.

"Yeah, me."

—

We've been waiting at Mr. Crowell's house for three hours when he finally walks into the living room with his cell phone pressed against his ear.

"Yes. Yes, great work. Okay, thank you." He puts his phone in his pocket. "That was the current police chief. He said they found her in an alley behind a local nightclub, but she's not conscious and her pulse is weak. He suspects she tried overdosing. They found traces of cocaine everywhere: on her clothes, under her fingernails. They're rushing her to Nashville General."

This is BS. God, this is BS.

Mrs. Coulter lays a hand over her heart. "Will she be okay?"

"There's no way to know until they get her to the hospital. Come on, I'll escort you."

I can't believe I left her. She was afraid of Percocets because of where they lead and instead of helping her, I left her. I pushed her past the gate. No, we both pushed her past the gate. I'm not going to give myself all the credit for this. We both erupted.

Somehow, all the chaos makes everything seem distant. Like, when I look out the back passenger window, I see nothing but Dez lying in the street calling for help. Noise? I hear nothing but dim echoes. Sirens. Talking. I hardly feel the seatbelt press into my chest as Mr. Crowell slams on the breaks when someone cuts him off.

The moment the Emergency Room glass doors slide open, every noise comes back. It's too much for my senses to take and I feel like I'm going to snap. Beeping. Emergency room silence. Hurt. Fear. Love. Fear. Beeping. Each time another noise or person enters my senses, I feel like the next will send me into a psych ward–worthy meltdown.

NOT AFRAID OF LETTING GO

In her room, I grab a chair and pick a spot by her bed. I refuse to move. I've left her once, and it was the worst decision I've ever made. I'm not going to do it again.

"Sir, visiting hours are over."

"That's nice. I'll let everyone know."

"Sir, you have to leave."

"No."

In the end, I'm pretty sure Mr. Coulter paid the nurse to let me stay.

The next three days are a mixture of blur and random detail. I know my phone's rung at least fifty times. I know that Christmas comes and goes in the most non-Christmas fashion, which isn't a surprise. Christmas isn't really for people lying in hospital beds after almost dying of a mixture of stolen pills, cocaine, and alcohol.

I don't know if the phone calls decrease, and I'm not sure if I've let go of her hand since I've sat down. I don't know if I've eaten, and I'm not sure if I've gone to the bathroom. What I do know is that Dez Coulter is beautiful, and I've felt her burn rippling up my shoulders. And even though Ray

Bradbury didn't mean it this way, I know it's a pleasure to burn with her. I tell her that, whether she's listening or not.

I don't know what day it is when I finally see life in Dez Coulter, my normal girlfriend, but it comes when her fingers slide between mine.

"I love you," I say. "I'm sorry. I'm so, so sorry."

She lifts her arm and the small plastic tube of the IV pulls taught. She tugs on my shirt and pulls my head onto her pillow.

"I'm sorry," she says, her voice scratchy and slurred. "If you'll have me, it'd be a pleasure to burn with you."

"Yes, please," I say.

She makes her fingers into a greater than sign and places them against my chest and just like that she's asleep again.

Three months later...

I'm on the shore next to the bridge of Deception Pass. The same place I stood when my family came here for their final vacation before the explosion of hearts.

This isn't a dream. I am here.

The sand is really beneath my toes. The water is definitely navy blue. Not black. The sky is sapphire blue, deep and thick with brilliance. A golden sun sets against the arches and crags of the various islands dotting the Puget Sound. I feel spring on the air. There's no darkness here. Just beauty.

"It's pretty," Addy says.

"Really pretty," Dad says.

"Brings back so many memories," my mom says, her voice breaking.

I swallow. I don't look at her, but I don't hate her.

"Thanks for suggesting this, Adam," Mom says. "Coming here for our first . . . family hangout is such beautiful symmetry."

"I know," I say, staring down the water.

"Come on," Addy says. "Let's head back before it gets dark. I feel the summoning of ice cream, somewhere."

The sound of sand crunching under feet surrounds me as my family walks back toward the tree line, but I stand staring at the water.

This is the point where deception meets reality.

The point where *I* choose what I believe about myself.

My body shivers with the fear of being alone, but I came to Deception Pass for this moment. There are no formulas here. There won't be, after this. There's nothing philosophical. There's only me and that Gollum-like voice telling me that I should walk toward the dark because it's safer. Telling me that being alone is better.

But I came here to swallow the dark.

I came to Deception Pass to turn around.

I swivel on my heel.

Leaving the water behind me.

My family has stopped a few feet ahead.

They wait for me.

Addy holds out her hand and motions for me. "Come on!"

I run to them.

—

The next day, I tighten my tie again and again. Eventually I realize nothing ever feels good enough for a funeral. I wipe the tears from eyes and look at my friends sitting beside me in their various states. Even though she's crying, Addy sits strong and present. Holding my hand like she always has. Trey's been crying since we hit I-5, and he's still going. Elliot's part-emo, so I feel like he's been sulking on the edge of tears since we met. All in all, we may now be the Knights of Vice Versa, but we're the same amount of mess as the Knights of Vice.

The Knights of Vice Versa is what Mr. Cratcher called us in his "Everyone" recording. He said, "Once you know what you are, you are no longer a human who struggles with addiction, but a human who struggles with being human. Therefore, I knight you all as new beings. You are now the Knights of Vice Versa."

I keep looking over my shoulder at the church doors, expecting Dez to come through them, but it's impossible. The minister stands and calls us all to order while my mind tries to concoct what complaints Dez would have about the cheesy photomontage playing against the wall via projector.

The church goes silent as "What Are You, Elias?" starts playing. I look at the doors again. I remind myself, again, she's not coming.

The doors creak as they swing open. A group of people—including my dad—walk down the aisle with the coffin.

Dad glances at me as he walks past. He wanted me to be a pallbearer, but I said no. It might be unfair, but right now I feel like I'm carrying enough weight without carrying death itself.

The pallbearers place the coffin at the front of the church and scatter to seats reserved for them on the front row. The minister looks at me and nods. I stand, but right before I step out of the pew, the church doors swing open and Dez runs down the aisle in black fur-lined boots, a yellow dress with white polka dots, and a black cardigan. In other words, she's as beautiful as beautiful can get.

The entire church is watching her, but she doesn't care. She stops by me, and we kiss for the first time since she went to rehab almost three months ago.

"You were going to take my speech, you ass. I've worked on it for hours," she whispers.

"You told me yesterday they weren't going to let you out," I say.

She puts a finger on my lips. "Shhh, you think too much."

I laugh. Only Dez would break out of rehab to go a funeral.

She walks up to where the minister's standing and lays a crumpled piece of paper on the podium. The minister gives me a "what's going on?" look.

Dez clears her throat and begins. "I've never found it necessary to read the stuff between the first and the last lines of books."

I chuckle along with the other Knights of Vice Versa.

"The reason for this is: I've never wanted to commit to working through boringness of everything that isn't the first and last line. However, being fresh from rehab—and by fresh, I mean being an escapee—I've been discovering that the middle's where all the life happens, and I've spent my tiny and pitiful seventeen years of life running from it. I had the stupid idea that if I ignored stuff that looked middle-ish—doing well in school, being okay with having money, having close friends, living day-to-day, working through hurt—I could live in the epic-ness of first and last sentences." She turns to us, the Knights of Vice Versa. "Turns out, this idea really just made me turn things that should be normal into epic things."

She takes a break, then a breath, and continues.

"Most of you know Mr. Cratcher was a mystic, but the one question he asked my friends and I the most was as simple and normal as it could get: 'What are you?' When he first asked me, I was sure I was only an addict, but I was only seeing myself in terms of a first and last line. To me, there wasn't a middle, but to Mr. Cratcher, the middle was everything. The middle meant we were human.

"Mr. Cratcher's question pushed me past my epic-ness obsession. He forced me to consider the middle, and my immediate observation was: the middle hurt like hell."

The Knights of Vice Versa laugh again, and this time a few people around us let out chuckle.

"However, in the middle, I found what I'd been looking for among the first and last lines: hope. I think if I told Mr. Cratcher that right now, he'd still think I was missing the point. He'd probably say something like, 'You can't have true life without living every part of it. The first, the middle, and the last are all equal parts beautiful, chaotic, and painful.' And if I disagreed with him, he'd repeat himself. And if I disagreed with him again, he'd repeat himself."

Finally, a hearty laugh flows through everyone. The why-is-this-girl-wearing-a-yellow-polka-dot-dress-to-a-funeral-and-talking-up-front awkwardness is defeated.

"I had the horrid pleasure of going on a miserable road trip with a group of addict friends. We went looking for a part of Mr. Cratcher's past, but we ended up finding the pain of our own. For me, the hardest part about the trip was the way everyone who'd known Mr. Cratcher talked about him like he'd changed their lives. I couldn't see how that was possible because I was certain life was fixed, that we are only as good as our first and last lines. I kept asking myself *how could this one man change so many lives simply by being in them?* More importantly, *how could lives change?*

"This next sentence will be taking advantage of a lot of untold backstory, but when I was lying nearly dead in a Nashville hospital, I realized that if change weren't possible, racial segregation wouldn't have been declared illegal. If change weren't possible, my friends wouldn't be turning into damn good men. If change weren't possible, love wouldn't have been a reason that made me want to stay alive."

She looks at me. I catch her blue eyes, and all I want to tell her is that I love her.

Just a normal "I love you."

"Mr. Cratcher's last words to me were in a message he'd left on a computer. He said, 'Your wholeness doesn't define your ability to love,' and that, to me, is one of the best last lines I've ever heard. With it, Mr. Cratcher invited me to be human. He invited me to change. He invited me to live in the middle, and I can never repay him for it. I can only be a holy and broken hallelujah, just as he was to me, and I'm sure if he was here, he'd tell me that'd be enough."

She walks down the stairs and squeezes between Elliot and me. I grab her hand and hold it, and this time, I'm not afraid of letting go.

HOW WE BLAZE

A sea of black swirls around me, but my eyes follow a blur of yellow polka dots. Dez runs up to me and throws her arms around me. Three months of nothing add up to now, and I hug her as tight as I can. I can hear her crying in my ear.

"I love you," I say.

"I love you, too." She pulls away and wipes a tear from her eye.

"So rehab is working, apparently?"

"It's amazing the things you can do when you aren't always half a human."

At the hospital, she spilled the true story of Dez Coulter. She'd been taking Percocet all along. She'd been drugged from the moment I met her.

"You look like a real Dez," Addy says over my shoulder. She lets go of Trey's hand, walks up to her, and they hug almost as tight as we did. Dez really does look like a real Dez. That girl I saw the night we walked down the Brentwood cul-de-sac. The one who hoped and dreamed and talked about a future. This girl in front of me wearing a yellow polka dot dress is her. She's someone I'd hoped for. Someone we're all capable of being.

Trey puts an arm over my shoulder and whispers, "Dude, Dez Coulter is hot."

I smile. "Yeah, she really is. Wait. Trey, you're dating my sister."

"I know! Isn't that awesome?"

"You are so confusing," I say.

"Tell me about it," Elliot adds, walking around the hug fest that is Addy and Dez. My two everythings.

Finally Addy and Dez split apart, but Dez is still crying. She comes over to me and buries her head in my neck.

"Do you think they're gonna make you stay longer because you broke out?" Elliot asks.

"I don't know. I'm just ready to be out."

"Are they coming for you? Are you like, a wanted chica now?" Trey asks. "Because that'd be pretty cool."

She sighs. "I don't know. I want to talk about something else besides my escaping from a rehab clinic. It's too first and last line. What were you guys going to do after the funeral?"

"Get some to-go milkshakes from Pritchett's and work on the album," I say. "We're working on 'When We Reach the City.'"

"My favorite," Addy adds.

Dez nods. "Well, I'd rather be captured recording an album than at a funeral. That'll look pretty weird to the white coats. Also, I thought of new name for the album while I was in the slammer. I think it sums up Mr. Cratcher's life better than *Hounds of Eden*."

"What is it?" Elliot asks.

"*Looking for Eden.*"

We're all silent for a few seconds, thinking through the name. We spent so much time looking for his album, *Hounds of Eden,* only to decide in the end that, even if it was in a box out in the garage, it didn't matter. We were going to remake the album without it, together, which is what I think he wanted me to do ever since he brought me into that studio. I thought he was recording the album for himself, but I realize now that he was simply facing the story of his life at the end of his days it so he could pass it onto me. All those times he tried to get me to write a song or said, "I don't think that'll be my decision," he wanted me to make the album mine. I didn't.

I made it ours.

Dez is right. *Looking for Eden* is perfect. His story. Our story. It all converges in that one name.

I grab her hand and walk toward the door. "That is the most perfect album title I've ever heard."

—

Addy calls in our milkshake order, and I'm nominated to go in and pick them up as she swings into the Pritchett's parking lot. Before I can get out of the car, Dez pulls me back to her and says, "I'll see you in a minute, forever?"

I nod. "Hell yeah."

She smiles. "Good. Don't mess up the order."

I run inside and stand at the hostess podium, waiting for someone to help me. A few seconds pass and no hostess shows, so I look around the diner, hoping to catch someone's eye, when I see them.

Daliah Howard, Bryonie Welch, and a few other girls. The Anti-Adam Order. I'd avoided them since I got back to school. Luckily, I didn't have classes with them and we sat no where near each other in the cafeteria. I wasn't proud of it, but I just couldn't look at them without feeling like utter dirt. Without feeling like I deserved to be alone. Like it was unfair to them that I was changing and getting better because I'd done them so wrong.

But I've been to Deception Pass, now. I turned around. I'm here. With my friends and sister waiting for me in the car. People who love me enough to tell me wise things that someday I'll understand. People who know the darkest me and haven't left.

I watch the Anti-Adam Order talk, laugh. I remember asking each one to have sex with me. I remember how right I felt in doing so.

"Sir?"

I look back to the podium, and there's a waitress standing in front of me.

"Uh." I wipe at my eyes.

"Can I help you?"

I look at their table again, and I know there's something I have to do, but to face them again . . . My feet feel like they weigh a million pounds. My mouth goes dry.

"What's taking so long, Frenchie?"

I turn around and see Dez standing in the door. She sees my face. My tears.

"Adam, what's wrong?"

"They're here," I say, looking back at the table of the Anti-Adam Order. "They're here and I can't just keep avoiding them."

Dez looks over my shoulder and points at Bryonie. "Is that them?"

I nod.

Dez grabs my hand and pulls me toward them. My heart lurches. I feel hot. I pull back, but she pulls me harder and says, "You can do this. You're my wife."

We walk up to the table, and, at first, the girls don't see me. They just see Dez, but when they do see me, their faces turn from confusion to anger and that's all it takes for me to start crying again.

"Sorry to interrupt, girls," Dez says, "but my boyfriend, Adam, has something to say to all of you."

She lets go of my hand and steps behind me. "Adam, take it away. I'm right here."

I can't look up. I'm so afraid to look up, and my tears keep spilling down my cheeks. They drop onto the floor with ear-splitting cracks. Then I feel Dez touch my back. A reminder that she's here. That Addy, my dad, Elliot, and Trey are all still here.

I look up at them. They're all looking at me, and I swear the entire diner is watching me, listening to me.

"I'm sorry," I finally say. "I'm so damn sorry. I—"

Silence.

"I hope—I'm sorry."

They don't say anything, and after a few seconds of silence, I feel Dez's hand slip back into mine. "Come on," she says. "That's good enough."

Dez brings me over to the bar area and sits me on a stool. She kisses me on the cheek and says, "I'm so proud of you. Now don't freak out. I'm gonna go get our milkshakes."

She walks back toward the podium, and while she talks to the waitress, I look back at the table of the Anti-Adam Order.

Bryonie Welch is staring at me. The other girls are laughing. I wipe my stupid leaking eyes for the millionth time I pull my hand down and lock eyes with Bryonie, she nods. She doesn't mouth anything after that. Just turns back to the girls.

And I'm filled with the beautiful kind of pain.

—

Dez stands at a microphone belting, "Come on reach the city. Come on reach the city lights."

Trey and Addy sit on the floor listening to her sing. Addy leans her head on Trey's shoulder and closes her eyes. Elliot practices his part downstairs in the kitchen. I put on the headphones and I hear the mix of everything we've recorded. As I listen to Dez, I think about Bryonie's nod and, for the first time since the divorce, realize I'm finally feel free. I think through the days I've spent searching for wholeness. I think about the nights ahead where I'll struggle with porn, but also think about the nights I won't. I think about my mom moving back to Bothell. I think about the days where I won't feel free, but I also think about the days made up of hallelujah moments like this.

Life is made up of two kinds of pain, the hurtful kind and the beautiful kind, and that's okay. Why? Because though I'm broken, I'm not an addict. Just because I have a hard night or week or month, it doesn't mean I haven't changed.

I might never be fixed, but that doesn't mean I can't be whole.

We're all variables of broken and holy light, and that's the only thing about the world that *doesn't* change. Addictions can never define Dez and me because they'll never have the chance.

We're never just one thing, but we can always choose to love.

And that's how we blaze.

CAST AND CREW

I've recently come to the conclusion that the people who've helped this book happen had a level of involvement more provided by a cast and crew than a village. This cast and crew have fought, read, and bent over backwards to help this book as well as books prior to this one, be holdable. Without further blah blah blah, here, readers, is the cast and crew responsible for TOA.

Original readers who read the first book I ever wrote (I'm so sorry)

Eric Graham, Brigitta Nortker (look at where we started, big shot editor), Charlie Rash, Clara Connis.

My very own Knights of Vice Versa

Pandrew, JM, Richards, Micah, DK, Andrew. You are all hallelujahs to me.

The Knights of Beta-Reading

AA Crystal Holland-dog, Cara Reed, Becky Valkenburg, Emily Mollenkof, Nic Stone, Jenna Kilpinen, Jay Coles, Joel Harris, Diane Connis, Clara Connis, Liz Feldman, Nic Stone, Zoraida Cordova, Jay Coles. Thank you for the wisdom of who you are & telling me things that are wise.

The Davids of YA Contemporary™

David Arnold & David Levithan, you've shown me what it looks like to author with kindness. Thank you.

Beta-Readers of Other Books I've Written but Still Hide in Dark Corners of Shame

Benjamin Brooks...Brooks Benjamin?, Daniel Kelly, Sangu Mandanna, Lizzie Cook, Mike Chen, Clara Connis (again), Gwen Cole, Wendy Macknight, Avalon Rowe (OMG, YOU'RE IN A BOOK! :D), Chyela Rowe.

The Whatever We Were 17s

We probably weren't swanky, but we survived. We learned. We made it regardless. I am thankful for all that you gave to me. Sara Biren, you're a warrior princess.

Mrs. Miyagi/My Mr. Cratcher:

Sara Zarr. Thank you for your friendship, persistence, and wisdom.

The Person Who Shall Not Be Named

Matt Landis

Bookish Peeps Who've Made Me Feel at Home in a Mind Made of Earthquakes

Sabaa Tahir, Becky Albertalli, Jenna Kilpinen, Hikari Loftus, Adam Silvera, Natalie Lloyd.

The Rock Crik Fellership Youth Group

Thank you for reminding me why I write, and letting me eat Doritos even when I'm doing a Paleo diet.

Guy Hoping to Sell the Binders Filled With First Book Drafts on Ebay

Charlie Rash. It's been an honor to be broken with you.

Biggest Fans/People Who've Always Seemed to Really Like My Music (still puzzling to me)

David and Chyela Rowe. Thank you. Thank you. Thank you.

People Who've Loved/Supported Me & Prayed for Me Since Birth

Mom and Dad. Your love is incredible. Sorry I killed that laptop with chocolate milk.

Agent/Slayer/Awesome Sauce

Eric Smith. You said "I love this" when I was about to say "I'm done." Thanks for helping me learn how to celebrate the now. (Nena, I see you. Thanks for telling Eric to follow his dreams and supporting me while you're at it.)

TeamRocks

May we slay together in all our waterfall glory.

That Indie Book Seller

Star Lowe, may Starline Books take over the world.

Editor with the Patience of a Saint

Nicole Frail, thanks for deciding TOA was worth it & for not killing me for the 80,000 emails I sent.

Sky Pony Team

Emily Shields, Katrina Enright, Ming Liu.

The Fam and Friends

There have been so many of you who've encouraged me and helped me along the way. Mom & Dad Demaster clan (babysitting $$$!), Mom and dad, thank you for all you've done.

The Looking for Eden Band

David Henry, Sammie Brown, Joel Harris, Noah Barnett, Hannah Lutz, John-Michael Forman, Spencer McGuire. The least I could give you was your own section.

One who Deserves Everything

Clara Connis. I can't even begin to write how much I owe you for all you've done to support and love me. Where others folded, you held strong. When I was obsessed, you were understanding. Never say I got the raw end of the deal, because this book, who I am, how I love, and my drive to be a better human is because of you. Here's to our years of blazing. Here's to our fighting. Here's to the times we have to apologize. Here's to the times when we don't. I love you.

The Real MVP

When I think I'm about to run out of words, I remember that you've got giant storehouses full. Thanks for dying for me. You didn't have to do it. When I'm prone to wander, you're prone to look for me. Thanks for being my inspiration/PR and marketing team/cheerleader/comforter/betareader. For teaching me to escape Deception Pass.

The Majestic Flailfuss

Asa, this book is dedicated to you. Do you really need to be here, too? Just kidding. Why I write makes so much more sense since you came along and I hope this book makes you proud.

Bucket

We love you. Have fun with your friends and see you soon.

Read the novel . . .

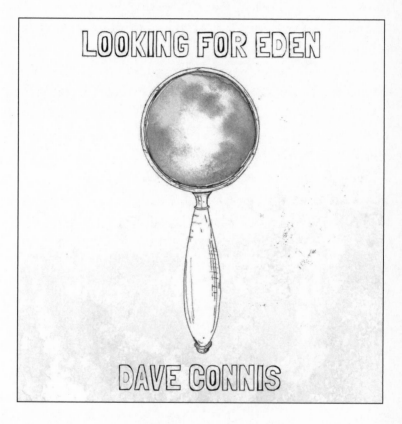

. . . hear the album:

Looking for Eden

Find the album on Spotify, iTunes,
and Google Play.